A legend of the deep guards
Dane Maddock just wants to num ... ...
his past behind. After a series of tragedies, the former Navy SEAL and his crew travel to the Bahamas in search of the wreckake of Maelstrom, the flagship of notorious pirate Riddick Blackwood. But what they find sets them on a hunt for one of the greatest legends of the New World—The Fountain of Youth!

But has their discovery unleashed something terrible upon the world? As the deaths mount, Maddock and his partner Bones Bonebrake must prevent a dangerous shadow organization from seizing the power that lies beneath the waters.

PRAISE FOR DAVID WOOD
AND THE DANE MADDOCK ADVENTURES!

"What an adventure! A great read that provides lots of action, and thoughtful insight as well, into strange realms that are sometimes best left unexplored." Paul Kemprecos, author of *Cool Blue Tomb* and the *NUMA Files*

"David Wood has done it again. Within seconds of opening the book, I was hooked. Intrigue, suspense,monsters, and treasure hunters. What more could you want? David's knocked it out of the park with this one!" Nick Thacker- author of *The Enigma Strain*

"A twisty tale of adventure and intrigue that never lets up and never lets go!" Robert Masello, author of *The Einstein Prophecy*

"Dane and Bones.... Together they're unstoppable. Rip roaring action from start to finish. Wit and humor throughout. Just one question - how soon until the next one? Because I can't wait." Graham Brown, author of *Shadows of the Midnight Sun*

"A page-turning yarn blending high action, Biblical speculation, ancient secrets, and nasty creatures. Indiana Jones better watch his back!" Jeremy Robinson, author of *SecondWorld*

"With the thoroughly enjoyable way Mr. Wood has mixed speculative history with our modern day pursuit of truth, he has created a story that thrills and makes one think beyond the boundaries of mere fiction and enter the world of 'why not'?" David Lynn Golemon, Author of the *Event Group* series

"An adrenaline-fueled thrill ride!" Alan Baxter, author of *Hidden City*

"Let there be no confusion: David Wood is the next Clive Cussler. Once you start reading, you won't be able to stop until the last mystery plays out in the final line." Edward G. Talbot, author of *2012: The Fifth World*

"I like my thrillers with lots of explosions, global locations and a mystery where I learn something new. Wood delivers! Recommended as a fast paced, kick ass read." J.F. Penn, author of *Desecration*

CONTEST

A DANE MADDOCK ADVENTURE
DAVID WOOD

ADRENALINE PRESS

Blue Descent- ©2019 by David Wood

The Dane Maddock Adventures™

All rights reserved

Published by Adrenaline Press
www.adrenaline.press

Adrenaline Press is an imprint of Gryphonwood Press
www.gryphonwoodpress.com

Edited by Melissa Bowersock

ISBN: 978-1-950920-07-5

This is a work of fiction. All characters are products of the author's imagination or are used fictitiously.

BOOKS BY DAVID WOOD

THE DANE MADDOCK ADVENTURES
Blue Descent
Dourado
Cibola
Quest
Icefall
Buccaneer
Atlantis
Ark
Xibalba
Loch
Solomon Key
Contest

DANE AND BONES ORIGINS
Freedom
Hell Ship
Splashdown
Dead Ice
Liberty
Electra
Amber
Justice
Treasure of the Dead
Bloodstorm

DANE MADDOCK UNIVERSE
Berserk
Maug
Elementals
Cavern
Devil's Face
Herald
Brainwash

The Tomb
Destination: Rio
Destination: Luxor
Destination: Sofia
Aztlan (short story)
Urban Legend (short story)

JADE IHARA ADVENTURES (WITH SEAN ELLIS)
Oracle
Changeling
Exile

MYRMIDON FILES (WITH SEAN ELLIS)
Destiny
Mystic

BONES BONEBRAKE ADVENTURES
Primitive
The Book of Bones
Skin and Bones
Venom

JAKE CROWLEY ADVENTURES (WITH ALAN BAXTER)
Blood Codex
Anubis Key
Revenant

BROCK STONE ADVENTURES
Arena of Souls
Track of the Beast (forthcoming)

SAM ASTON INVESTIGATIONS (WITH ALAN BAXTER)
Primordial
Overlord

STAND-ALONE NOVELS
Into the Woods (with David S. Wood)
The Zombie-Driven Life

You Suck
Callsign: Queen (with Jeremy Robinson)
Dark Rite (with Alan Baxter)

DAVID WOOD WRITING AS DAVID DEBORD

THE ABSENT GODS TRILOGY
The Silver Serpent
Keeper of the Mists
The Gates of Iron

The Impostor Prince (with Ryan A. Span)
Neptune's Key

FROM THE AUTHOR

More years ago than I care to remember, I published *Dourado*, the first *Dane Maddock Adventure*. I'd had the rough outline of the plot kicking around my head for years, but it wasn't until I came up with Dane Maddock and his partner "Bones" Bonebrake that I felt ready to write it. I tried to take the things I loved about classic pulp adventure, Indiana Jones, early Dirk Pitt, and many other influences and combine them all into an adventure set in the modern world.

Since then, the Dane Maddock universe has grown exponentially, with twelve volumes in the main series, ten in the *Origins* series, and many more in the ongoing *Universe* series. The Maddock books have also spawned three spinoff series, the *Bones Bonebrake Adventures*, the *Jade Ihara Adventures*, and the *Myrmidon Files*, along with three connected series, the *Jake Crowley Adventures*, the *Sam Aston Investigations*, and *the Brock Stone Adventures*. Many of the books are now available in non-English translations, and the audiobooks are narrated by Jeffrey Kafer, one of the best in the genre. Needless to say, I didn't anticipate any of this back when *Dourado* was first released.

The problem with having a series that's been around for a very long time is that new readers usually want to start with book one. While I think *Dourado* is a fine book, and readers seem to enjoy it, in no way does it reflect the writer I am today.

And so, I present to you *Blue Descent*, book "zero" of the *Dane Maddock Adventures*. This book takes place shortly before the events of *Dourado*, and serves as an introduction to the main characters and the universe. As always, I've made a few changes to actual locations, and played with the timeline of a few locations in order to make this the most fun and entertaining read possible. If you're already a Maddock reader, I think you'll enjoy the little Easter eggs I've sprinkled throughout the story. If you're new to the Maddock universe, welcome and I hope you enjoy the adventure!

Yonder sea, great and wide, therein are creeping things innumerable, living creatures, both small and great. There go the ships; there is leviathan, whom Thou hast formed to sport therein.
   Psalm 104:25-26

PROLOGUE

1691- Off the Coast of New Providence

Riddick Blackwood stood over his vanquished foe and breathed in the odor of gunpowder and fresh blood. It was a hot, sunny day on the Caribbean Sea, with no breeze to wash away the stink of battle. He didn't mind. There was nothing like dancing with death to make a man truly feel alive. He wondered how his crew would feel if they knew that, for their captain, the loot came second to the fight. Always.

"The fight is over, Captain." Rax, his quartermaster, stood over a fallen enemy. Blood dripped from his sword.

"That was fast," Blackwood said, looking around in hopes of spotting some enemies still in the fight. He saw none. Regretfully, he sheathed his cutlass. "I must confess I am sorely disappointed."

"Most sailors turn yellow when they see *Maelstrom* on the horizon. You do your job too well, Captain." Rax knelt and began rummaging through the dead sailor's pockets.

He wasn't wrong. Blackwood had developed such a notorious reputation that few captains were willing to stand and fight with him. It was always a chase, and far too often, an unconditional surrender.

"I'm going to take a look around, see if anyone is still resisting." Blackwood tried to sound bored, but his bloodlust was up and he was itching for another fight. *Please, let someone do something foolish,* he prayed.

No such luck. The crew of the captured ship had surrendered. He looked them over. A few appeared to be in good health. They could be sold in the slave markets. The rest were a sorry lot. No good to him.

Stiles, his first mate, joined him.

"What's the report?" Blackwood asked.

"We'll be well-provisioned for a while, but no gold. Sorry it was all for so little, Captain."

"Nonsense. We needed a fight to keep the crew sharp." He turned to the captives and raised his voice. "Any man who swears not to lift a hand against us will not be harmed." Everyone hurried to swear the oath. "Excellent. You will obey my first mate, Mister Stiles as you would me." Stiles made a mocking bow. "Mister Rax also should be obeyed. Not because he speaks with my voice, but because he's a dirty bastard who will stab you if you make him angry."

A few of the captives managed a nervous laugh. Most merely stared at the deck.

Blackwood turned to Stiles. "Have them transfer anything of value onto our ship. Once they've finished, lock the good ones in the brig and set the others free."

"Aye aye, captain." Stiles grinned broadly. What their captives did not know is that, on Blackwood's ship, "set free" meant "tossed overboard and told to swim to the nearest island." None were in sight.

Blackwood hadn't lied. His crew would do no harm to these men. The future slaves would be confined and well fed. The others would only get a bit wet. What happened to them once they left *Maelstrom* was between them and the sharks.

"Captain!" One of the captured crew, a skinny man with more eyes than teeth, called out to him.

Rax stalked over to the man and kicked him in the ribs.

"You don't speak directly to the captain."

"I'm sorry," the man grunted in pain. "There's something he will want to know."

"What is it?" Rax said.

The man looked around nervously. He was a twitchy sort, the kind that made Blackwood itch just by looking at him.

"He wouldn't want anyone else to know."

"Fine. Come with me." Rax grabbed the fellow by the hair and dragged him across the deck to where Blackwood and Stiles waited. "You can stand now," Rax said. "But if you try anything, you'll get a knife in your back. And I know just where to stick it."

"That's what you told that cabin boy in Port Royal," Stiles said.

Rax clenched his fists and rounded on Stiles, but Blackwood raised one finger, bringing the man up short. Rax froze, arms at his sides, but he still trembled, his eyes burned with rage. But he dared not disobey his captain. On most pirate crews, the captain was first among equals, a man or woman who ruled by consent of the governed. A few, however, were absolute monarchs. Riddick Blackwood was one of them.

"Tell him you're joking, Stiles."

"Just a jape," Stiles said immediately.

Rax gave a curt nod. "Fine. I won't kill you today, Stiles." He grinned. "Mayhap tomorrow."

"The two of you see to the captives. I can handle this."

Stiles began barking orders and soon the two pirates had the captives hard at work.

Blackwood turned to the skinny, toothless man, and smiled. "What is your name?"

"It's Garth, Captain." The man's Adam's apple bobbed as he swallowed hard.

"And what is it you need to tell me?"

Garth looked around, then lowered his voice.

"I want to be a part of your crew."

"And what do you have to offer?"

Garth leaned in close and whispered two words. "Eternal life."

1

Off the coast of Andros Island, Bahamas

The sun beat down on the crystalline waters. A gentle sea breeze ruffled Dane Maddock's short blond hair. The skies were clear and the seas calm. It was a perfect day for treasure hunting. But not everyone was happy.

"For the last time, it's not an imaginary ship." Dane Maddock raised his hand to silence the complaints of his crew. The most vociferous of them was Bones Bonebrake, his best friend, business partner, and former colleague in the Navy SEALs. "It's true that Riddick Blackwood and his ship, *Maelstrom*, were characters in a famous fantasy novel, but they were based on historical fact." He'd told them all this before, but they still seemed more than a bit skeptical.

"All right, fine. I'll shut my hole." Bones mimed pinching his lips closed. It didn't last. "But when we're finished up here, I think we should go after the lost treasure of Frodo Goblins, or whatever his name is."

"Leave the Tolkien references to people who know how to read," Corey Dean snapped.

Bones and Corey couldn't have been more different. Bones was a six-and-a-half-foot-tall Cherokee, massively built, with long black hair he typically wore in a ponytail. Corey was a ginger with a ruddy complexion, average in just about every physical aspect, except for his mind. The only non-veteran among the bunch, Corey was a tech wiz and a valuable asset to the crew.

"I knew how to read the note your mom slipped me last night," Bones said.

"Man, that's disgusting," Willis Sanders chimed in.

Matt Barnaby, the final member of the crew, didn't miss a beat. "I know what you mean. I've met Corey's mom. She looks just like him, except she can actually grow a beard."

Like Bones and Corey, Willis and Matt were a mismatched pair. Willis was another former SEAL. He was almost of a size with Bones, with dark brown skin and a shaved head. Matt, by contrast, was a light-skinned, brown-haired Minnesotan, who'd served in the Army Rangers.

"Screw you guys," Corey said. "Now, do you want to hear about the hit we just got on sonar?"

That shut everyone up. Maddock grinned. He already knew what Corey had found.

"There's definitely a ship down there," Corey continued. "It's wooden and is located very close to the spot Maddock predicted it would be."

Maddock flashed a knowing smile. He hadn't by any stretch been confident in his guesswork. He'd found no primary sources on the sinking of *Maelstrom*, and instead relied on stories handed down. Hopefully he hadn't missed his mark.

"How does the wreck look?" Bones said.

"We sent *Uma* down for a look," Maddock said. *Uma* was the nickname Bones had given to their unmanned miniature submersible camera in honor of actress Uma Thurman. "The condition doesn't appear to be great, but at least parts of it are intact. I think it's worth checking out. Fingers crossed."

Over his crew's demands that they play Rock, Paper, Scissors to decide who made the first dive, Maddock announced that he and Bones would go first.

"Sure, play favorites." Matt winked.

"More like, the dudes who are paying your salaries go first," Bones said.

Matt turned to Willis and frowned. "When was the last time you got paid?" he deadpanned.

Willis scratched his smooth scalp, sweaty and

gleaming in the Caribbean sun. "Man, I ain't ever got paid. I'm afraid I'm going to have to start shopping at the Dollar General."

"There's nothing wrong with that store," Maddock said as he strapped on his gear. "Bones buys all his clothes there."

"You ever been to a Dollar General in Detroit? It's a war zone."

Maddock laughed. Willis had grown up in a poor section of Detroit, and had escaped poverty by joining the Navy, eventually becoming a SEAL and a longtime comrade of Maddock and Bones. He'd made his home in Key West since joining Maddock's crew. The treasure hunting game was famine or feast. They didn't starve, but Willis never missed a chance to "po mouth," as he called it.

Willis turned to Matt. "Did you have a Dollar General in Lake Wobegon?"

Matt rolled his eyes and turned away. He cocked his head. "Anybody seen the binoculars? Looks like there's a boat on the horizon."

"I've got them here," Corey said. He raised them to his eyes but Maddock took them from Corey's hands without a word. "That was polite."

Maddock ignored the jibe. He trained the binoculars on the distant object. A tiny sailboat came into focus, crewed by an attractive young couple.

"Just people on vacation," he said. "Nothing to worry about." In the treasure hunting business, there was always a concern that other treasure hunters might try to horn in on your dive. Or pirates might snatch your loot. The latter wasn't typically a problem in the Bahamas, but the former was a constant threat.

"I don't think we've got anything to worry about," Bones said, reading Maddock's thoughts. "Nobody else is looking for Captain Hook."

Maddock let the comment roll off of him. He was eager to dive on the wreck. "You ready, Bones?"

"That's what your old lady said last…" Bones fell silent, his complexion turning a deep shade of red. "Sorry, I didn't actually mean…"

Maddock swallowed a lump in his throat. His wife, Melissa, had died a little over a year earlier. It had been a sudden, shocking death, coming on the heels of the loss of his parents. Now, the only family he had left were the people on board this boat.

"It's cool. I know it's just an insult."

"It's an idiom, which is figurative language," Corey said. "Which is, by definition, not to be taken literally."

"Don't you have a diary entry to write?" Bones said.

"It's not a diary; it's a journal, and it's for professional records." Corey scowled, then retreated into the cabin.

Ten minutes later, Maddock and Bones were outfitted in their SCUBA gear and diving through cool, clear water. Shafts of sunlight lanced into the shadows as they dove deeper. A sand shark swam past. It was barely the size of Maddock's arm, and neither party paid much attention to the other. Each had his own business to attend to.

Down they went deep into watery twilight. Here, Maddock could forget the world above the surface. He had no choice but to sharpen his mind and focus on the task at hand. What they did was dangerous, and demanded full concentration. And he loved it. He was his own boss, unless you counted the IRS and his mortgage company. He went where he wanted and chose his own jobs. For the first time in years he was not a weapon in someone else's hands. He was his own man.

They clicked on their forehead-mounted dive lights, and soon the outline of the wreck appeared in the dim glow from above. To the untrained eye it would have been easy to miss, much of it covered in silt and aquatic growth. As they swam closer he scanned the seabed, looking for stray artifacts, but nothing leapt out at him. It was no matter. They'd begin with the wreck and then work their way outward later in the process.

When they reached the wreck, Maddock's heart sank. It wasn't a pirate ship, or any other ship that was likely to be of any value. It was small, probably a coastline-hugger. He looked at Bones, wanting to offer an apologetic shrug, but continued to bear down on the wreck.

Good old Bones. When he was bored, he had the attention span of a hummingbird. But set him on a treasure hunt and he could lock in with single-minded determination. Bones would also be feeling guilty about the "old lady" jibe, and wouldn't want to do anything to make Maddock feel worse. It was the right play. No point coming all this way without even checking out the wreck.

It didn't take long to search the wreckage. They came away with some shards of pottery and what looked like a clay egg. Bones held the strange object up so they could inspect it.

It surface was engraved with rows of pictographs. Some had worn away, but others appeared to tell the story of a sea voyage. Fascinating! But whether it was of any value remained to be seen. Discouraged but intrigued, Maddock placed the egg in a mesh dive bag and he and Bones made their slow return to the surface.

Back on board, they described what they had found. The others were interested until they learned that Maddock and Bones had found no treasure. The fragments of pottery were interesting, to be sure, but they all had bills to pay. The egg garnered more attention.

"Do you think there's something inside of it?" Willis asked.

Maddock shrugged. "That would require equipment we don't have. But I suppose it's possible."

"What do you think it is?" Bones asked.

Maddock shook his head. "Egg decoration predates Easter by tens of thousands of years. And many cultures valued different types of ceramic eggs. Decorated eggs were even found at a 55,000 year-old site in South Africa."

"Could it be local?" Matt asked.

"I'm not sure. That ship didn't look like it could cross an ocean."

"Says who?" Bones said. "Sailors from the Ancient World visited the Americas."

"You never missed an episode of *In Search Of* when you were growing up, did you?"

The big Cherokee shook his head. "Nope, and I still catch it on reruns. But seriously, don't close your mind completely to the idea."

Maddock was formulating a mocking reply when a sudden scream pierced the calm.

2

Maddock spun around and saw that the sailboat they'd spotted earlier had capsized. The young woman was treading water and shouting. Her companion was nowhere to be seen. Still wearing his dive gear, Maddock sprang into action, but Willis was faster. Determined not to be left out again, the big man made a graceful dive, broke the surface, and swam toward the capsized craft with powerful strokes.

Maddock hit the water seconds after him and followed behind. His flippered feet drove him forward and he caught up with Willis in a matter of seconds.

"You need me?" Bones shouted from the deck.

"Have Corey bring the boat around and we'll see!" Maddock shouted around a mouthful of salt spray kicked up by Willis as he swam.

Sea Foam's engines roared to life just as Maddock and Willis reached the capsized sailboat.

"My brother, Kyle!" the frantic young woman said as the men reached her. "He was messing around and capsized us and now I can't see him anywhere."

"You just hold on to the boat," Maddock said. "We'll find him."

I don't see him, Willis mouthed.

That left somewhere under the water. Maddock bit down on his regulator and sank beneath the waves. He spotted Kyle immediately. He was trapped beneath the capsized boat. His arms and legs thrashed wildly, but something was holding him fast. At least he was still alive.

Willis swam in front of Kyle and tried to gain his attention. He kept his distance for the moment. In his panic, a drowning man often took his would-be rescuer down with him. Kyle finally noticed him and when Willis made a placating gesture, he calmed down.

Maddock swam up and offered his regulator. Kyle must have dived before because he knew exactly what to do. Renewed by a fresh breath of air, he gave a thumbs-up and then pointed at the back of his neck.

He wore a crystal on a thick cord which had become wedged into a crack in the boat. Maddock took out his knife and cut the man free.

As the cord was severed in two, Kyle grabbed the crystal in both hands before swimming to the surface. Bones was now in the water, helping Kyle's sister onto the boat.

"Thanks, broseph," Kyle said as they swam over to *Sea Foam*. "Thought I was a goner for sure."

"You're welcome," Maddock said.

"You got that blond hair and dive suit and you're all buff," Kyle continued. "I was like, 'Dude, that is totally Aquaman.'"

Willis heard that and laughed. "You got a green and orange suit, Maddock?"

"No."

"Hey, what's up, Shaft?" Kyle said to Willis. The young man was surprisingly upbeat and not even winded after his underwater ordeal.

"What did you just call me?" Willis asked.

"I don't think he means anything by it," Maddock said. "I'm Maddock. This is Willis. The guy helping your sister is Bones. I wouldn't advise calling him by any other nickname than that unless he gives you express permission."

"Word." Kyle flashed a peace sign, then allowed Matt and Corey to help him up onto the *Sea Foam* where his sister waited.

"Thank you so much," the young woman said. She had light brown skin, a smattering of freckles across the bridge of her nose, and curly, shoulder length black hair. She was tall and willowy. Her brown eyes were filled with an intelligence that wasn't quite there with her brother. "I'm Raeána Franklin, Rae for short. And, as you know, that's my brother, Kyle."

"Everybody calls me Dogtown," Kyle said, already lounging on the deck as if he were on vacation.

"Nobody calls you that," Rae said. "You can keep trying to make it happen, but you'll never get that nickname to stick."

Maddock looked from one to the other. Aside from the curly hair, which wasn't even the same color, the two looked nothing alike. Kyle was the stereotypical surfer dude, with a deep tan, sun-bleached dirty blond hair, and vacant blue eyes.

"Same mom or same dad?" Willis asked.

"Both," said Kyle, while Rae responded, "Neither."

Maddock scratched his head at the odd response. Of the two, he figured Rae was the more reliable, so he flashed a quizzical glance in her direction.

"We were in the same foster home from junior high through high school," she said. "We're not blood relations."

"You don't need that to be family." Bones shot a glance at Maddock, then looked away. He and the rest of the crew had been saying things like that ever since Melissa had died. Maddock appreciated it, but was more than ready for them to stop treating him with kid gloves.

Kyle stretched luxuriously, yawned, and turned to gaze at the capsized sailboat. "How are we going to get Echard's boat back to him?"

Rae turned and gaped at him for a full second before smacking him on the back of the head.

"Echard? That's the person whose boat we borrowed? You said it belonged to Val."

"Did I?" Kyle rubbed the back of his head and

frowned.

"Who is Echard?" Bones asked.

"A local creep. He's always hanging around, ogling all the girls. He sells crappy trinkets, like the crystal Kyle almost died for. Rumor is he's into some shady stuff, too. Kyle's the only one who can stand him."

"He's not so bad. I mean, he lent us this boat for fifty bucks."

Rae let out an exasperated sigh and looked up at the heavens. "If you pay for it, it's not a loan, Kyle. Do you even know for certain that the boat belongs to him? I could totally see Echard charging you to take someone else's boat out."

"He said it was his."

"It'll be all right," Maddock said. "Matt and Willis have righted more capsized sailboats than I can count."

"We have?" Matt asked.

"And they've been dying to get into the water all day," Maddock said loudly.

With an assist from Bones, and a series of useless, shouted instructions from Kyle, they quickly righted the small craft and bailed out most of the water. Once they'd lowered the sail and secured the rigging, they secured the boat to *Sea Foam's* stern and towed it behind them as they returned to the island.

Kyle was a self-described Renaissance Man, although he pronounced it 'Renee's ants.' To hear him tell it, he was a musician, a poet, and a collector of stories.

"But most of all," he proclaimed, "I'm a man of the sea."

"You definitely remind me of some seamen I've known," Bones said, eliciting a choked laugh from Matt and a sharp glance from Rae.

The insult bounced right off of Kyle, who went on to explain that he was also a deep dive competitor. "I'm competing in Blue Descent. It's a deep dive competition, and they're holding it right here on Andros in one of the deepest blue holes in the world. You should check it out. They even have a beginner's competition tomorrow just for fun."

"Dude, Maddock and I are totally down for that," Bones said.

Maddock frowned and slowly turned toward Bones. "Are we?" He enjoyed diving, but only when there were sights to see or treasure to find.

Bones draped an arm around Maddock's shoulders. "Absolutely we are."

Kyle smiled and turned to Willis and Matt. "How about you two legends? Care to take the plunge?"

Willis gave a slow shake of his head. "That sounds like the kind of thing white people who burn a lot of incense are into."

Matt shrugged. "Sorry, I don't own any incense."

Kyle gave a nod of understanding and turned back to Maddock and Bones. "Guess it's just a threesome, then."

Maddock squeezed his eyes shut and counted to three, but when he opened them again, Kyle was still an idiot. He was already regaling the others with stories of the powers his crystal held. According to him, it could store up energy, be used to heal someone, or be used as a weapon.

"Crystal power," Bones said. "Imagine believing in that."

As they made their way back to the island, Maddock chatted with Rae. Unlike her brother, she was intelligent and clear-thinking. Maddock liked her from the start.

She and Kyle had grown up in Southern California. She'd been the studious, responsible one, and he the lovable buffoon who constantly stumbled into trouble.

"How did you end up in the Bahamas?" Maddock asked.

"I teach at the College of the Bahamas," she said.

"The pay isn't great, I don't have tenure, and on a good day all the old men in my department try to treat me like their Girl Friday instead of a colleague. But I love the islands. It's worth it just to be able to live here."

Maddock understood completely. He, too loved his home in Key West, Florida and had never given serious consideration to living anywhere else. His work as a treasure hunter was unsteady, always hit or miss. But the struggles and challenges were more than worthwhile if it allowed him to live his life in the islands and at sea.

"So, what's your story?" Rae asked.

Maddock briefly sketched out his life history for her. His time in the Navy SEALs, the death of his parents, followed by the death of his wife, and his new career as a treasure hunter. Sympathy welled in Rae's eyes as he spoke, and when he finished, she reached out and gave his arm a squeeze.

"I'm so sorry," she said. "I can't imagine what that feels like. My birth parents died so young I hardly remember them, and I've never been married."

"Someone with your brains and beauty? That's hard to believe," Maddock said, giving her a wink. God, he was acting like Bones.

Rae didn't seem to mind. "Thank you," she said, flashing a shy grin. "I imagine the ladies are beating down your door now that you're single."

"Are you freaking kidding me?" Bones said from the doorway. "If anyone's beating on his door, it's the women on the inside who are trying to get out."

"Your mom never wants to leave," Maddock said.

"Right," Rae said, looking from one man to the other with the expression of a weary schoolteacher. "Do you think Kyle is okay? I mean, he seems like himself, but who knows?"

"I don't think there's any permanent brain damage, but how would you be able to tell?" Bones said.

"Come on, now. I know he's a goofball, but he's still my brother. He's a dummy, but he's kind and has a good heart. I've kept him alive for over fifteen years. I can't lose him now."

"Bones doesn't mean anything by it," Maddock said. "He's a smart ass by nature. As is the rest of the crew."

"Yeah, I picked up on that. It's okay."

They lapsed into an awkward silence. Maddock racked his brain for something to talk about. Damn, Melissa hadn't been gone for much more than a year and he had already lost the ability to carry on a conversation with a woman. "Is the weather always this nice?" he asked and immediately felt like an idiot. The weather? Really?

"Yes, it is." There was a twinkle in her eye that said she knew he was struggling and she was enjoying it. She had no intention of letting him off the hook.

"So, what do you teach?" That was a little better.

"Biology, but my real passion is marine archaeology." She bit her lip. Anticipation brimmed in those sparkling brown eyes.

The slowly grinding gears of Maddock's brain began to turn a little faster. "I'm a marine archaeologist, too. My dad was obsessed with Captain Kidd. He was always traveling around, looking for his lost treasure. He researched other pirates too, but Kidd was his passion."

"That would be amazing," Rae said, "to have a dad who could instill that kind of passion in you. Did he include you in his treasure hunting?"

"Not really," Maddock said. "I was in school, and he traveled a great deal. But we talked about it a lot. I think that's where my interest comes from." A sudden thought occurred to him. "Say, we actually found something today that we can't identify. Would you like to take a look?"

Rae smiled broadly. "Of course I would. What is it?"

"I just told you, we don't know for sure. That's why I'd like your expert opinion." Maddock grinned.

"Fair enough. Let's see it."

Maddock led her below decks to the small cabin where they cleaned and preserve the artifacts they recovered. The egg lay in a tank of seawater. Rae drew in a sharp breath the moment she saw it.

"That is amazing," she said. "Is it okay if I touch it?"

"I think that's the first time a woman has ever asked Maddock that question," Bones said.

Rae ignored him. At Maddock's nod of consent she put on gloves, reached in, and took out the egg. Her eyes gleamed with fascination as she turned it over, closely examining every inch of its surface. Maddock could see the passion in her eyes, a passion that he shared. Perhaps he had found a kindred spirit.

"It definitely looks Old World to me," she said

"Who called it?" Bones said pumping his fist. "Nothing but net!"

"The humility is overwhelming," Rae said flatly. She returned her attention to the egg, her eyes drinking in the sight of it. "Many cultures made ceramic eggs, as I'm sure you already know. This one, though..." She weighed it in her hands. "It's so heavy, I can't help but wonder if there is something in here."

Maddock looked at Bones and nodded. The two of them had wondered the same thing.

"We thought so, too, but we're reluctant to cut into it without knowing for sure."

"If you don't mind," Rae continued, "we could take this to the college. We've got a scanner that we could use to see what's inside. We might also be able to get a better picture of what's engraved on the surface."

"That would be fantastic," Maddock said. "When would you like to do it?"

Rae considered for a moment. "Tell you what, we

can go tomorrow after you guys compete in the amateur dive competition." She smiled expectantly.

Maddock wasn't sure what to say. Free diving beyond safe distances for no good reason seemed like a bad idea to him. But something about Rae's smile made him want to give it a go.

"That's my condition," she said.

"You see, Maddock?" Bones said. "You've got to do it. It was meant to be."

Maddock shook his head. He didn't believe in fate or destiny, but he did believe in science, and right now, they needed access to Rae's lab equipment. The fact that he would get to spend a little more time with her was a bonus.

"All right, I'm in."

3

Andros Island, Bahamas

Andros Island was the largest of the Bahamian islands, boasting a land area greater than the other seven hundred islands combined. Andros consisted of three major islands: North Andros, Mangrove Cay, and South Andros. Over a hundred miles long and forty miles wide it its widest point, Andros was divided by "bights," estuaries that split the island into three and connected its east and west coasts. One of the least explored of all the islands in the chain, its largest industry was tourism. Most of the tourists were divers drawn by the Andros Barrier Reef, the world's sixth-largest, and to its many blue holes, water-filled cave systems. It was one of these blue holes, just offshore, where the Blue Descent dive competition was being held.

"I can't believe I let you talk me into trying this." Maddock stood on the shore and looked doubtfully out at the cobalt depths of the blue hole. Nearby, contest organizers sat behind a folding table, taking care of last-minute registrations. Deep divers from all around the world milled about, chatting amiably and swapping dive stories.

"I can't believe I had to talk you into it. It's a chance to dive in a freaking blue hole!" Bones reached out and gave Maddock a condescending pat on the head. "Don't worry, little guy. I'll take care of you."

Maddock smacked his hand away and spat a half-hearted curse. At a hair under six feet tall, Maddock was hardly little, but one couldn't help but appear diminished standing alongside the giant Cherokee. And Bones loved to rub that in.

"Seriously, though, do you know how dangerous this

is?" Maddock said as he scrutinized the platform that bobbed in the water. Around it, swimmers were positioning a rope ring supported by buoys. "People die in blue holes all the time. It's as bad as the fresh water caves back home."

Blue holes were large marine sinkholes or caverns that formed in limestone or other carbonate bedrock. Some were as deep as three hundred meters, while others led to submerged cave passages. They were fascinating and potentially deadly.

"Sure, a few people die. Idiots who don't know what the hell they're doing," Bones said. "Which is not us."

"Also, people who take too many risks. Which is all you, buddy."

Bones shrugged. "What you call risky, I call awesome."

"Story of our lives."

"Maybe we'll find gold down there," Bones said.

Maddock winced. The remainder of the crew had gone out to make another dive on the wreck they'd found. They were not pleased that it had not turned out to be a pirate ship laden with gold and jewels.

They made their way to the registration table. Behind it sat an impatient-looking woman with ebony skin and braids adorned with seashells that clacked when she turned her head. She was shaking her head and jabbing her finger at a sunburned man in a floral print shirt.

"Echard, I am not going to tell you again. You may not sell your trinkets here. This is a serious diving competition, not a beach party."

Maddock looked the man up and down. So this `was the allegedly shady character who had sold Kyle the magic crystal. He didn't look like a criminal, just a middle-aged white guy in a bucket hat, Hawaiian print shirt, and sandals. His leathery skin said he'd lived among the islands for a long time and hadn't bothered with sunscreen.

"Come on, Val," Echard said. "They're going to need all the luck they can get. What harm can a simple charm do?" Echard held up a handful of carved wooden fetishes on leather cords. To Maddock they looked more like something out of the South Pacific than the Caribbean.

Bones raised his hand like an attentive pupil. "Yo, dude. Didn't one of the kids on the Brady Bunch almost drown because he went out in the water with an idol around his neck?"

Maddock frowned at Bones. "The Brady Bunch? How old are you? Eighty?"

"Screw you, Maddock. The mom was hot."

Maddock groaned.

With one last, forlorn look at the competitors, Echard held up his bunch of carved idols in a gesture of faint hope. "Last chance." When no one replied, he shrugged and wandered away.

"What's his damage?" Bones asked.

"He's a local eccentric," the man in line in front of them said. He was a stocky fellow in his early thirties with a shaved scalp, prominent brow, and a shortage of neck. He spoke with a slight Russian accent. "They say he is annoying but harmless. That's what they say," he repeated.

"You don't think so?" Bones asked.

The man shrugged. "Something is wrong about him. I cannot say what."

Bones flashed a side-eyed glance at Maddock. "I think it's the shirt. He just doesn't fill it out like Magnum P.I."

"Your knowledge of popular culture is disturbingly dated," Maddock said.

"Not my fault. I stopped watching TV when I realized girls were more fun."

The Russian laughed at this and introduced himself. His name was Alexei, and he taught Russian at a small college near Tampa, Florida.

"I wouldn't have pegged you as a schoolteacher," Bones said.

Maddock agreed. Whatever Alexei's current vocation, he couldn't hide the telltale signs of military training. His posture, his manner, his way of moving all stood out to Maddock's experienced eye.

"It is a new career for me." Alexei didn't elaborate.

While they waited their turns, Alexei filled them in on Blue Descent. While such competitions were nothing new, this was one was special. The field was large, with top divers from around the world making the trip. The disciplines included: Constant Weight with Fins, Constant Weight No Fins, and Free Immersion. Although there were several beginners here, like Bones and Maddock, most of the competitors were serious, dedicated freedivers. All were hoping to break world records or records for their own nations. Alexei was aiming for the Russian record in Free Immersion.

"Dos Equis is actually sponsoring the contest. They provided some prize money and free t-shirts."

"You hear that, Maddock?" Bones asked. "Dos Equis. It's a sign." The beer was a staple among the crew of *Sea Foam*.

When Alexei asked, Maddock and Bones explained that they were beginners at deep diving, and were mostly interested in the challenge and the experience of diving in a blue hole.

"We won't be breaking any records," Maddock said.

"Speak for yourself," Bones said. "You never know what I might manage."

"Isn't that the truth."

As they continued to chat, Maddock's eyes drifted in the direction of the blue hole. He saw Kyle make a swan dive from the floating platform into the water. *Must be getting warmed up for tomorrow, when the serious divers take their turn*, Maddock thought. Categorizing Kyle as serious in any respect felt wrong. Just then, a sharp voice called out to him.

"You two, come here." The woman called Val looked up from her work at the table and pointed at them with a cheap ballpoint pen. "I need to speak with you right now."

Bemused, they made their way up to the table.

"Did I hear you correctly? You're not deep divers?"

"We're not deep divers but we've dived deep," Bones said. "Even in the water, sometimes."

"What my friend is trying to say," Maddock began, shouldering past Bones, "is that we're novices to competitive diving, but we're experienced professional divers."

Val was uncertain about the wisdom of the two men participating.

"It's a novice competition, but we like for contestants to have some experience."

Maddock gave her the high points of their diving experience and she eventually came around.

"If you two were SEALs, surely you've got at least a modicum of common sense." She paused, glanced at Maddock. "Well, blue eyes here looks like he's got common sense. I'm not sure about ponytail." She pointed her pen at Bones. "I've got a bad feeling about you."

Bones leaned forward, rested his elbows on the table, and smiled. "In that case, I think you should get to know me better. Drinks are on me."

Val rolled her eyes and let out a tired sigh. "Just don't give me any trouble. I've already got Dogtown to worry about."

"You mean Kyle?" Maddock asked.

Val nodded. "That's the one. His sister had to leave, but she asked me to keep an eye on him." Val suddenly frowned. "Where has that dummy gone?"

"I saw him diving from the platform." Maddock turned and scanned the water. He saw no sign of Kyle.

"Oh, no! That idiot said something about practice, but surely he wouldn't try it when…" She rose from her chair and hurried toward the water, stripping off her shorts and t-shirt as she went.

Maddock and Bones were faster. In a matter of seconds the two men were in the water and making a beeline for the dive platform. They reached it quickly, and paused only a few moments for breath before diving.

The dark blue water seemed to go on forever. Maddock had never looked into such an abyss, at least, not a literal one. Even with Bones swimming beside him, the sight made him feel strangely alone.

Maddock saw no sign of Kyle, but he kept swimming, his eyes searching the darkness. He pinched his nose and forced air into his ears to equalize the pressure. Invisible coils seemed to wrap around his chest, squeezed tight. What they were doing right now was dangerous, reckless even, but they had to try.

He kicked harder, driving himself deeper and deeper. His throat was feeling tight. He could hold his breath longer than most, but everyone had their limits. Down below was unending waters of deep blue. No sign of the missing diver.

And then the young man was there, eyes closed, floating up toward him. Maddock grabbed the unconscious man around the chest and swam for the surface. Seconds later, Bones joined him. Even with their combined efforts, it was a struggle to carry the man's weight.

Maddock saw spots in front of his eyes. Oxygen deprivation was getting to him.

Almost there, he told himself.

And they broke the surface. The heat of the sun was a welcome sensation on Maddock's face as he emerged and sucked in precious air. Two more people came to their aid—Val and Alexei. The four of them hauled Kyle's limp body onto the platform.

"I cannot believe this dude keeps trying to drown himself," Bones said. "That's two days in a row."

Maddock performed two rescue breaths and then began chest compressions. In most cases of near-drowning, constriction of the larynx prevented much water from entering the lungs, which meant almost all of it ended up in the person's stomach.

"Come on, you big dummy," Val said. "Rae will kill me if I let something happen to him."

Seconds later, to Maddock's great relief, Kyle sucked in a long, wet breath. He rolled the young man over on his side as Kyle vomited what seemed like an ocean of sea water. Finally, he caught his breath and flopped onto his back, arms splayed.

"Whoa! That was awesome!" He opened his eyes. "Hey, guys! Long time, no see!"

"Good thing we were here…again," Maddock said.

"Isn't that the truth. I knew my crystal would bring me good luck."

"Crystals," Bones mumbled. "Looks like Rae is back."

Maddock turned to see Rae standing on the shore, hands on hips. She wore a loose-fitting tank top over a two-piece swimsuit. He would have liked to sit and admire her for a minute, but the concern on her face urged him along.

"Let's get back to the shore so your sister can yell at you," Maddock said.

"I can't wait."

By the time they got Kyle back to the shore he was showing no ill effects of his near drowning and was, in fact, in good spirits.

"Don't worry about me," he said. "I'm fine. Really."

"Yesterday was an accident, but what you did today was dumb. I thought you were an experienced diver," Bones said.

"I am. I was just going to go down about twenty meters, just to get a feel for the place. Then I saw something." He trailed off

"What did you see?" Rae asked.

Kyle shook his head. "Forget it. You'll just laugh at me."

"Bro, I hate to tell you, but that ship has sailed," Bones said, grinning at Maddock.

Maddock gave a small shake of his head then turned to Kyle. "Go ahead. We're listening."

Kyle took a deep breath and sighed. He sat down on the sand, knees pulled to his chest, arms folded around his shins. He gave a small shake of his head.

"It was weird," he said. "I was just getting ready to come back up when I looked down and there was a girl there.

"A girl?" Rae asked, her tone neutral.

Kyle nodded. "Look, I know how that sounds. But I really did see her." He paused as if waiting for someone to argue. When no protest came, he continued. "Anyway she was, like, motioning to me like she needed my help." He made a beckoning gesture. "I didn't think, I just went after her. She wasn't too far away and I thought I could get to her quickly. But the harder I swam, the farther away she seemed to get. Not, like, a long way away, but just a little. I could almost touch her and then she'd be just out of reach. Over and over again. And then, next thing I knew, I didn't know anything," He shrugged, held up his palms.

Maddock saw no harm in taking his story seriously. "What did the woman look like?"

"Yeah, was she hot?" Bones grinned.

"She was pretty. Really pretty. At least that's how she looked from what I could see. It was pretty dark down there. Not much sunlight that deep."

"Can you tell us anything else about her?"

Rae flashed Maddock a frown, obviously puzzled as to why he appeared to be taking the story seriously.

Kyle squinted, concentrating. The effort appeared to be painful. "Light skin. Long hair. I'm not sure the color, but it wasn't brown or black. Maybe red or dirty blonde." He thought for a few more seconds and then his face brightened. "She was holding something. I think it was a knife."

"Was she wearing scuba gear?" Bones asked

Kyle shook his head.

"Let me get this straight. You saw hot chick way the hell down under the water holding a knife and trying to get you to swim deeper. She didn't have any scuba gear on. And you thought it would be a good idea to just swim on down to her." Bones folded his powerful arms across his chest and waited for the reply.

"That is this about the size of it, my angry red friend. She looked like she was in trouble so I went to help her. When somebody's in danger, Dogtown doesn't waste time thinking."

"That's redundant," Bones said.

"I didn't realize you even knew that word," Maddock said.

"Screw you, Maddock."

"Seriously, though," Maddock went on. "You aren't exactly known for thinking things through when action is called for."

"Fair enough, but I'm not going to let some chick lure me to my death, no matter how hot she is."

Maddock smothered a cough with his fist. He resisted the urge to throw in a little comment. Bones had done plenty of foolish things when an attractive woman was involved.

"I'm sure you'll be fine," he said to Kyle. "Just rest here for a little while." He turned, took Rae by the hand, and they walked a short distance away until they were out of earshot.

"Do you really think he's all right?" Rae whispered. "And please, no wisecracks about brain damage."

"I think he will be. I've seen people stay under much longer than he just did and end up being fine."

"But what about this vision of a woman? Should I be worried that something happened to him?" She tapped the side of her head.

"It was probably a hallucination brought on by lack of oxygen. It's not uncommon. It's sort of like the supposed after-death experiences of people die briefly on the operating table. As they're dying, the synapses in their brain begin to rapid-fire. It causes strange visions, the mind dreams the same sort of dreams they've heard about other dying people having. The person only believes they've had after death experience because they have no way of knowing at what moment the vision actually happened."

"Should I take him to a hospital?"

"Do you think he would even agree to go? Look at him." Maddock glanced in Kyle's direction. He was already on his feet and asking for a beer.

Rae's shoulders sagged. "I guess you're right. I love the guy, but he is high maintenance. If I took him to the E.R. every time he hurt himself, I'd be bankrupt."

Maddock consulted his dive watch. "What do you say we catch the ferry to Nassau? If we leave now we can get the early boat."

Rae shook her head. "No way, buddy. Not until the novice contest is over. That was the deal."

"That's not how I remember it."

"I don't care how you remember it. You want the use of my lab, you compete in the contest."

"Why do you care so much?"

"It doesn't matter why. It only matters that I do care." She winked at him and smiled.

For a moment, Maddock lost his train of thought. She was so beautiful. And then another thought came to him unbidden. Melissa. She hadn't been gone all that long and here he was flirting with a girl. What was wrong with him?

"Are you all right? I'm sorry if I upset you. I was only teasing."

"No, it's fine. I want to make the dive. Who knows? Maybe there really is a mysterious woman down there."

"Great! And I promise that as soon as the competition is over, we'll take a peek inside this egg of yours."

The egg! Maddock had been carrying it in a backpack, but in the excitement, had dropped it somewhere. Where was it? He looked around but didn't see it.

"Hey, Bones! Have you seen my bag?"

"That's not a nice thing to call your girlfriend," Bones said. His grin vanished almost as quickly as it had appeared. "You mean the one with the egg?

"Yes. That one."

They both began to scan the crowd. Bones' sharp eyes quickly picked out someone moving away from the group. It was a man in a floral shirt, and he was carrying an orange and blue backpack. It was Echard

"Yo, Echard! Get back here with that!" Bones deep voice boomed across the noise of the gathered divers. The man did not pay any attention to them. He kept walking at a leisurely pace. He might not have heard Bones, but Maddock doubted it.

Maddock took off at a sprint and closed the gap

quickly. He was almost on top of his quarry when Echard finally turned around.

"What the hell, man? Why are you chasing me?" Echard demanded, holding his hands up as if he were under arrest.

"That's my bag you are stealing."

"I'm not stealing anything." Eckert looked down at the bag in his hand. "You mean this? This is mine."

"I don't think so." Bones a caught up with him, snatched the bag away, and held it up in front of Echard's face. "Unless your driver's license says Maddock." He pointed to Maddock's name written in black marker near the top.

"Oh." Echard frowned. "I thought it was mine. I've got one just like it. Sorry," he added belatedly.

"It's all right," Maddock said, though he did not in fact think things were all right. He thought Rae and Alexei were right about this fellow. He was sketchy.

Echard made an apologetic wave, then turned and continued to walk away from the beach.

"Don't you need to go find your bag?" Maddock asked.

Echard stumbled, then glanced back over his shoulder, still walking. "No, I just remembered I left it at home." With that he turned and hurried away.

"Right," Bones said, his voice dripping with sarcasm. "And the Pope doesn't crap in the woods."

Rae looked at Maddock and frowned.

"Don't try and make sense of Bones. Just give him some attention. That's all he really wants."

"What I really want," Bones said, "is the attention of that Japanese chick over there. Call me when the contest starts."

Rae shook her head as he walked away. "I'm sure he's going to make it far calling women 'chicks' and the like."

"He says things for the shock value. He insists his favorite football team is the Redskins. He's been known to wear a Redskins t-shirt when he goes home to the reservation, just to piss people off." Bones had grown up on the Cherokee reservation in North Carolina, where the rest of his family still lived.

"He is one of a kind," Rae said.

"That's true," Maddock agreed. "And thank God for that. I love the guy, but I wouldn't want two of him."

"And that," Rae said, "is exactly how I feel about my brother." She gave him a quick, impulsive kiss on the cheek. "Come on," she said, "I want to see you dive."

4

By the time the dive contest began, Maddock still was not quite sure about it. He'd done plenty of diving in his time, but with proper equipment. On the rare occasion he had attempted a deep free dive, it had always been for a good reason — usually a life or death situation. But to attempt what they were about to try solely for sport seemed absurd.

"I can tell what you're thinking," Bones said. "Just trust me for once."

"Why do you always say that? We've been putting our lives in one another's hands for years, but you act like I never listen to you."

"You're right. And you're still alive, aren't you? So shut up and do the dive. If it's too tough for you, you can go down a few feet and wuss out. I won't stop you." Bones flashed a grin and glanced back toward the shore where Rae and Kyle stood. "Of course, your girlfriend will be disappointed in you if you don't give it your best effort."

"Come on, Bones you know it hasn't been that long since Melissa…" He couldn't bring himself to say it.

"Look, Maddock, I get it. I loved her, too. I was there the moment you two met. It sucks that she's gone, but it's been more than long enough." When Maddock opened his mouth to object, Bones spoke over him. "Almost two years," he said slowly.

Maddock frowned. Had it really been that long? "How did the time go by so fast? What have I been doing?"

"Working your ass off. Having no fun."

Maddock nodded. "Oh, what the hell? Okay, let's do this."

They swam out to the platform where they received their final instructions.

The divers would descend straight down, holding on to a rope. The diver would descend as deep as he or she was able. Upon returning to the surface, the diver was required to remove all facial equipment, give a visual "okay" sign and a verbal okay in order for the dive to be complete. Scuba divers would be all around, keeping an eye on the contestants, ready to provide aid if needed.

Maddock glanced over at Bones, who was keeping pace with him. The pair were a good five meters deeper than the other amateur divers. It looked like one of the two former SEALs would be the winner. Maddock's heart raced. He was actually excited. Sure, it was a stupid contest, but no more foolish than his and Bones' constant attempts to beat each other at rock climbing. It was a passion the two shared, and they seldom missed an opportunity to race to the top. Well, they'd see if Bones could beat him this time.

He continued his slow steady descent. He was beginning to run out of air. His chest constricted, his heart thudded, his throat was tight. He stole another glance at Bones and could tell that his friend was experiencing similar symptoms.

This is going to be tough. He's too stubborn to quit. Then again, so am I.

And that was when Maddock saw her. Saw something, anyway. It looked like a human shape, coming closer. Higher and higher it floated. He saw dark eyes, a gaping mouth, a halo of hair spread out around its head. And then darkness.

Maddock's eyes snapped open. Through the stinging, cold saltwater, he saw a diver swimming toward him. He felt strong arms around his chest. Bones had a hold of him. He tapped Bones arm twice to let him know he was okay and felt his friend release him. The diver, one of the competition's volunteers, removed his regulator and handed it to Maddock. They buddy breathed their way back to the surface, where Maddock swam to the platform.

"Second place as usual," Bones said. "Too bad, Maddock."

"Your buddy beat you by less than a meter," Val said. "You guys got some serious depth. I just wish you'd come back up before you blacked out. That was close."

Maddock nodded. He'd rather them believe he blacked out than tell them what he thought he had seen. Bones, however, wasn't fooled. He frowned and Maddock gave a small shake of his head.

"Sorry about that," Maddock said. "My mistake."

Val patted him on the shoulder. "It's fine. Just glad you're okay."

Bones leaned over and whispered, "What's going on?"

"I'll tell you later." Maddock turned to see Rae standing on the beach, looking in his direction and clapping. She had no idea what had happened. "Actually, I'll make a deal with you. You babysit Kyle while Rae and I go to the lab, and I'll tell you what I saw."

"So you saw something down there? Tell me it wasn't the girl Kyle saw."

"No comment. You going to babysit for us or not?"

Bones stared at him his eyes narrowed speculatively. The two had been best friends for so long that sometimes they could read one another's thoughts, but the thoughts Bones seemed to be reading had nothing to do with the mysterious figure under the water. There was a sudden twinkle in his eye.

"That's what I'm talking about!" Bones slapped Maddock on the shoulder. "Take her out for a drink. If all goes well, the egg can wait until morning. I'm sure there are plenty of empty hotel rooms on Nassau."

That was way too much for Maddock to think about right now, but he played along.

"We'll see how it goes." The truth was, he thought he would enjoy spending some time with Rae. He was also eager to see what, if anything, was hidden inside the egg. But try as he might, he couldn't get the thought of that spectral figure out of his mind.

5

Brigadier's Restaurant was a seafood bar located on the northwest coast of Andros just off the Queen's Highway, just a few miles from Blue Holes National Park. The indoor dining area was situated at the end of a pier, offering picturesque views of the sea.

Bones chose an outdoor table and ordered a round of mojitos while he and Kyle waited for the remainder of their party to arrive. It wasn't his usual drink but at the end of a hot day, he couldn't deny the minty concoction of white rum and citrus was refreshing. The gentle rush of the waves and the whisper of the breeze rustling the palm trees made for a pleasant atmosphere. He could almost allow himself to relax. But there was Kyle to consider.

"How deep do you think the water is down there?" Kyle asked, peering over the rail.

"Six feet maybe? Why?"

"When I have a few too many, I've been known to dive. Mostly from hotel balconies."

Bones shook his head. "Babysitting a grown man," he grumbled.

"What was that?" a voice asked. He turned to see Val, followed by Alexei and an attractive woman of Japanese descent, whom Val introduced as Koharu Shimizu, another freediver.

"What disciplines are you competing in?" Bones asked Shimizu, trying to start a conversation with the attractive young woman.

"I've competed in all three," she said. "But I'm just here for fun. I'm expecting, you see."

"Oh, congrats."

"Thank you. I'm trying to choose the perfect blue

hole for giving birth."

"What was that?"

"I'm going to give birth in a blue hole," she said. "Babies are aquatic creatures. I can't think of anything more fitting than giving birth underwater. My boyfriend is a diver, too."

"You do realize babies can't breathe underwater after they're born," Bones said.

"I know. I'm still working that part out," she said.

"Buddy breathing?" Kyle asked. "You know, with a SCUBA tank?"

The pair launched into a discussion of alternative childbirth methods.

"Those two are a pair," Val said. She bought a round for the table, which raised her several notches in Bones' book. Now that she was no longer stuck running the registration table at Blue Descent, Bones found that he enjoyed her company. She was bright and seemed to love the ocean as much as he did.

"You seem a little antsy," Val finally said. "Do you need a dose of Ritalin?"

"Oh, don't pay any attention to me. It's just that my friend ditched me so he could hang out with a girl while I'm stuck babysitting her brother."

Val pursed her lips and frowned. "If you're his age and you still need babysitting, you need to examine your life."

"You should meet some of my students," Alexei said. "Old enough to fight and die for their country but ask them for a five-page paper and they act like they're living through the siege of Leningrad."

"Cheers," Bones said, chuckling. They clinked bottles and drank deeply.

"So, what brings you to the islands? Not an amateur dive competition, I'll wager," Val said.

Bones explained that he and Maddock were marine

archaeologists, and that they were searching for the wreck of legendary pirate Riddick Blackwood's ship, *Maelstrom*.

"So you are a treasure hunter."

"Is that a bad thing?"

Val considered for a moment, then shook her head, the seashells in her braids clicking. "Not necessarily."

"That's good, then. I don't want to get on the bad side of the only woman at the table with a fully-functioning brain." He glanced at Kyle and Shimizu who were discussing the relative merits of various crystals.

"Did you know you can grind up rose quartz and drink it with water as a treatment for kidney stones?" Kyle asked.

"I think that's more likely to cause kidney stones," Alexei said.

"Not if you do it right," Kyle said seriously.

"Are you going to drink that?" Alexei pointed to the crystal around Kyle's neck.

"I don't know. Echard wasn't sure what its powers are. I need to wait and see what, exactly I've got here."

Bones rolled his eyes, then took another drink. "I don't suppose any of you know any good pirate legends, do you?"

Val frowned, considered. "Legends? Not sure about that. But I can tell you a little history."

Bones resisted the urge to let out a groan. Maddock was the history nerd. But, he liked Val and didn't want to give offense so he flashed a smile and nodded.

"Nassau, or New Providence as it was known then, was once the home of the Republic of Pirates," Val began.

Bones perked up. The Republic of Pirates? This might be one history lesson that was actually worth paying attention to. "Never heard of it."

"It was a sort of confederacy among pirates and self-described privateers in the region. It lasted about ten years until just after the turn of the eighteenth century. It wasn't an official republic, not in the technical sense, but they did work together under a unified code of conduct."

"Are you freaking kidding me? Even pirates have to behave? It's not grade school."

Val grinned and shook her head. "No, it wasn't like that. It was a set of guidelines on how they went about their business. Not just the way they interacted with one another, but how crew members should be treated, how plunder was shared, and how a captain could be deposed."

"That's... unexpected," Bones said. "I thought things would be a little more cutthroat than that. No pun intended."

"Sometimes it was. The interesting thing about the Code of Conduct is that it was a way for pirates to guarantee better working conditions onboard their ships than did most merchant and naval vessels. In a pirate crew, an African or an Irishman was equal to an Englishman or any other. Several mulattos even became captains during that time."

Bones nodded. He was not surprised that pirates would treat their crews better than the Navy treated its sailors. He'd been there, done that.

"It's really a fascinating time period," Val said. "Lots of colorful figures. The two most famous, and the two who dominated the Republic, were pirate captains named Henry Jennings and Benjamin Hornigold."

Bones nearly spewed his drink all over the table. He took a moment to clear his throat. "Hornigold?" he rasped. "Seriously? I mean, I get excited at the thought of treasure but come on."

Val's small, pitying smile was almost enough to embarrass him. Almost.

"How old are you?" Val asked. "I nearly didn't say

his name because I expected a reaction of that sort."

"And yet you brought him up anyway. On some level you find me amusing."

"Keep telling yourself that. I mentioned him because so few people know about him, yet he was a significant figure in history."

"I do not understand this joke," Alexei said.

"Horny is an American idiom for sexual arousal," Val said.

"Oh, a pun," Alexei said. "I understand. A joke, but a small one, I think."

"That's the only thing small about me."

"Lots of guys say that, but none of them live up to the advance billing."

Bones laughed, then returned to the subject at hand. "Tell me about Hornigold."

"Well, he was a mentor to Edward Teach."

"Blackbeard," Bones said.

"Yes. Thanks for interrupting. Also Sam Bellamy and Stede Bonnet. And Jennings was a mentor to Charles Vane, Calico Jack Rackham, and the so-called 'pirate queens' Ann Bonny, and Mary Read."

"Pirate chicks," Bones said approvingly. "Feminist buccaneers."

"Do you ever stop with the lame comments?" Val said, signaling the server for another drink.

"Think of me as Mystery Science Theater. Most of my jokes are weak, but when one lands, it's a thing of beauty."

"Right now, I think of you as a bit of a misogynist."

"No, just a smartass. I'll shut up now."

Val raised her eyebrows. Though she was a foot shorter than Bones, she managed to appear as if she were looking down upon him. "I doubt that. Anyway, even though they were rivals, the two pirates formed the so-called 'Flying Gang' and quickly became famous for their exploits. At one point, there were over a thousand pirates living in Nassau, and only a few hundred inhabitants. Eventually they became powerful enough that they dared to challenge the Royal Navy on occasion."

"I'll bet that didn't go over well across the pond."

"Definitely not. King George the First appointed a governor of the Bahamas, a man named Woodes Rogers, to bring an end to piracy in the islands. He came to the Bahamas with a fleet of ships and an offer of pardon to any pirate who turned themselves in and vowed never to return to piracy. Hornigold took the deal." She paused, but Bones didn't offer any more one-liners. "Although some pirates, like Charles Vane and Blackbeard, escaped capture, Hornigold managed to take ten of his former comrades prisoner."

"Hold on. He didn't just take the deal, but he flipped to the other side?"

"No honor among thieves, or pirates. Anyway that ended the pirates' dominance in the Bahamas but not in the rest of the Caribbean. As the remaining pirates fled, they spread out across the region. That began what is known as the Golden Age of Piracy."

"That's actually a really cool story. I don't suppose you know anything about Riddick Blackwood, do you?"

Val frowned for a moment. "No, sorry."

Bones shrugged and took another drink. It had been a shot in the dark. Of course he couldn't possibly get that lucky.

"Excuse me," a delicate voice said from behind him. "But I heard what you said, and I happen to know a lot about Riddick Blackwood."

He turned and could not help but suck in his breath sharply at the sight before him. It was a woman, and a drop dead gorgeous woman at that. She had long red hair, so impossibly red it couldn't possibly be natural. Her creamy skin was out of place among the dark-skinned locals and sunburned tourists. She had big green eyes that sparkled like emeralds, and a few other assets he was trying very hard not to stare it, but her form-fitting tank top and shorts made that a challenge.

"I'm sorry, what did you say?" He blinked twice. There was something about her that made him feel dazed.

"I said, I know a lot about Riddick Blackwood." Her voice was almost musical. "And if you'd like to buy a girl a drink, I'll tell you all about it."

Bones was about to accept the offer, but then he remembered that he was supposed to be keeping an eye on Kyle.

Val read his expression immediately. "You go ahead. I'll keep an eye on him." She gestured with her chin in the direction of Kyle, who was extolling the virtues of homeopathy to Koharu, who was listening intently. The pair glanced in their direction and Kyle frowned at Thel, blinked, then turned away.

"Are you sure?" Bones asked. "He literally might jump over the rail at any second if he thinks there's something interesting down there. He's already considered it."

"I have three younger brothers, all of them knuckleheads. I've got this."

"I can help," Alexei said. "I've got nothing better to do until tomorrow."

Bones thanked them and told them where *Sea Foam* was docked. "After dinner, if you'll hand him over to my friends on the crew, that would be great. I don't know when to expect Maddock and Rae." On impulse, he gave Val a quick, around the shoulder hug. "You are the man."

Val turned to the redhead. "Good luck with this one. He never knows the right thing to say."

Bones introduced himself to the woman, who said

her name was Thel.

"Short for Thelma?"

"No. It's short for Thelxiope. It's Greek."

"It's pretty," Bones said, unable to find a mental footing. This was crazy. Thel was hardly the first beautiful woman he chatted up, but there was something about her that he found intoxicating.

"Thank you. You have nice eyes." The simple complement sent shivers down his spine.

"So, what's your poison?" He inclined his head in the direction of the bar.

"Oh, I didn't mean buy me a drink literally. That stuff really is poison. I was thinking we could take a walk."

"Sounds good to me." Bones offered his elbow and she hooked her arm in his. Her touch was electric. It reminded him of the sensation he'd felt the first time he'd held hands with a girl. But that had been a long time ago and him just a kid. He found himself both excited and unsettled to have such a reaction now. Before he realized what he was doing, he leaned down and gave her a quick kiss on the lips.

She smiled and took a step back. "Slow down, Casanova. We just met. But it was a very nice kiss."

"Sorry. I just like you a lot."

"I like you, too."

She took his hand and they strolled along the pier back toward shore, basking in the glow of the afternoon sun. Bones tried to make conversation, but Thel didn't seem to want to talk.

"So, where are you from?"

"Here." She didn't elaborate.

"Lived here long?"

"A very long time."

For a girl who, moments before had come right up to him and boldly asked him to buy her a drink, she sure seemed closed-lipped now. A thought occurred to him. Holy crap, what if she was a hooker and this was a business transaction? He'd made that mistake before.

"What kind of work do you do?"

"I'm a recruiter."

"Corporate?"

She shrugged. "It's a small organization. We conduct genetic research. I would tell you more about it but I..." She paused, thinking.

"Signed an NDA?" Bones finally asked.

Thel nodded vigorously. "That's right," she said, smiling. "Sorry, I'm a little out to lunch." Her smile evaporated.

"Are you here on business or for pleasure? Or a little of both?"

Thel's brow furrowed as if the question confused her. "I'm attending a conference at the resort up the road," she said quickly. "It's just that I don't like to talk about my job. It's not much fun and I hardly get any time away from it."

"You said you could tell me about Riddick Blackwood," Bones said, changing the subject.

She frowned. "Blackwood? Oh, yes." She let go of Bones' hand, turned, and leaned against the rail. The afternoon sun sparkled in her eyes and on her fiery hair. She suddenly looked sad. "Riddick Blackwood is a rapacious man. His appetites can never be satisfied."

Bones thought the use of the present tense was odd. The girl had a flair for the dramatic. "Did those appetites include treasure?"

Thel nodded but didn't elaborate. An odd flask was hooked to her belt. Somehow, Bones hadn't noticed it until now. The woman really muddled his senses. It was a rustic looking thing, made of clay and stoppered with an old cork.

"That's cool? Is that some kind of antique?

Thel glanced down at the flask and her cheeks reddened. "Not an antique, but you can't buy it at Woolworth's."

Bones scratched his head. "I don't think that chain is around anymore."

Thel winced and looked away. She seemed to be debating something. Then she hastily unhooked and unstoppered it, took a drink, and then offered it to him.

"You should try this," she said quickly. "It's the best water in the world."

"I don't know about that. I grew up in the Appalachians. Have you ever taken a drink from a mountain spring?"

"I'm not joking," she said. "This stuff is groovy." She thrust the flask into his hands, rose up on her tiptoes, and whispered in his ear. "I promise you. It really is the best water in the world."

Bones felt goosebumps on his neck where her warm breath caressed his skin. He looked down at the flask. Not only was it made of clay, but the inside was lined with something green. Moss or seaweed or something like that.

"This thing is handcrafted."

"I made it myself. It's one of my hobbies." She put a finger under the flask and tilted it up toward his lips. "Now, drink."

Bones drank. The moment the water touched his lips he knew Thel had been right. This was the best water in the world. It was like nectar of the gods. Tingled in a refreshing way, and he felt a tingling sensation all over his body. His head, already swimming just for being this close to the beautiful young woman, began to drift into a beautiful daydream that involved the two of them, an isolated beach, and lots of tanning oil.

Thel snatched it away almost immediately. "Not too much," she said.

"Whoa, these edibles have got a kick," he joked.

She frowned. "It's water."

He began to explain that he'd only been kidding, but she ignored him.

"Let's get out of here," she said.

"Could I have another drink, first?" He'd only gotten a taste, not even one good swallow, but he was dying for another drink.

"Maybe later. Let's keep walking."

He couldn't explain why, but he wanted to do whatever this young woman said. It wasn't just that she was beautiful. She was… persuasive.

They took off their shoes and walked in the surf. Bones did most of the talking. He began with the broad strokes, family, friends, his time in the service. But soon he was revealing deeply personal things, stuff he didn't even talk to Maddock about. He was aware of what he was doing, but he couldn't stop himself.

For her part, Thel said little. Oddly, her vocabulary was peppered with outdated idioms like groovy, hip, and I can dig it. He didn't mind. Her presence was intoxicating.

He felt as if he were flying, and he looked down to make sure his feet still touched the sand. He was surprised to see that despite that heat of the late afternoon, fog was rolling in off the sea. He looked around. He couldn't see the sun, or the sky for that matter. All he could see was Thel's smiling face.

"This water is kicking my ass," he said. "In a good way." He wondered if he ought to be concerned. This couldn't be ordinary water. She must have dosed him, but looking into her eyes, he didn't care.

"It's trippy the first time you drink it," she said. "But don't worry. It's just very good water."

"Are you sure?" he said. "This is nothing like a mountain spring."

"You are not what I expected," Thel said quickly.

"What do you mean?"

"The truth is, I thought you were all brawn and no brains. Good breeding stock."

"You make me sound like a prize stallion," he said. "But don't get me wrong. I like to have a good time as much as the next guy, but I'm not interested in reproducing any time soon."

Thel gazed at him for what felt like an eternity. Her eyes were narrowed in concentration. She bit her lip.

"You all right?" he asked.

"How do you feel?" she asked, tension filling her voice.

"Like I'm floating in a cloud." He paused. "My mouth tastes weird. Really, really dry."

"We'll get you something to drink."

"You've got water."

"No!" she said abruptly. "You shouldn't have too much. It's a bad idea."

"Okay, no worries." He couldn't hide his disappointment. He could think of nothing but another drink.

"Oh, don't look like that. I'm sure there's something else we could do." She smiled and batted her eyelashes like an actress in an old movie.

"What did you have in mind?"

"Come on. I know a place."

Wandering in a half-stupor, Bones allowed her to lead him away. He didn't know where they were headed, but right now he'd follow this girl to the gates of hell.

6

Nassau, Bahamas

The College of the Bahamas was located in the capital city of Nassau on the island of New Providence, just a short ferry ride from Andros. The main building was a two-story structure, its entrance done in Greek Revival style, with a pedimented gable supported by four massive white columns. Palm trees flanked the entrance, swaying in the breeze. Three tall, arched wooden doors provided access inside.

Classes were not in session, so the building, like the rest of the campus, was eerily quiet. Rae led the way along a series of corridors and up a flight of stairs to a door simply marked *Laboratory*. She looked around nervously.

"Is something wrong?" Maddock asked.

"No. It's just that… It's not that I'm not allowed to be in here, it's just that I don't normally work in this lab. I'd rather not have to explain to anyone what I'm doing."

"But you're on the faculty?"

"Yes. I'm a female faculty member in a department of male academics in the field of Biological Science. That doesn't garner me a lot of respect."

Just then, they heard the sound of footsteps approaching. Rae hurriedly unlocked the lab door and ushered him inside. Leaving the lights off, she closed the door behind them and they waited listening.

The footsteps came closer.

There was a small window in the door and Maddock peered out. All he could see, however, was the outline of a figure silhouetted in front of a large picture window.

"Can you see anything?" Rae whispered.

"It's a man," he said softly. "But I can't tell much else." He didn't feel as if they were in danger. But he also didn't want Rae to get into trouble while doing a favor for him.

"Let me look." Rae slipped in front of him and he took a step back so she could look outside. "And there he goes, whoever he is." She turned and smiled. "Must've been one of the maintenance staff. We ought to be okay. I didn't see a single light on in any of the offices." She flipped on the light. "I don't know what I was so nervous about. I have a right to be here, even if certain people don't think so."

"Anyone in particular?"

"Yes." She flashed him a dark look but said no more and Maddock didn't press.

Rae took the egg out of the backpack and carried it over to a device that Maddock did not immediately recognize. It was a metal square with a hinged door on the front, like a smaller version of a dishwasher you'd find in a commercial kitchen. Except it was connected to a keyboard. She opened the door and carefully placed the egg in an upright position with its base in a concave stand at the center of what looked like an old record turntable.

"Are we going to play it like a phonograph record?"

"Ha ha, funny guy. This is a knockoff version of a 3-D scanner. The object slowly rotates and this row of lasers," she pointed to a vertical strip of tiny lights running up one side of the interior, "casts light on the surface. The instrument reads the wavelengths of the reflected light and the results are transferred to the computer over here." She pointed to a monitor a few feet away. "It's essentially the modern way of making a plaster cast of something. But it's much more accurate. The lasers record lines that have mostly faded away, and it doesn't damage the instrument."

Maddock had heard of this technology but had never seen it in action. "Interesting. I've been wanting to see one of these."

"It's funny you mentioned phonograph records," she said as she closed the door on the scanner. "Back in the eighties, 3-D scanners used what they called contact probes, sensors that actually touched the artifact, like a record needle touched the spinning record, and recorded the bumps and dips. This way is much more accurate and there's no risk of harm to the artifact." She tapped a few keys and the computer flared to life. A few more commands and the scanner began to hum.

"How long does the process take?" Maddock asked.

"Not long at all. It's not a large artifact and it appears to be in decent shape."

They stood in silence, watching the computer screen as if waiting for a cake to rise. After a few minutes he began to feel a little foolish.

"You know what they say about a watched pot," Maddock said.

"You're right. We need a way to kill time." Rae thought for a moment. "Tell you what. You tell me something you've never told anyone else."

"Does that include Bones? Because I gave up trying to keep anything from that guy a long time ago. He is ridiculously nosy."

Rae made a disapproving frown. "Do your best."

Maddock considered the question for a moment. There were plenty of things he had never told anyone, but in most cases there was a very good reason for his silence. Hell, a lot of the stuff he wasn't even allowed to talk about.

"I found the wreckage of Amelia Earhart's plane."

Rae gaped at him for a full three seconds before she started laughing.

"Come on. Take the game seriously."

"All right. I'll come up with something else." Of course she didn't believe him, even though it was true. Maddock thought quickly. "When I was a kid, my dad went to Nova Scotia for a few weeks every summer. He was a treasure hunter too, but one of the academic variety. He was interested in all sorts of pirate treasure but his great passion was Captain Kidd. I always wanted to go along with him but he would never let me and he wouldn't explain why."

"Oh, that's tragic." Rae mimed a shocked face, pressed her fingertips to her cheeks. "How horrible it must have been to have to call your dad on the phone a few weeks a year. Sorry. That was mean of me."

"It's fine, but that's not it," Maddock said laughing. Of course someone who grew up in the foster care system would have trouble mustering much sympathy for the middle-class kid with two loving parents who didn't get to go on a particular vacation with his dad. "It wasn't about missing the trip. The summer I turned thirteen, he was up in Nova Scotia, and a letter arrived from one of his treasure hunting buddies. Inside was a small section of an old map. I was feeling spiteful so I burned it." He hung his head at the admission. "I always wondered if maybe I had thrown away the key to him finding Kidd's treasure."

"First of all," Rae began, "I'm horrified that you threw away a piece of history, even if it wouldn't have led to anything significant."

"Believe me, I feel the same way."

"Second of all, don't beat yourself up. I once stabbed one of my foster dads. Of course, he deserved it."

Maddock didn't need to ask what the man had done. The look in her eyes said it all. He wasn't certain how he should reply. He was saved when the computer monitor flared to life. A series of images began to scroll up. Maddock gazed, mesmerized at the pictures. It was like watching an ancient world comic strip.

In the first image, a giant sea monster destroyed a sailing ship. As they went on, Maddock recognized images from Greek mythology. He pointed to an image that showed a ship in peril, with a sea monster off its port bow and a whirlpool to starboard.

"Scylla and Charybdis," he said.

"You consider me a young apprentice," Rae sang.

"I hate to break it to you, but that's something Bones would do. But you have a much nicer voice."

"Thank you." She indicated another image, this one of a serpentine creature with tentacles and a long muzzle swimming toward a woman chained to a rock. Above her, a warrior held out his clenched fist.

"Cetus and Andromeda," she said.

Maddock tilted his head. There was something about the picture that was a little bit off.

"I think so, but if that is supposed to be Perseus, something is missing."

She gasped. "He ought to be holding Medusa's head."

"He's going to have a tough time beating the giant sea monster without it."

"Pretty cool, huh?" Rae asked, grinning.

"It's baffling is what it is. We've got what appears to be an ancient world ship, carrying an egg engraved with scenes out of Greek mythology. Can we get a print out of that?"

"Absolutely." She tapped a few keys and somewhere behind them the printer began to whine. She opened the scanner and took out the egg. "Now for the good stuff!"

Next, she placed the artifact in a CAT scan machine. CAT was an acronym for computerized axial tomography, although Rae said that academics had begun simply referring to it as a CT or computerized tomography scan. Primarily used in the medical field, the scan should give them images from all angles of anything that might be hidden inside the egg without damaging the artifact.

When they got the results, they examined them on a different computer monitor. Each image showed a dark shape inside the egg, right at its center.

"There's definitely something in there," Rae said.

"I can't tell what it is. It's just kind of a mass."

"Maybe one of these other angles will give us a clearer picture." She cycled through several more images and then a distinct shape appeared. They couldn't make out a lot of detail, but it was definitely ring-shaped, with irregularities that suggested it had been sculpted. "It's made of metal. And I think this," she tapped a lighter spot on the image, "could be a jewel, but we won't know for sure unless we…" She bit her lip.

"Open her up?" Maddock asked.

Rae nodded. "Should we, though? It seems so wrong."

Maddock ran a hand through his hair. He also didn't like the idea of cutting the egg open. But what else were they going to do?

"I hear what you're saying, and I agree. But we aren't going to learn anything more about what's inside without opening the egg. And you've done a good job of recording the images on its surface." He inclined his head at the computer.

"Let me think about it." Rae busied herself printing out the results of the CAT scan. She tucked all the papers into a manila envelope, sealed it, and handed it to Maddock. "Okay, I think I'm ready to try it."

Somewhere in the distance, a door slammed and the sharp click of footsteps on the tile floor approached rapidly.

Rae's eyes went wide. "Kill the lights. I'll turn these off." In a few seconds they stood in darkness. The only light was a dim sliver from the small window in the lab door. Rae peered out. "It's Professor Sternan," she groaned. "He's my department head. I think we should just go on out and speak to him. I'd rather him know I was in the lab without a good reason then for him to catch me hiding here at the dark as if I'm up to something."

"Would it help if I punched the guy?"

Rae grinned. "No, but it's sweet of you to offer. Let's go." She led the way out.

"Hello Ms. Franklin." Sternan was a large, florid man, with thinning white hair. Despite the heat, he wore a suit and tie. A single jacket button strained to contain his girth. He had an inappropriately loud voice and his face was contorted into a perpetual sneer.

"Hello Professor Sternan."

"Doctor Sternan," he corrected.

Maddock smirked. So he was one of those. Why was he not surprised?

"May I asked what business you had in the lab?"

"I was just showing my friend around. This is Dane Maddock."

"Pleasure to meet you." Maddock stepped in close, a little bit too close. He crushed Sternan's soft, moist hand in his own and bared his teeth in a wolfish grin. He saw Sternan's eyes go wide, felt the man try to pull away. "Rae says she loves working here and is so grateful for all that you've taught her." He released his grip and gave the man a pat on the shoulder. He almost laughed as the professor sighed with relief.

"Well, that is gratifying to hear. Ms. Franklin is one of our rising stars." His face white as a sheet, he managed a small smile Rae's direction and a nod before waddling away.

"Nicely done," Rae whispered, her shoulders shaking with silent mirth as she gazed at the man's quivering backside as he rounded the corner at the end of the hallway. "I didn't take you for a bully."

"I don't know what you're talking about," Maddock said. "I was perfectly pleasant."

Rae giggled, snaked arm around his waist, and gave him a squeeze. "Sure you were. But I think we should open this in my office. I think I have the tools we'll need." She took him by the hand and led him away.

7

Echard slipped into the janitor's closet and waited silently until the fat man in the suit had passed by. He counted to twenty, opened the door an inch, and peered out. Nothing. He listened intently. Still nothing.

Feeling safer, he moved out into the hall and closed the door behind him. He had heard the girl say something about a lab. That must've been where she and Maddock had gone. A quick search led to a door with a sign that read Laboratory. This must be it.

He tested the door and found it locked. That was not a problem. He took out his lock-picking tools and was inside in no time. He flipped on the light and looked around. Nothing seemed to be out of order, and he didn't see the egg Maddock had carried with him to the dive competition earlier in the day. They must have it with them. He supposed it had been too much to hope that they had left it behind.

"This could be a problem," he mumbled. He doubted he could take the egg from Maddock through brute force. He had to hope the pair got careless with it, or maybe Maddock would leave the artifact with Rae. Short of that, Echard was going to need help.

He was about to leave when something caught his ear. It was the soft whir of a computer fan. He looked at the nearest computer and realized that someone had turned off the monitor but had left the base unit running.

"Now that was not very smart."

He hit the power button and the monitor flickered to life. What he saw there puzzled him. They were 3D renderings of what appeared to be scenes out of myths. All included sea serpents.

"I knew it!" He pounded his fist on the desk, then froze, looked around. "Calm yourself," he said. But he couldn't calm down. This proved his theory was correct.

He printed out all the images, and then checked the other unit, the one attached to a CT machine. It had been given the same treatment; monitor shut down but the unit still running. Sure enough, there were images there, including the strange, ghostly shape of a ring. His heart thrummed in his chest and the thrill of excitement sent a shiver down his spine.

"Now, what are you?" he whispered. He printed out the CT images, added them to the others, and tucked them all inside his shirt. Next, he deleted the images from both machines and turned them off before shutting out the lights and slipping out the door.

Cold sweat was dripping down the back of his neck. He was closer now than he'd ever dreamed. For the first time ever, he might have found a way back in. If he was right, this would be something they'd definitely want to get their hands on. He had to find a way to take it from them!

He considered for a moment. Rae was obviously an employee here at the college, so perhaps she had an office nearby. He supposed there was no harm in looking around. At least, as long as Maddock didn't catch him.

He searched around and soon found a staff directory hanging from the wall. It was a simple board with surnames and office numbers in plastic letters. He picked out Franklin, Room 315. That should be just around the corner.

When he found Rae's office, he smiled. The light was on and he could see movement through the small window. Perfect!

He pressed his body against the wall, slid up to the door, and peeked inside.

The egg was laid out on a cloth on top of a desk.

Maddock and Rae hovered over it, wearing gloves, masks, and safety glasses. Their full attention was on the artifact. They had no idea Echard was watching.

Rae held a cutting tool with a fine circular blade in a firm grip. The two of them leaned down over the clay egg as Maddock traced a straight line in pencil around the middle. This was where she would make the cut. His heart pounded and his stomach felt queasy. He didn't like what they were about to do, but he had to know what was inside. As long as they were careful, they should be able to preserve the two halves, which could then be restored in a museum.

She glanced up at him. Beads of sweat glistened on her brow and excitement twinkled in her brown eyes. Maddock gave her the thumbs-up. Her shoulders rose and fell as she took a deep breath and let it out slowly.

And then the high-pitched sound of the cutter filled the air. Gently, Rae pressed the blade to the edge of the egg. Fine dust filled the air as the blade sliced through the ancient clay.

Maddock winced as he watched. *Please don't let it fall apart.* Focusing, he gradually turned the egg as Rae continued the cut around the circumference.

Finally, she completed the circuit. She set the cutting tool aside, then used compressed air to clear any remaining dust from the groove. Finally, she took a fine chisel and small hammer and gently worked at the bonds that still held the halves together.

In less than two minutes the egg came apart in Maddock's hands. Inside was a mix of sand and clay, still slightly damp. As he pulled the two sections apart, the mixture on the inside crumbled, finally revealing its secret.

"There it is," he said.

A glint of silver shone beneath the fluorescent lights. Carefully, she and Maddock brushed away the silt until the artifact was fully exposed.

It was a metal ring approximately four inches in diameter. It was formed in the shape of a sea serpent biting its tail. The metal was some sort of strange silver alloy that Maddock did not immediately recognize. Despite what might have been a few thousand and more years lying at the bottom of the sea, its surface was not tarnished.

Its eyes were inlaid with aquamarine jewels. The piece was exquisitely carved with fine scales, fins, and sharp teeth.

"What is it?" Rae asked.

"It's an ouroboros," Maddock said. "An ancient amulet that depicts a serpent or a dragon eating its own tail. It was first seen in Egyptian iconography, but spread to the ancient world. The term comes from the words *oura* and *bora* in the ancient Greek."

"And what does that mean exactly?"

"Literally tail food."

"Do you think this is of Greek origin?" she asked.

Maddock held the artifact up to the light. He had to admit he had never seen its like.

"Honestly, I have no idea where this originated."

8

It was late afternoon when they boarded the ferry to return to Andros. They chose seats on the starboard side and sat swapping stories. Maddock regaled her with tales of Bones' misadventures, while Rae recounted the times Kyle had nearly killed himself, never intentionally, of course.

"We really are a couple of caretakers," Rae said. "The difference is, I suspect Bones can take care of himself if need be. Kyle is a different story."

"He's stayed alive so far," Maddock said.

"True, but there have been a few close shaves."

"Maybe he's the kind of person who will rise to the occasion of you give him a chance. I've known plenty of people like that in my time. They never know what they're capable of until they're forced to become self-reliant."

Rae's eyes flashed. "Don't tell me how to be a big sister. You don't know him like I do."

Maddock held his hands up. "I'm just saying."

"I know, and I'm sorry." Rae took his hand and gave it a squeeze. "I can't explain our connection. It's not romantic. It's more like he's my son."

"Well, I don't have a sibling or a child, so I don't know what that's like."

"I really want to find out what this thing is," Rae said, abruptly changing the subject. She pressed her hand to her chest, where the ouroboros, which she had begun referring to as the amulet, hung from a cord between her breasts. "I almost suggested that we stay the night in Nassau so we could go directly to the library first thing in the morning."

Maddock's heart skipped a beat. "We can still do

that." He saw her cheeks immediately go red and felt his own do the same.

"No. I mean, not because I don't want to. I can't because of Kyle. He nearly drowned two days in a row."

"Does anyone keep an eye on him when he's not visiting the islands?"

"Not usually. I'm afraid that's going to be his downfall if I can't help him find something to focus on. Diving is the first thing he's showed any real passion for." She gave a slow shake of her head, a sad smile turning down the corners of her mouth. "I know I can't fix him, but I feel like I need to do the best I can for him. Maybe he can get a job at a surf shop or a resort, something that will keep him close. And what better place to work on his freediving?"

"Sounds like a plan." Maddock wasn't sure what to else to say. And then someone caught his eye.

"Echard," he whispered.

"Where?" Rae stood and looked around.

"Sit down." Maddock took her by the shoulder and gently pressed her back down into her seat. "No sense calling attention to ourselves. He was just leaving the dock and heading toward town."

"Must not have anything to do with us," she said.

"Let's hope not."

The engines let out a throaty rumble and the deck vibrated beneath Maddock's feet as the craft headed out to sea. It followed the coastline, affording them a distant view of sparkling beaches. Maddock soon found himself relaxing and enjoying the company of this intelligent, beautiful woman.

"What sort of creature do you think this is?" Maddock said. "It doesn't quite look like a dragon or snake, does it?"

Rae shook her head, her brown curls brushing her cheeks. "Neither. I think it looks like a sea serpent."

"Let me see it again." He leaned a little closer.

"You just want to take a peep down my shirt, don't you?" Rae's eyes twinkled with mischief and she didn't lean away. Her eyes flitted to the left and then the right, then she reached inside her shirt and took out the amulet. "At first glance, it does look a bit like a dragon, but look closer at a couple of things. Take a look at the head, for example." She covered every part of the amulet except the head. "If you had never heard of an ouroboros, and you weren't predisposed to see this as a dragon or snake, what would it look like to you?"

Maddock frowned, squinted, tried to see it for the first time. There was something about it….

"What if I uncover this?" Rae moved her hand a fraction of an inch, just far enough to reveal one of the triangular plates that ran along the spine.

And then Maddock saw it. "It looks a little bit like a shark. That plate looks like the dorsal fin."

"That's what I think, too. And you see this pattern running along its sides? I thought it represented oddly rounded scales but I think they are actually tentacles. Look at where the serpent bites its tail."

Maddock leaned even closer. She was right. What he had taken to be the frill around the dragons neck appeared, in fact to be the tips of many tentacles. "That's weird. A sharktopus?"

"Dude, I can literally feel your breath on my cleavage."

Maddock jerked back so suddenly he nearly wrenched his neck. "Sorry. I didn't realize." He began to scoot away, but Rae wrapped her arms around his shoulders and pulled him back.

"I wasn't complaining. Are you always this uptight?"

Maddock turned and looked her in the eye. "Absolutely, I am."

She laughed and gave him a quick kiss on the cheek.

"We will just have to…" She froze in mid-sentence, eyes wide.

"What's wrong?"

"Maybe nothing. There are two guys hanging out by the stern, port side. I know who they are and they are bad news. Thugs for hire, and they will work for anybody."

Maddock discreetly glanced over his shoulder and spotted the two immediately. They were tall, lean men with athletic builds. And each wore a pistol concealed beneath his clothing. The untrained eye might not have noticed the weapons, but Maddock spotted them immediately.

"Are they watching us?" he asked.

"I caught one of them staring at the medallion while I was holding it up. He turned away quickly and they both started talking and stealing glances back at us. Now it looks like they're going out of their way to act like they are not looking at us. I don't know, maybe I'm being paranoid."

Maddock didn't think so. Echard had already tried to steal the backpack with the egg and amulet once. And if these men were willing to work for anybody…

He looked around, searching for a place to hide but the ferry was a small one. Besides, taking refuge would mean they were cornered. If these men truly were after them, no sense leading them to a place where there were no witnesses or any possible help. He ran through scenarios in his mind. Bones would have suggested creeping up on the two and assassinating them. Of course, Maddock didn't know for certain that they were after him and Rae, and even then, he was no murderer. That, and the boat afforded no cover he could use to sneak up on the pair. He patted the Recon knife at his side, his only weapon, but it brought him little reassurance.

His eyes drifted to the coastline, not too far away. They had left New Providence behind and up ahead was a strip of empty beach and lush forest. He had an idea.

"Rae? How well do you swim?"

9

Quietly, trying not to draw attention, Maddock and Rae stood and made their way toward the stern. From the corner of his eye, he saw one of the men eyeing them. The man's partner glanced their way, too, then both looked away quickly.

"They think we're trapped here," he said. "Probably waiting until we get back to Andros before they make their move."

"Are you sure about this?" Rae asked.

"I'm sure it's a safer bet than me trying to disarm both of them."

She glanced nervously down at the turquoise water sliding past them.

"Okay, let's do this."

They waited until no one was looking, then vaulted the rail. Maddock hit the water, followed a second later by Rae. Before he could begin to swim he was startled by what felt like a tremor passing through him. It was an odd feeling, like feeling a bass note played through a stock of amps at a concert. It was gone as soon as it had come, so fast that he wondered if he'd imagined it. But he knew it had been real. He still felt the vibrations. What had it been? But there was no time to ponder the question. After a quick glance in Rae's direction to make sure she was doing all right, he struck out for the shore.

They swam underwater as far as they could, a much greater distance in Maddock's case. When he finally came up for air, he looked back at the ferry. The two men were nowhere to be seen. They must have already noticed Maddock and Rae's absence. Nothing he could do about it except continue to swim.

It wasn't long before he realized they had a problem.

"They're coming after us," he said.

The two men who had been stalking them had spotted their attempted escape and were now in pursuit. At the rate the pair were going, they could've been Olympic swimmers.

"What has someone been feeding these guys?" Maddock said.

He and Rae continued to swim but the men were closing the gap. They were bogged down by their waterlogged clothing and the clay egg Maddock carried in his backpack.

"Are they going to catch up with us?" Rae gasped.

"Just keep swimming."

A shot rang out and Rae let out a squeak.

"Where did that come from?"

Maddock stole a quick glance behind them. One of the men was still charging hard, but the other was now treading water and taking aim for a second shot.

"Get down."

They submerged just as Maddock heard the dull pop of a gunshot. As he plunged into the water, now as dim as twilight as the sun fled toward the western horizon, the beginnings of a plan formed in his mind.

Those plans dissolved as a huge figure suddenly loomed in front of him. He was a tall, dark man armed with a spear. And he was just standing there.

That's not right, Maddock thought.

Beyond it he saw the outline of a Stonehenge-like structure. Odd thoughts flashed through his mind. All of Bones' conspiracy theories echoed in his head. Atlantis. The Bermuda Triangle. Frogmen.

He continued to swim but the figure didn't make a move.

Because it wasn't alive.

This was an underwater sculpture garden. He'd heard about these. They provided a destination for snorkelers, with some of the simpler parts of the installation intended to serve as the foundation of a new coral reef. Too bad there was no time today to explore it. He would have loved to check it out. And then his idea returned, but now it was fully fleshed out. He saw Rae surface for air and he swam over to her.

"Here, take the pack and swim for the shore as fast as you can." He shoved the backpack containing the egg into her hands.

"What about you?"

"I'll catch up. Just go."

To her credit, she didn't waste time arguing or questioning him, but set off toward the shore with renewed vigor.

Maddock heard the sound of splashing behind him. Their pursuers had almost caught up. He was nearly out of time.

He submerged again and swam for the shelter of the giant warrior. Taking up a position behind it, he grabbed hold of its thick neck, set his feet against its back, and tensed to spring. He gripped his Recon knife tightly. For a moment, he felt as if he would be sick. He'd had his fill of killing, believed he'd left it behind. But the men had fired on them. Hostilities had commenced, and through none of his doing. He had no choice if he and Rae wanted to live through this.

The man appeared in a matter of seconds, driving through the water with forceful kicks and sloppy strokes. He was tiring, and that was fine with Maddock.

Maddock waited until the man's dark outline was almost directly above him and then he sprang.

He shot through the water like a torpedo and came upon his unsuspecting quarry from below. The man had no idea Maddock was there until the former SEAL plunged his knife into the man's gut. Maddock pulled the knife free and the man shoved him away and pressed his hands to the wound. That left his throat unprotected and Maddock made him pay. A crimson cloud spread out around them and Maddock kicked away from the dying man, who was now frantically trying to grab hold of Maddock. He was out of the fight, but could easily drag Maddock down with him.

Now to find the other man.

Maddock surfaced and looked around. Listened.

Nothing.

Where the hell did you go?

Either the second assailant was underwater or he'd drowned. Maddock doubted he could be that lucky. On the upside, Rae was almost to shore. That was what mattered most.

Wanting to keep her safe, Maddock swam for a spot farther down the beach. He didn't go underwater this time. This way would get him there faster and hopefully draw the enemy in his direction.

He finally reached the shore, waterlogged and weary. He still saw no sight of the man who had been following them. Summoning his reserves of strength, he sprinted across the beach, all the while waiting for a gunshot that never came. He scrambled over the sand dunes that separated the beach from the tree line and stopped to catch his breath.

The beach was deserted. He looked up and down, but all was quiet. The gentle flow of the surf, the breeze. This would've been a great place to spend some time alone with Rae were it not for that pesky problem of someone trying to kill them.

Now he needed to find Rae.

He worked his way east along the coastline, keeping his eyes peeled for any sign of her or the man who followed. Soon, he spotted tracks leading up from the water, across the beach, and into the dunes. The footprints were smaller than that of the average man. It had to be Rae. He moved a little faster, still careful to keep quiet as he hurried along.

To his right, through the trees, he saw the dark outline of crumbling walls. It was difficult to make out details in the evening light, but they were ruins of some sort. As he moved closer he saw a figure scramble over a wall. He could tell immediately it wasn't Rae. The person was too tall and moved with the grace of a high-level athlete.

"Dammit. I can't let him get to her first."

He made a mad dash for the spot where he had seen the man. The low, crumbling stone wall was no challenge for the former SEAL. He scaled it with ease and dropped down to the other side to find himself in the ruins of a Colonial era plantation. Nearby stood a single wall of what must have once been one of the finest homes on the island. It was made of gray brick with the doorway and arched window still visible. The history buff in him want to explore, but that obviously wasn't an option. He supposed he could come back later, but there were more pressing issues right now and he chastised himself for letting his thoughts stray for even a split second when someone was in trouble. He had lost some of his focus since he left the service. Bones claimed that there were other reasons for Maddock's occasional lapses, but what the hell did Bones know?

Up ahead, on the other side of a crumbling outbuilding, a scream rang out, followed by a gunshot.

"Rae!" Maddock shouted.

Another gunshot.

"Where are you?" he yelled as he continued to run in the direction from which the sounds had come. He didn't care if the man heard him. In fact, he preferred the man come for him instead of Rae.

Two more gunshots and another cry of fear and alarm. They came from farther away now. Good. That meant Rae was still alive and she was on the run.

He poured on the speed. He had to get there in time. He had to.

Another shot. This time he didn't hear the sound of Rae's voice. But that didn't mean she was dead. Maybe she simply didn't want to give away her location. That had to be it.

He kept running. His chest was tight, his legs weary from the long swim in sodden clothing.

The way ahead grew brighter and he broke through onto a service road. Its surface of sand, broken seashells, and fine gravel seemed to glow in the dying light. He heard footsteps running in his direction and then something buzzed past his face like an angry hornet as he heard the boom of a gunshot.

He had a moment to hope the man was carrying a six shooter, and then the attacker was upon him. The man managed to seize Maddock's right wrist, the one in which he held a knife. His big hand swallowed Maddock's wrist. Meanwhile, Maddock controlled the man's right wrist, keeping his pistol at bay. As Maddock had feared, it was an automatic, so he had to assume there were bullets remaining in the magazine.

They grappled wordlessly, each trying to gain the upper hand. The loose surface of the road gave way under Maddock's feet, and he barely managed to regain his balance. The fellow grinned, his teeth glowing white like the fangs of a vampire.

"Give up." He spoke with a slight island accent. "I lettered in three sports at the U."

"Any of them combat sports?" Maddock answered. The assailant crinkled his brow and then Maddock drove his knee into the man's ribs, and followed with another knee strike, this one to the groin. The fellow grunted and his knees wobbled. Maddock leaned back and drove his head forward, smashing the fellow's nose with his forehead.

"Dammit!" The man squeezed his eyes closed and tried to turn away. Clearly he was accustomed to shooting people from a distance. He was no fighter.

Maddock seized the advantage, and while his opponent was off balance, flipped him backward. They hit the ground hard. Maddock's opponent bore the brunt of it. His breath left him in a rush as he landed flat on his back. On a harder surface he might've cracked the back of his skull, too, but on the somewhat softer sand-and-gravel drive, the blow was cushioned although Maddock knew it still had to hurt.

Still controlling the man's gun hand, Maddock raised up and then drove his elbow into the man's forehead. It wouldn't do a lot of damage, but it was painful and the forehead tended to cut easily. The man let out a grunt of pain and blood poured down his face. Maddock pressed the fine edge of his Recon knife to the fellow's throat.

"Listen very closely. You've probably been told I'm a civilian. You'd be wrong." He moved the knife a fraction of a centimeter and the man winced. "I know exactly where to cut you and I've ended better, harder men than you. So you can cooperate, or I finish this right now."

"All right. I give up. Just stop." The man let go of the weapon without being asked. His eyes darted from side to side.

"If you're looking for your friend, I've already dealt with him."

The man's shoulders sagged and the remaining fight seemed to go out of him.

"Who do you work for?"

"I don't know his name. The white man who sells the trinkets."

Echard had been selling carved amulets at the dive competition.

"What does Echard want with the egg?"

"Look, man, I don't know if his name is Echard and I know nothing about an egg, or what he wants with any of it. He hired us to do a job."

"Which was?" Maddock thought he knew the answer but he wanted confirmation.

"You have a metal ring. An amulet, he thinks. Shaped like a serpent."

Maddock frowned. How did Echard know that?

"Our job is to take the amulet and kill you if necessary." He flashed a wicked smile. "There was a bonus if we killed you."

"How did he know about the amulet?" Maddock and Rae had only discovered the amulet a short while before. Had Echard been spying on them?

"Like I said, we just took the job and did as we were told. The only thing I can tell you is Echard doesn't just want to possess the amulet, as you call it."

"What does that mean?"

"He mentioned some big players, a powerful group. I guess he used to be a part of it, but he definitely said that this could be his ticket back in."

"What kind of group? Black market antiquities?" That was what made the most sense in Maddock's mind. The amulet they had found must be of great value. If Echard had once been a part of one such ring and later fallen out of favor, a rare enough artifact might be a way back in.

"No idea. I swear to you, that's all I know."

Maddock believed him. Now, what to do with the man? He didn't have any rope to tie him up with. And should he leave the man behind? He was an assassin, a weapon to be pointed at anyone, by anyone who could afford the price. Was it a bad idea to leave him alive?

The decision was taken out of his hands when the man did the stupidest thing possible. He tried to fight.

He threw his hips up, attempting to buck Maddock off of him. At the same time he snatched at Maddock's knife.

But the blade was already pressed against his flesh, right at the jugular. The sudden movement, coupled with Maddock's weight being thrown forward, drove the knife into the hired assassin's throat.

Maddock rolled off of him, snatched the pistol and waited for the man to die.

It was over quickly. But despite watching this man's final moments, Maddock felt nothing at all. That bothered him.

"Rae, it's me. Everything's okay now!" he shouted.

"I'm coming." Her voice sounded from the woods on the other side of the road. He heard a rustling through the underbrush and then she appeared.

"You're okay?"

"I'm fine." Her eyes fell on the dead man and she let out a whimper.

"I gave him every chance to live. I was going to let him go."

To Maddock's surprise, Rae wasn't squeamish about the corpse. She helped him hide the body in an old well at the edge of the old plantation. As they worked, he explained what had happened, including the information the man had revealed. Rae agreed that it sounded like Echard was hooked up with black market antiquities dealers.

"What is this place, anyway?" Maddock asked, looking around.

"Clifton Heritage National Park," Rae said. "This place was originally inhabited by the Lucayans, island natives. Later it was colonized by American Loyalists and their slaves."

"And that statue?"

"It's a new art installation called Ocean Atlas. I've been meaning to snorkel it but this wasn't the way I imagined it."

"Story of my life." Maddock gave a rueful shake of the head. "How long do you think it will be before the body is found?"

Rae shrugged. "They don't maintain this area, so no one really comes here. And I don't think there'll be much smell since he's down in the water." She shivered. "God, I can't believe this is happening. It feels so wrong to be hiding a body and speculating about whether or not it will be discovered."

Maddock nodded. They had agreed that contacting law enforcement would be a bad idea. There were layers upon layers of corruption in the bureaucracy of the Bahamian government, and neither of them could afford the bribes that might be the only guarantee of their freedom. Still, he understood how she felt. At least, he remembered a time when he would've felt that way.

"I get it, but I really think this is the right thing to do. The safe thing. We don't know who is connected with whom. For all we know, those guys might have done some work for people in the local police department or the prosecutor's department."

Rae nodded. "But what happens when the other body washes ashore?"

Maddock thought about this. "If these guys are as shady as you say, it won't be that big a surprise when he's found, will it? And if we're lucky, as long as the body in the well goes undiscovered, the authorities will assume that one partner murdered the other and dumped his body in the water."

"But what about Echard?"

"What about him? Yes, he can connect them with us, but is he really going to tell the police that his hired hitmen disappeared after failing to complete a robbery and murder he hired them to do?"

"Okay, that makes sense. As guilty as I feel about

this, I'm starting to feel a little better. I mean, the guys did try to kill us." Rae visibly relaxed. She wrapped her arms around Maddock, rested her head against his chest, and gave him a squeeze.

"Thank you," she breathed.

Maddock smiled and held her tight. "Don't mention it."

"What do we do now? We're in danger because of this artifact." She tapped the spot between her breasts where the amulet hung beneath her shirt. "But if we report it to the authorities, that could lead to Echard."

"Which would connect us to the two dead men. I think you're right. We're going to have to find out for ourselves what this thing is, who these people are Echard is trying to get back in with, and why everyone wants it so badly they're willing to kill for it."

10

Andros Island, Bahamas

Bones awoke with a splitting headache. His mouth was dry and his ears were ringing. Above the tinny sound, he heard someone moving around. He stared up at the cracked ceiling, lit by the yellow glow of artificial light that shone in between the cheap curtains. The place stank of cigarette smoke and mold. It took him a minute to realize where he was. He and Thel had gotten a cheap motel room.

He rolled over, the movement making his head spin. Thel was no longer in bed. He listened, but didn't hear a sound. Must not be blowing chunks in the bathroom, which he felt like doing right now.

"Thel?" He pushed himself up on one elbow and flipped on the bedside lamp, bathing the room in the weak glow of a twenty-five watt bulb. A stray cobweb dangled from the dusty shade.

"I'm right here." She was standing by the door, a nervous look painting her face.

"You're not leaving, are you?"

"Yes, I need to go. It's after midnight and I should have already been back." She froze as if she'd said something wrong.

"That's cool." Bones said it out of sheer reflex. He'd enjoyed plenty of these one night stands and it was always easier when neither party tried to cling to the other. But for some reason, he didn't want her to go. "You could at least come over here and say goodbye."

Thel managed a weak smile. She approached him slowly, almost reluctantly, and planted a gentle kiss on his forehead. Bones could've sworn that in the one spot where her lips touched him, his headache went away.

"Thank you for a wonderful night. You are not at all what I expected."

"In a good way or bad?"

She smiled sadly. "Very good. It was so wonderful how you opened up to me, told me about your family, all the problems you had growing up, what you went through in the SEALs, your drinking problems. Most men can't show that kind of vulnerability in front of a woman, especially not one they just met."

Bones sat up fast. The effort sent a bolt of pain stabbing into the base of his skull. He winced and let out a pained grunt. "Dude, I don't remember that, or not much of it. It definitely doesn't sound like me. I've never even watched Oprah."

"It's all right. I think you and I have a special connection." Thel reached out and brushed a lock of hair out of his face. "You don't show it, but you are a deeply spiritual person. You're different."

Bones tried to process her words but they didn't make sense. Still, he knew instinctively that something odd had transpired between them. He only wished he could remember what it was. Had they even hooked up or had they just... talked? If that was all it had been, he couldn't let Willis and Matt find out. If that happened, Bones would never live it down.

"Say, can I have another drink of that water before you go? That stuff is awesome." His mouth was dry as the Mohave and he remembered how it seemed to sparkle on his tongue when he drank it. How alive he had felt. He could certainly use that kind of pick-me-up right now.

"No!" Thel sprang to her feet and backed away, her hands guarding the clay flask at her hip.

"Okay, sorry. I didn't know water was such a big freaking deal around here. I guess I shouldn't expect anything from a chick who was going to ditch me in the middle of the night."

Thel flinched. "I wish I could explain. I'm sorry, but I really do have to go. It's for the best."

She opened the door crack and Bones saw that it was still dark outside.

"At least let me walk with you. You don't know who you might run into out there on the streets. Just give me a second to get dressed." He stood on wobbly legs and looked around for his boxers.

"No, you can't come. It's very important that you don't."

"Oh, come on. It won't do any harm for me to walk you back to your resort."

Bones reached out to take Thel by the hand. Next thing he knew, he was lying on his back, staring up at the ceiling. His ears rang and the back of his skull burned. Thel had seized him by the wrist and performed a perfect judo hip toss on him. He was tired and groggy, to be sure, but what the hell? Bones could count on two hands the number of people who had managed to do that to him. Maddock, Willis, his sister once and only once, and a few others, trained men, most of whom were no longer alive. And now add a hot redhead to that list.

Their eyes met. "I wish I could make you understand. Please, just let me go."

Bones sat up and rubbed the back of his head. "I would love it if you would start making some sense right about now."

"If only I could. You've got to trust me. I'm doing the right thing for you. And I assure you I can take care of myself." She took one step out the door, then paused and looked back. "And for what it's worth, I think you should find your father. If you can't find it in your heart to forgive him, at least give him the chance to explain."

The words were like a dagger to his heart. He gritted his teeth and rose on shaky legs.

"Get the hell out of here," Bones growled. He glared at her, immune to the hurt he saw in her face, the tears welling in her big green eyes.

"Goodbye," she whispered. Gently, she closed the door.

Uttering a curse, Bones hurled himself onto the bed and soon descended into fitful sleep.

11

Alexei closed the door of his cheap motel room and locked it behind him. More out of habit than any real concern he made a quick inspection of the space. Still the same faded yellow walls, the same cheap art print of a beach scene. Nothing seemed to be out of place. He didn't know why he was worried. No one knew what he was doing here. What was the American saying? Old habits die hard.

"You are safe here. This isn't Russia," he told himself. It was something he had to remind himself of daily.

He climbed up onto his bed, took out his Swiss Army knife, and opened the screwdriver attachment. He used it to remove the air-conditioning vent cover, reached inside, and took out a Ziploc bag and dropped it on the bed.

Air-conditioning, he thought as he replaced the vent cover. It hadn't worked since he had arrived. What was the point of even having it?

When everything was back in its place, he sat down and opened the bag. He spread the items out on the bed. This motel was so cheap it didn't even offer any sort of desk or table, save the small one at the bedside.

"Maybe someday you can afford better," he said as he picked up his legal pad, flipped to the first empty page, and wrote down a pair of names. He stared at the page for a full minute, wondering if he was doing the right thing. Of course he was. He had always trusted his instincts and he was still alive.

He picked up the phone, dialed a number he knew by heart.

She answered on the third ring. "*Allo?*"

"Did I wake you?"

"*Zho-pa.*" Despite her obvious annoyance, she delivered the curse in an affectionate tone. "What is it you want from me at this early hour?"

"Early?" He laughed. "Here in the islands, the evening has only just begun."

"If that is the case then why are you talking to me? Shouldn't you be out romancing the island women?"

Alexei laughed. "You know me. I have too much work to do."

"And I assume this work is the reason for your call?"

"You know me too well. I need you to perform a background check on a couple of people for me."

A long, slow exhale. And then silence.

"Are you there?"

"You know I am really not supposed to do this. I can't lose this job. They would send me back."

"I know. I promise this is the last time I will ask." This time, her curses carried a touch of heat. Alexei made a placating gesture even though he knew she couldn't see him through the phone. "I'll make it up to you."

"Of course you will. Hold on, let me get a pen."

Alexei felt guilty even making the request, but it was important. He needed more information on these two, because he was certain they were not what they seemed.

"All right. Give me the names."

"Dane Maddock and Bones Bonebrake."

"Did you say Bones? Like *skelet*?"

"That's it exactly. Sorry, that is his nickname." He racked his brain, trying to remember the name Bonebrake had written on his Blue Descent entry form. It had been something from the Bible. Something unusual. "Uriah Bonebrake. That's it."

She laughed. "I understand why he prefers to be called Bones. What can you tell me about them?"

"They both live in the Florida Keys. They served together in the Navy but I don't know in what capacity. Bonebrake is a Native American in case you didn't guess from the surname."

"Interesting. Anything else?"

"Only if they are treasure hunters."

"All right, I see."

They made a few minutes of small talk. Alexei made some grand promises about where they would go for dinner and how he would go about repaying her.

"By the way," she said before they hung up, "I am still working on that other thing for you. Nothing to report yet."

"You are the best."

They ended the call and Alexei began his work.

He hadn't been completely honest with Bonebrake. Alexei had, indeed, been conscripted into the Russian Army, but his career didn't end after his mandatory two-year term. And he had been more than a simple grunt. He had a feeling the same was true of Bonebrake. It was easy to tell that the big Indian had seen and done some things the average person could scarcely imagine.

Alexei had been involved in covert operations for the Russian Armed Forces. On one particular mission, his squad had been sent to assassinate a high-level member of the Turkish Hezbollah, a man known only as Cemal, in his compound in northwest Turkey near the Greek border. Cemal had apparently been a collector of rare antiquities. Many priceless artifacts, doubtless acquired on the black market, had been taken home to Russia by Alexei and his men. They'd received commendations for their efforts. Someone above his rank had probably kept the artifacts. Probably added to the president's private collection.

There had been one prize Alexei couldn't take. Rather, there had been a collection of prizes—texts in

Ancient Greek carved in stone, wood, and on parchment. These had been carefully curated, framed, and hung all around Cemal's secret trophy room. Alexei could read enough ancient Greek to know that these texts had not been collected at random. They all told pieces of a single story. The fact that they were all connected led Alexei to conclude that the fragments of ancient maps that had also been framed and put on display were connected, too.

Unable to carry them away, he'd made a thorough photographic record. That decision had set him on a course that had brought him here today. He was certain he was on the right path, and had come ninety-nine percent of the way. It was the last one percent that was proving a near-impossible task."

He took out a folder which contained printouts of all of those photographs, as well as his translation of the text. He knew it nearly by heart, but he liked having it by his side as he searched for clues. Tonight's project was an old book of local legends he had stolen from Balcony House Museum. He hoped something in here would match up with something in the text.

He began to read. Page after page went by but nothing rang a bell.

He looked at the clock. It was one o'clock in the morning. Frustrated, he decided to give up for the night. He took a minute to hide his research, before deciding to take a walk.

The night was refreshingly cool, with a pleasant breeze blowing in off the sea. He relaxed, taking it all in. With no particular destination in mind, he wandered along, enjoying the moonlight and the peace and quiet. As a professor he didn't get much of the latter.

He soon found himself hiking at the edge of one of the many blue holes that pockmarked this section of the island. He couldn't recall the name of this one. Captain something, he thought. A wooden gazebo sat at the edge of a twenty-foot, mangrove-covered ledge. To his left, a staircase led down to the water. He descended, took a seat, and tried to relax.

"That is nice," he sighed. His time outside the diving competition had been consumed by his project, his nights troubled by insomnia. The rational part of him knew that he was safe, but he couldn't seem to stop looking over his shoulder. The product of growing up in the old Soviet Union, he supposed.

As his eyes adjusted to the dark, they took in his surroundings. The light gray walls of the blue hole made a nearly perfect circle. Here and there, mangroves grew from cracks in the stone. The jungle grew right up to the edge of the precipice, making a ring of black beneath moonlit sky.

In the distance something, caught his eye. He squinted peering into the darkness. The water was calm like mirrored glass. A band of moonlight shone across its surface. And then he saw it again a ripple. No, not a ripple. It was larger than that.

And then something massive broke the surface. Only for a second, and then it was gone. Instinct told him he should stand, but for the first time in his life, he was frozen in place by sheer shock. It had been there, hadn't it? Now he wasn't so certain. It was late and his sleep-deprived brain was focused on his research. He had imagined it. Still, he wished he had brought his camera, just in case.

He waited. His eyes began to droop. His body felt heavy.

Perhaps I will just sleep out here. It's cooler than my motel room.

There it was again! A disturbance on the surface of the water, as if something huge were down in the blue hole. He sprang to his feet, wide awake now.

He racked his brain. There had to be an explanation. What could make a shadow that large? A whale? No, this was an inland blue hole, if not far from the water. Many underwater passageways connected the network of blue holes to the sea, but no explorer had ever found a passageway large enough for something of any decent size to swim through. An octopus, maybe.

Octopus!

He felt as if he'd suddenly been doused with cold water. Goose flesh rose along his arms. His heart raced. Invisible hands wrapped around his throat. He couldn't breathe. A voice inside his head told him to run, but the rational part of his mind told him to relax. Estimating the size of something beneath the water was difficult enough up close and in broad daylight. If there was something down there, it wasn't a monster.

Gradually, he relaxed. What was he? A coward? He was a seasoned veteran, a man who had faced certain death on many occasions, and had lived to tell the tale.

"You are working too hard, Alexei, and your mind is making a fool of you." He didn't know why, perhaps to prove to himself he wasn't afraid, he sat down, removed his shoes and socks, and dipped his feet into the water. He took a deep breath, trying to relax.

"Remember it is not all about the work. You have the dive contest. You have new friends." He felt foolish talking to himself but he found that his calming thoughts were more effective when spoken aloud.

He looked up at the moon and smiled.

"Life is not so bad."

And then something clamped down on his leg.

12

Bones awoke at sunrise. His head no longer hurt but he felt groggy, much more so than a night of restless sleep could explain. He downed two cups of cheap motel coffee but it didn't help much. Finally, he made the long, slow trek back to the docks where *Sea Foam* was tied up.

Along the way he kept catching himself looking around for Thel. Every time he heard a woman's voice, and once when he saw someone with red hair, he perked up.

"What the hell is with me?" He never got this hung up on a woman like this.

Willis and Matt were sitting on the stern deck of *Sea Foam* drinking coffee when Bones arrived. They greeted him with laughter and catcalls as he approached.

"Heard you met a girl," Willis said. "Looks like she kept you out late."

"How did you know about that?"

"Your little buddy told us all about it." Matt pointed at what looked like a heap of dirty clothes lying against the bulkhead. It was Kyle, sound asleep. "Val brought him back last night."

"Great," Bones said as he climbed aboard. He was embarrassed to have forgotten all about the young man, and about promising Maddock he'd look out for him.

"Hey, you didn't ask permission to come on board," Willis said as Bones vaulted the stern rail.

"Screw you. You're not captain. Where is he, anyway?"

Willis and Matt exchanged impish grins.

"What's the joke?" Bones asked.

"You're not the only one who stayed out all night," Willis said. "I had a feeling about him and Rae."

"It's about damn time. That dude has been basically celibate since, you know. Good for him." Bones probably meant it but he was feeling too crappy to care one way or the other. He slumped to the deck and rested against the bulkhead. "Got any more coffee?"

"Coffee?" Matt inclined his head. "You look like you need hair of the dog. What did you drink last night?"

Bones frowned. "Just water."

Matt and Willis gaped then broke into laughter.

"If all you had to drink was water, that must've been one heck of a girl to leave you looking a mess," Willis said. "What was her name?"

"Thel. It was short for something, some Greek name I'd never heard before. And yeah, she was pretty awesome. At least I thought she was." He hated to admit that he didn't remember. "So, what's on the agenda for today?"

"Waiting for the boss to show up. Or to call in and give us our marching orders."

"Corey is monitoring the radio in case he reaches out," Matt added.

"Say, you don't think we ought to be worried, do you?" Willis asked. "I can't remember the last time Maddock stayed out all night for a fun reason."

"No idea," Bones grumbled. God, he felt horrible. "How about you guys get your asses in gear? We can dive without Maddock if we have to."

"All right, man, chill." Willis frowned. "You don't seem like yourself. Are you sure you're all right?"

"I'm fine." That wasn't true. He couldn't get his mind off of Thel and it was pissing him off. "I'm his partner, so it's not just Maddock's money you're pissing away, sitting around doing nothing." He paused when he saw Willis and Matt's bemused expressions.

"Don't mind me. I just feel like crap."

"It's cool. It was worth it to see you get all cake eater

on us," Willis said, using the naval slang for an officer.

Bones managed a smile. "I'm going to have some coffee and anything round or oval I can find in the medicine cabinet. One of you wake Kyle up. The dive competition starts today."

Just then, a voice called out from the dock.

"Doesn't anybody have a work ethic these days? We need to earn!" It was Maddock. Rae was with him.

"I was just telling them that," Bones said.

"Sure you were." Maddock gave a shake of his head as Rae boarded and went to wake Kyle, who had managed to sleep through the loud conversation.

"You two have a good time?" Bones waggled his eyebrows.

"Would you call being chased and shot at by hired thugs a good time?"

Bones was surprised but could only manage a shrug. "I wouldn't call it boring. What happened?"

Corey emerged from the cabin bearing a fresh pot of coffee and three empty mugs, and they all sat on the deck and listened as Maddock and Rae recounted the events of the previous day.

Bones tried to concentrate, but his thoughts were slippery. What was with Thel's odd behavior? And how had she gotten so freaking strong?

"Rae and I are going to a local museum to see if we can learn anything about the artifact. I need somebody else to do some legwork for me. Find out what you can about Stanley Echard, see where he goes, what he gets up to, and who he's working for."

Bones perked up. "I can do that. I'll hang around here and see what I can dig up."

"Seriously? You want to do that instead of going back out to the wreck?"

"He's hoping he'll bump into the girl he met last night," Willis said.

"Wait," Maddock said. "You met a girl and you still want to talk to her the next day?"

"That girl was seriously hot," Kyle said, finally perking up. "Hair like fire, eyes like gems, skin like alabaster. Those are also lyrics from a song I'm writing, but that's what she looked like."

"Can I at least count on you to investigate Echard while you're pining for your lost love?" Maddock asked.

"I'll be fine," Bones said loudly.

"I'll go with him," Kyle said. "I've got a few hours to kill and I know some of the places he hangs out."

"And the rest of us will get back to work," Willis announced.

"I don't need any help," Bones said hurriedly. "I'm good."

Kyle reached out and clapped Bones on the shoulder. "It's cool, Amigo. I've been wanting to learn more about our red brothers for a long time now. Like, why do you guys put curry in everything?"

Bones looked to his friends.

"Anybody want to trade jobs? I'll even say please."

Everyone just smiled.

13

The Poseidon Resort was a seaside hotel on the island of Andros a short distance from the dock where *Sea Foam* was tied up. It was painted bright white and shone like a pearl in the morning sun. A statue of the Greek god from which the hotel drew its name guarded the entrance. Poseidon stood on a rock in the middle of a fountain, holding his trident aloft. Bones and Kyle made the short trek, Kyle filling what should have been a quiet walk with inane chatter. Bones let the sound wash over him like white noise. If he stopped listening to the actual words, the sound of the young man's voice was actually comforting. Kyle feared nothing, worried about nothing, and was curious about everything.

"Yo, Skeleton Man. Did you hear me?"

"What was that?" Bones said, already tired of the clever nickname Kyle had given him.

"Do you think Poseidon was like, a real dude? Not the guy in the cartoon, but the guy from mythology. Do you think he was based on a real person?"

"No idea." Bones paused at the front door. "Can you wait for me out here?"

Kyle stuck out his thumb and pinky to form the "shaka sign," commonly known in surfer culture as "hang loose."

"No problemo. I'm going to sit by the fountain and commune with Poseidon. Or is it Neptune? Which one is which?"

"They're the same guy," Bones said over his shoulder as he opened the front door to the resort.

A wave of cold air blasted him as he stepped inside. He was suddenly aware of how much his casual clothing stood out among the business persons milling about in the lobby, but he did not let that deter him. He headed to the concierge desk and flashed his most winning smile at the young woman working there.

"I'm looking for a friend of mine who's attending a conference here I don't know the name of the conference, but it's for corporate recruiters or something like that." He looked around, then leaned forward and in a stage whisper added, "She left something behind in my hotel room. I think she'll want it back." He winked.

The young woman smiled knowingly. "I understand. Luckily, we're only hosting one conference at the moment. The details are there." She pointed to a placard on a stand behind him. At the top it read in bold letters, Women in Business Conference. Ballroom C.

He almost skipped as he made his way down the lush, carpeted halls, buoyed as he was by the thought of seeing Thel again. Strangely, he wasn't thinking of those beautiful eyes, that stunning red hair, or any of her other positive attributes. Instead he was remembering the strange flask and the glorious water inside. His body craved it.

"Get on your game, Bones. There's a hot chick just down the hallway and you're thinking about water."

When he reached the ballroom, the door was standing open. It must have been a break time. Attendees were milling about in small groups, chatting, drinking coffee, and dining on fruit and pastry.

"Can I help you?" The speaker, an attractive brunette in a power suit, made her way over to him. Bones guessed she was about ten years his senior and she moved with a confident grace. Another day and time, he would be trying to get her number, but not today.

"I'm looking for a friend," he said. "She told me she was attending this conference."

The woman's smile flickered. "Oh, I see." Disappointment rang in her voice. "What's her name?"

"Thel." Bones suddenly realized that he not only did not know her last name, but couldn't remember her actual first name. "It's short for something Greek. A weird name. I'm drawing a total blank on her last name."

"Well, I'm the organizer of the conference, and I can tell you we don't have anyone here by that name, or any name similar to that. It's a small group. This is everyone." She glanced over her shoulder. "Do any of them look familiar?"

Bones scanned the crowd again. Thel was not there. He felt his throat clench. He couldn't summon the words so he merely shook his head.

"I'm sorry I couldn't help you." The twinkle in the woman's eye belied her words. "I'm Lana, by the way."

"I'm Bones," he said.

"Nice to meet you." She shook his hand firmly, then relaxed her grip and covered his big hand in both of hers.

"Oh, don't look so glum. Do you really expect me to believe you've never given a girl a fake name or number?"

He had to laugh at that. "Fair enough. It's weird that she specifically mentioned the conference here."

"Maybe she's a guest here. She saw our sign and used it as a cover story. Maybe if you hang out you'll bump into her."

"That's okay. I can take a hint. It's weird though. I thought she and I had a pretty good time, but then she got really weird all of a sudden and just left."

Lana winced. "I hate to say this, but have you considered the possibility that she's married and she was having a touch of buyer's remorse? I coordinate events like this all over, and I see it a lot, especially in a remote place like this. You feel like you're in another world. Then you do something stupid and reality comes crashing down on you." A brief downcast expression suggested that Lana might be speaking from experience.

Bones had not considered that possibility, but something told him that wasn't the case. "Maybe," he said noncommittally.

"Could it have been the girl who disappeared?" someone nearby asked. A short blonde with big teeth and lots of makeup sidled up to them. "I heard that one of the hotel guests went out for an early morning swim and didn't come back."

Lana rolled her eyes. "Well that's just a wonderful thought, Tammy."

Tammy shrugged. "I'm just saying. It's not like I hope that's what happened. Actually, I heard talk at the front desk. Apparently there were a few disappearances last night."

The words were like a dagger to Bones' heart. He hadn't wanted Thel to walk home by herself, but he'd let his anger get the better of him. Why had he just let her go like that?

"One man drowned," Tammy continued. "He was out for a night swim. His friends were sitting on the dock, watching him, and he just disappeared. They said it was like something just yanked him under the water. One moment he was there, and the next…" She held out her hands, palms up.

"I'm going to go out on a limb and suggest alcohol might have been involved," Lana said.

Tammy shrugged.

"Listen, I've got to go," Bones said. "Thanks for your time." Heart sinking, each step seemingly heavier than the one before, he made his way out into the hall.

"Bones, wait." Lana caught up with him just outside the door and grabbed him by the arm. "Listen, I hope I'm not out of line, but if you don't find your friend, I'll be in the hotel bar after six."

Bones thanked her but said he could make no promises.

"Well, I hope you can work me into your schedule." She gave his biceps a quick squeeze then returned to her conference.

Despite his disappointment, Bones couldn't help but watch as she walked away. He loved her confident stride along with several other things about her.

"That," he said to himself, "is one hell of a woman."

14

Nassau, Bahamas

The Pirates of Nassau Museum was a wax museum on New Providence near Nassau's Straw Market. Its convenient location made it a popular destination for tourists, especially cruise ship passengers. Maddock and Rae navigated crowds of sunburned families in flip flops and air brushed t-shirts as they browsed the exhibits.

The Quay Side was a model shanty town where museum visitors explored the lamp-lit dockside at twilight. The smells of tar and salt water mingled in the humid air. Throughout the exhibit were signs sharing details about the pirate's life.

"You almost feel like you're really there," Rae said.

They explored a model of the pirate ship *Revenge* and exhibits devoted to some of the most notorious pirates of the region, including Ann Bonny, Mary Read, and Blackbeard himself, Edward Teach. Maddock couldn't help but let his mind drift at the sight of the pirate. He could tell these people a few things about Blackbeard's fate, and the fate of his treasure, but no one would believe him.

Rae glanced at him. "Earth to Maddock."

"Sorry. Just admiring the wax figure."

"Come on. Riddick Blackwood is this way, and the guy we're looking for should be around here somewhere."

Riddick Blackwood's wax figure was striking, tall with dark hair and intense brown eyes. His hand rested on the hilt of his sword, the corners of his mouth twisted into a permanent smirk.

"He was cute," Rae said.

"That's one way to describe a guy who was the

scourge of the Caribbean for years."

Rae shrugged. "I'm just saying."

The sign that accompanied the exhibit offered no information they didn't already know. Blackwood hadn't only preyed upon European ships, but on the native populations. He robbed, kidnapped, murdered, and enslaved the locals for years until his death.

"Excuse me, but are you interested in Blackwood?" A tall, thin man with leathery brown skin and short, almost white hair approached. He wore a three-piece suit and a name tag that read OLIVER LAWSON. This was the person they were looking for.

According to Rae, Lawson was born and raised in the islands and was considered a local expert on pirates and associated legends. She had never met him but knew him by reputation. They hoped he could help them understand the find Maddock and his crew had made.

"We are," Rae said. She introduced herself as a local professor and learned that she and Lawson had a few mutual acquaintances. They chatted amiably for a few minutes before getting down to the subject at hand. "Do you know much about Blackwood?"

Lawson shrugged. "I suppose I'm considered a local expert. Is there anything specific you'd like to know?"

Maddock really wanted to ask him about the ouroboros and the egg, but thought they should build up to it. A ship and an artifact that appeared to hail from the ancient world lying in the waters off of Andros seemed so improbable that he felt he should ease into the subject by asking about something more commonplace, less controversial. Besides, he still hadn't given up hope of finding Blackwood's treasure.

"I've done a lot of research about Blackwood, but are there any local legends about him that we might not find anywhere else?" Maddock had done a lot of digging but had found it difficult to find much beyond the stories everyone knew. Even his friend Jimmy Letson, a journalist and hacker, had not been able to find much. Blackwood was an enigma.

Lawson smiled. "This was Blackwood's old stomping grounds. Well, Cat Island was his home base, but the locals who know the old stories could tell you plenty. You'll hear all sorts of crazy stories, each one more a little more farfetched than the others."

"The crazier the better," Maddock said. If he could guide Lawson into the realms of the absurd, he'd find it easier to bring the discussion around to the actual reason for their visit.

"I guess the craziest one would be that Blackwood is still alive."

"That would be crazy," Rae said.

"According to the most commonly accepted story, the one with which you're probably already familiar, Blackwood was hunted down by the turncoat Benjamin Hornigold. Hornigold and his men tracked Blackwood and his crew to his lair on Cat Island. Blackwood's crew surrendered, but the captain would not go quietly. They engaged in an epic duel. Blackwood had been wounded in the leg, which was the only reason Hornigold eventually won the fight. He cut off Blackwood's head to make sure he was really dead, and brought it to the governor, who displayed it in the streets for all to see."

Maddock nodded. This was precisely the story Jimmy had turned up, although the detail that the fight had taken place on Cat Island was new.

"Is he walking around like the Headless Horseman?" Rae asked.

"According to the legend, the head belonged to one of Blackwood's crew," Lawson said. "Few people actually knew what Blackwood looked like. He was so reviled, even among pirates, that he seldom came into port. Most who saw the man up close didn't survive to tell the story.

So, when Hornigold delivered a head matching Blackwood's general description, the governor was none the wiser."

"That part of the story is plausible," Maddock said, "but how is it that he's still alive today?"

Lawson grinned. "The legend holds that Riddick Blackwood found the Fountain of Youth."

"In Florida?" Maddock asked. The Fountain of Youth was a legendary spring that supposedly restored the youth and vigor of anyone who drank its waters. There had been plenty such legends over the years, even appearing as far back as the writings of Herodotus in the fifth century BC, and the Alexander Romance, a mostly fictional story of the life of Alexander the Great, written in the third century AD. The legend gained prominence during the Age of Exploration. The most famous name associated with the Fountain was Juan Ponce de León, the first governor of Puerto Rico.

Lawson shrugged. "Ponce de León never mentions the Fountain of Youth in any of his writings. In fact, the legend of Ponce de León searching for the Fountain in Florida seems to have originated with *Gonzalo Fernández de Oviedo's Historia General y Natural de las Indias*, written 1535. It's been suggested that Oviedo's account may have been politically inspired to generate favor in the courts."

"If the Fountain isn't in Florida, where is it?"

"According to the native islanders, the Fountain of Youth can be found in the land of Bimini, a place of health and wholeness."

"I assume we aren't talking about the islands we now know as North, South, and East Bimini?" Maddock asked.

Lawson shook his head. "No, but there is a place in North Bimini called The Healing Hole. It's a pool that can only be accessed through a network of winding tunnels. Underwater channels pump mineral-laden fresh water into the pool. Because this well was carved out of the limestone rock by ground water thousands of years ago it is especially high in calcium and magnesium, a mineral associated with improved longevity and reproductive health."

"So, if the mythical Bimini actually existed, it could be anywhere," Rae said.

Lawson nodded. "One native, an Arawak chief named Sequene, was so obsessed with the legend that he took a crew and sailed off in search of it, never to be seen again. But the general consensus is that Bimini is hidden somewhere among the islands, and that Blackwood now guards it."

"Guards it against what? Or who?"

"Against whom," Rae said, giving him a nudge with her elbow to show she was teasing.

"Against anyone foolish enough to try and find it."

"Like the knight who guarded the Holy Grail in the Indiana Jones film?" Maddock asked. It felt odd to be discussing these legends as if they were true.

"More like Smaug the dragon guarding his treasure trove. Blackwood was a greedy man. He wouldn't want to share something as priceless as the Fountain of Youth with anyone else. Even if there were water to spare, the idea of him alone possessing it for all eternity would have been intoxicating to one such as him."

"Any idea as to the source of the legend? How did Blackwood come to be associated with the Fountain?" Maddock asked.

"According to legend, he makes an appearance every few decades, probably to stock up on rum and women. He's been blamed for many disappearances here. Always a beautiful, young college girl, a tourist. Blackwood charms them and takes them back to his lair where they join his immortal harem. The occasional local girl has even been known to blame her surprise pregnancy on Blackwood." Lawson's eyes twinkled.

"An immortal pirate with a constant stream of young, beautiful women? Sounds like a story written by a teenage gamer geek."

"Are you a gamer?" Rae asked.

"No, I was thinking of my crewmate, Corey. He's the biggest nerd I know."

"I know it sounds mad," Lawson said, "but several years back someone actually captured a photograph of a man they claimed was Riddick Blackwood. This man, whoever he was, was one of the last people seen with a particular missing girl. And I have to admit, it looks a great deal like the old paintings of Blackwood."

Maddock nodded thoughtfully. Too bad Bones hadn't come along. He loved this sort of thing. Ancient mysteries, far-out legends, and attractive women.

"You said Blackwood was greedy. Any legends about lost treasure or sunken ships?"

"When it comes to Blackwood's treasure, there are basically two schools of thought: those who say he spent every penny he ever stole, and those who say he hoarded his treasure, either in a hiding place among the islands, or with him at the fountain."

"How about the wreck of his ship *Maelstrom*?"

"Only that it was taken down by a sea monster."

That was interesting.

"Could it have been a creature with a shark's head and the tentacles of an octopus?" Rae asked.

Lawson quirked an eyebrow. "You're talking about the Lusca." When Maddock and Rae exchanged quizzical glances, he went on. "According to legend, the Lusca is a giant octopus with the head of a shark. It lurks in blue holes and hauls people down to their deaths."

"Did it look like this?" Rae reached into her shirt and took out the amulet.

When he saw it, Lawson gasped and his eyes went wide. He quickly smoothed his expression into one of indifference, but Maddock hadn't missed the initial reaction. It was a look of recognition and alarm.

"Perhaps," Lawson said. "But that's really all I know. I've heard the broad strokes and nothing more. I mean, a shark-octopus hybrid? That's about as realistic as the Fountain of Youth." He forced a nervous laugh.

"Any idea where we could learn more?" Maddock asked.

"About the Lusca? No idea. I've spent my life gathering local stories and legends, and what I just told you is all I know."

"This might sound strange, but have you heard any legends of explorers from the ancient world coming to the islands?"

"None," Lawson said flatly. He made a show of checking his watch. "I'm sorry, but I really have to go. I hope you enjoy your visit to the museum." With that, he turned on his heel and hurried away.

Rae turned to Maddock. "Was it me or did he clam up after I showed him the amulet?"

Maddock nodded. "Something spooked him. He knows more than he's letting on."

15

Andros Island, Bahamas

The local police precinct was a two-story block building that dominated the narrow street on which it stood. The interior was no more impressive. The walls were a dull green and sorely in need of a fresh coat of paint. What had once been a white tile floor was now cream and on its way to light brown. Half the fluorescent bulbs had burned out, and a few more flickered annoyingly. The place was neat and clean, with a strong smell of cleaning solution and burnt coffee.

The officer on duty, a tall, skinny young man, greeted them with a tired smile. His name tag read *M. Gomez*.

"How may I help you?" he asked.

"A friend of mine is missing," Bones said. He wasn't quite certain that was true. In fact, he had no idea if Thel were missing or had simply ditched him. But he couldn't shake the feeling something was wrong.

The young man's shoulder sagged. "I'll need you to fill this out." He handed him a clipboard and pen.

Bones frowned. He couldn't complete this form. Feeling foolish, he handed the clipboard back to the officer.

"See, here's the thing. I don't actually know her name. At least, not her full name. But I can describe her and tell you where she was staying."

Gomez closed his eyes and rubbed his temples.

"Sir, I'm terribly sorry if this seems rude but we really can't help you if you are unable to give us the information we need."

"Just answer me this. Have you had any reports of a woman named Thel going missing? Caucasian, red hair, big green eyes, fair skin, perfect lips. About this tall." He held his hand out just below shoulder height.

"Chick is drop dead gorgeous," Kyle added. "She swept this dude off his feet in no time flat."

"Is this a joke?" Gomez's demeanor, which had conveyed fatigue and perhaps a touch of impatience, had suddenly gone downright hostile.

"I don't understand," Bones said.

"Don't play dumb. Every year about this time, we get at least one tourist who comes here and tries to file a missing person's report for a friend who was last seen with the Little Mermaid. Or at least someone who looks just like her. Every once in a while someone falls in love with her but can't find her again. They get so desperate that they show up at the precinct fishing for information."

"That's not what's going on here," Bones insisted. "Come on. A freaking cartoon?"

"I didn't mean that literally." Gomez fixed him with a long look. Slowly, his facial features relaxed. "You seem sincere, so I'll give you the benefit of the doubt. The thing is, it's become sort of an urban myth around here, and tourists pick up on it. It happens like clockwork. About this time of year somebody comes in here and makes a report involving this girl. A couple years ago she stole a guy on his honeymoon. He and his new bride were having drinks at Brigadier's. She ran to the ladies room and when she came back, her husband was talking with a beautiful redhead. She said there was something like madness in his eyes. The girl hurried away, but the guy got all twitchy, like he was jonesing for her. At least, that was how his wife described it. Said he suddenly hopped up and took off. She never saw him again."

Bones suddenly felt dizzy. He couldn't deny that his desire to find Thel felt very much like the deep craving an addict might feel when denied their drug of choice.

"This urban legend," he began, trying to distract himself, "is there anything to it? Like, is there a source? Was there an original redhead who disappeared?"

Gomez cast a nervous glance over his shoulder. "Sir, we're really busy."

Bones looked around. He was literally the only civilian in sight. And something told him Gomez wanted to talk about this.

"I know you're busy and I don't mean to waste your time." In truth, it appeared the only thing Gomez was busy with was a cheese Danish, which sat half-eaten on his desk. "The truth is, I love this sort of thing. I grew up on *In Search Of* and now I can't get enough. And we really did meet a girl last night who might be missing."

The young officer's eyes went wide. "Really? I'm a huge fan of that show! What's your favorite episode?"

"Like I could ever pick just one. But if you're going to force my hand, I'll have to pick the episode with Nessie."

"I love Nessie! Have you ever heard of the Lusca?"

"No. What is it?"

"A local legend. A giant water monster that drowns swimmers in blue holes."

"Blue holes, plural? How does that work?"

Gomez grabbed a legal pad and began to sketch. He drew the side profile of an island in the sea.

"Andros is filled with blue holes." He drew lines going straight down through the island. "They're connected to one another by a network of underwater passages." He began sketching horizontal lines. "Most are small, impassable to anything larger than a fish, but not all of them. And some even connect to the sea." He drew more lines, these connecting to the water.

"What about the offshore blue holes? Do those connect?"

"Probably. At least some of them. Those are some of

the deepest blue holes in the world and the bedrock is like Swiss cheese in places."

"Has anybody ever swam from an offshore blue hole to one on the island?" Kyle asked.

"No, and It would be suicide to try it," Gomez said, glaring first at Kyle, then at Bones.

"I have no idea what you're talking about," Bones said.

"Don't give me that. I saw the way your eyes lit up when your friend was talking."

Bones chuckled. "You got me."

Just then, a man in a rumpled suit entered from a door at the back of the room. His hair was mussed and he had dark circles under his eyes.

"Is everything all right here, officer?"

"Absolutely, Detective. I'm just warning these gentleman away from some risky diving locations."

"Good." The detective looked from Bones to Kyle. "Listen to the officer. People regularly drown on and around Andros, and in many cases we never find their bodies." He stared until the two men each acknowledged him.

"Understood," Bones said.

"Word!" Kyle added, flashing a peace sign.

When the detective left, Bones lowered his voice. "If you never found the bodies, you can't really know for certain they're dead."

Gomez rolled his eyes. "Don't say that loud enough for Detective Lane to hear. He's an ass at the best of times, but he's been up all night investigating several disappearances. It's been one hell of a night for our department. We don't need anyone else to go missing." He frowned pointedly at Kyle, who nodded vigorously. "He also hates my fascination with cryptozoology."

Bones smiled. He loved meeting a kindred spirit. They chatted for a few minutes about their favorite legendary creatures. Gomez told them he'd actually compiled a great deal of information on local cryptids. Bones said he'd love to learn more, and they made a plan to meet that evening. Maybe, if they were lucky, Gomez might know something about the shipwreck they'd found and the strange artifacts they'd recovered.

"Don't worry about me," Bones said after Gomez had warned him for a third time about the dangers of diving in and around the blue holes. "I was in the SEALs. I know the hazards."

"Please promise me you won't go down there," Gomez said. "You have no idea of the paperwork involved, and it would all get dumped onto me. Also, I want to hear more about the Florida Skunk Ape. That's a new one on me."

"You won't be hauling my corpse out of a blue hole. That I promise." Bones paused. "That is, if you'll tell me all you can about the urban legend. The one about the missing girl."

Gomez glanced back in the direction of the captain's office. "To tell you the truth, it's sort of a hobby of mine, along with my cryptid research. Most of what I've collected I can't show you."

Bones didn't miss the guilty look on his face. It looked as if someone had been copying official documents.

"But I can show you one thing—a newspaper clipping about a girl who went missing in the seventies. I think she might be patient zero, so to speak. The girl whose disappearance spawned the legend. Hold on a minute."

Gomez hurried over to the door from which Detective Lane had emerged, opened it, and peeked through. Apparently satisfied, he returned to his desk, dug deep in the bottom drawer, and pulled out a large three-ring binder. He flipped through, took out a page, and left the room. Bones heard the rumble and whir of a copy machine. When Gomez returned, he handed Bones a sheet of paper, still warm from the copier. It was folded in half.

"Okay, you two get out of here. Don't look at that until you're well away from the station. I don't want to risk Lane finding out what I just did."

"Fair enough. Thanks for your help and we'll see you at the boat tonight. You bring your cryptid research, I'll provide the beer."

"Count me in," Kyle said.

"No," Bones said, then winked at Kyle to show he was kidding. Well, he was sort of kidding.

He folded the paper a couple more times and tucked it into his pocket. He wasn't entirely sure why he couldn't let go of the thought of finding Thel again. She was hardly his first one-night stand. But she was different. The craving inside of him was driving him to distraction He had to know who she was, where she had gone.

Out on the street, when they were well away from the police station, he finally took a look at the article. The headline read, SEARCH FOR MISSING COLLEGE STUDENT ENTERS SECOND WEEK. There was a photograph of the missing girl. When he saw it, he stumbled and nearly fell. He was suddenly dizzy.

Kyle grabbed him by the arm and steadied him.

"Whoa, man. You okay?"

Bones couldn't speak. Instead, he handed the paper to Kyle, who took one look and gasped.

"Bro, you have got to be kidding me."

16

Nassau, Bahamas

Lawson lost himself among the museum visitors, then doubled back. He spotted Rae and the blond man who hadn't introduced himself. They were making their way toward the exit. He followed them outside and watched as they turned the corner onto Bay Street and disappeared from sight. He breathed a sigh of relief. He'd thought he'd given himself away when they'd pulled out that amulet, but they didn't seem to have noticed anything.

He returned to the museum, hurried back to his office, and locked the door behind him. It was a tiny space, with only a single window to elevate it above the level of janitor's closet.

"I thought Echard was full of it," he muttered as he searched for Echard's phone number. It took him a minute to find it. He'd hidden it in a bottom drawer tucked inside the pages of his favorite novel, *Atlas Shrugged*. He'd never actually read the book, but had heard enough of it discussed on talk radio that it was now near and dear to him. He'd found this copy in a secondhand store and fallen in love with it. It was a battered hardcover that looked to have been read through many times. He kept it close, like a good luck charm. It was also where he hid his emergency cash, although that was a bit light of late. He'd been participating in a poker group Echard organized, and he wasn't doing well.

There it was. A scrap of paper with the name Bill Jones scribbled at the top. Echard had called him the previous night and promised a financial reward, plus forgiveness of his gambling debts if he should ever come across an artifact like the one Rae had just shown him. His first instinct had been to snatch it, but that wouldn't have gone over well with her friend. The man had been friendly enough, but there was a coldness in those blue eyes that gave Lawson the creeps.

He had explained to Echard that theirs was an experiential museum, not one that emphasized the collecting and curating of artifacts. Still Echard had insisted that Lawson contact him should he ever come across such a piece.

He punched in the numbers with a trembling finger. Why was he so nervous? He was just passing along information. Echard should be delighted.

The person on the other end picked up on the third ring.

"Yeah?"

"Echard, it's me." Long pause. Silence. "Lawson from the museum."

"Yeah, sorry. Didn't sleep much last night. I'm pretty out of it."

"You sound like you're getting sick." Lawson thought Echard's voice sounded deeper, gruffer than he remembered. Of course, they'd never actually spoken over the phone.

"Yeah, maybe."

Lawson hurried on. "I don't actually have the artifact in my possession, but I know who does."

"Really? Tell me."

"Raeána Franklin. She teaches at the college. I didn't catch the name of the guy she's with, but he looks military to me. They just left here, headed toward Prince George Wharf."

"All right. Thanks for letting me know. Anything else?"

Lawson frowned. "Well, there's a matter of payment. You promised..." He let his voice trail off. Technically,

Echard had said he'd pay for the artifact, and all Lawson had to offer was information. Still, that had to be worth something.

"Yeah, I'll come by later. Thanks." Echard hung up.

Lawson hung up the phone, then sat down to catch his breath. The sight of the artifact, the phone call, they had unsettled him. He was certain something was going on here that he didn't understand.

Twenty minutes later, there was a sharp knock at the door. When he opened it, he was surprised to see Echard.

"That was fast."

Echard frowned, scratched his head. "I wanted to give you a heads-up. There's a girl named Rae Franklin and a guy called Dane Maddock who have been poking around, asking questions about my business. If they show up here, give me a call right away."

"What are you talking about? I just called and told you they were here with the artifact." He scratched his head. "Wait a minute. How did you get all the way here from Andros in less than a half an hour?"

Echard's face went scarlet. He seized Lawson by his necktie, pulled it tight, and slammed him backward into the wall.

"You had better start making sense, and fast," Echard snarled. "Or else I'll sell your gambling debt to some friends of mine who sell human organs on the black market."

Lawson didn't know if it was an idle threat but he wasn't about to take any chances. Quickly, he recounted Rae and Maddock's visit, and his subsequent phone call.

"It sounded like you," he lied. "And I know I dialed the correct number."

Echard's gaze seemed to burn into Lawson. How had he ever believed the man was a mere beach bum? The rage, the intensity Lawson saw in Echard's eyes frightened him even more than Maddock's cold stare. But what was worse was Echard's obvious zeal. He was obsessed with this artifact and that made him deadly.

"It was not me." Echard said each word with the force of a punch to the gut. "So who the hell did you talk to?"

"I don't know."

Echard tightened his grip around Lawson's throat. With his other hand, he lifted up the hem of his Hawaiian print shirt to display a pistol tucked into the waistband of his cargo shorts.

"Tell me exactly what was said. And don't leave out a single word."

Bones hung up the phone and turned to Kyle. "That was a guy from the pirate museum in Nassau. He thought I was Echard."

Kyle had guided him to Echard's apartment. They'd skulked around, and once satisfied that the man was not home, Bones had picked the lock. It was a skill he'd developed as a teenager. They had just closed the door when the phone rang. Bones had answered on impulse.

"What did he say?" Kyle asked.

"He was calling to let Echard know that Maddock and your sister have the artifact."

"Hold on." Kyle scratched his head. "You dudes just pulled that thing up from the bottom of the sea, didn't you?"

Bones nodded. "And it was hidden inside a clay egg until yesterday afternoon."

"So what does that mean?"

"It sounds like Echard was already aware this thing

existed before we found it. He's been keeping an eye out for it. At least that's what makes the most sense."

"But, how did he know they'd take it to the museum?"

"What else would you do with an artifact? He's probably got connections at all the local museums."

Bones looked around. "Let's give this place the once-over. Shouldn't take too long."

Echard lived in a small apartment above a restaurant, so the whole place stank of curry. It was comprised of a single room plus a small bathroom. It didn't take long to search every inch.

They didn't find much. Echard owned little in the way of personal possessions except for a box of the wooden fetishes he'd been hawking on the beach. Bones was amused to see that they'd been manufactured in China.

"Do you think this dude is a Mormon?" Kyle said. He held up a copy of the *Book of Mormon*.

"Maybe," Bones said. "That might have come with the room."

"Dude, this is not a hotel. Besides, it's got his name written inside." Kyle held the book open to show the name inscribed on the reverse side of the front cover. Stanley Echard.

"Why didn't you say that in the first place?" Bones snatched the book away from Kyle and flipped through it. A number of passages were marked.

"There's a Bible here, too. It looks pretty old."

"We'll steal them both in case these passages he's marked are important."

"You don't think he's just doing some Bible study?" Kyle asked.

"Does Echard seem like the kind of guy who studies the Bible on a daily basis?"

Kyle's expression was grave. "Dude, when you're

brought up in the system, one of the things you learn is that the people who act the most righteous on the outside are the ones hiding the darkest secrets on the inside."

"I heard that," Bones said. It was the first truly wise thing he'd heard come out of Kyle's mouth. "You find anything else interesting?"

"Not really. You can hardly tell anybody even lives here. If this was my place, I would have trashed it within a day."

"I give you full marks for self-awareness." Bones weighed his options. The search of the apartment had been fruitless. He supposed they could hang around, wait for Echard to come back, and try to beat the truth out of him. Of course, there were a million things wrong with that plan. He filed it away as a last resort.

Kyle consulted his watch. "I've got to bail if I'm going to get checked in and ready to compete. If you want, I can tell you which bar is Echard's favorite. He's usually there this time of day."

"It's the middle of the day. And I thought you said he was a Mormon."

Kyle grinned. "I didn't say he was a good one."

17

Off the Coast of Andros Island

The sun hung high overhead, beating down on the men who plied the decks of *Sea Foam*. The gentle breeze did little to quell the oppressive heat.

"I don't think we're going to find anything in this grid." Willis gazed balefully at the chart spread out on the console in the bridge. "Me and Matt gave it the once-over. It don't look there's anything down there. I think we should try over here." He tapped a spot well away from the sections they'd already worked.

Corey looked up at him and frowned. "Maddock won't like it. You know how he prefers to do things."

"Gotta love Maddock and his grids," Matt chimed in. He was sprawled in a chair, staring at the sonar screen.

"When Maddock ain't here, Bones is in charge, and when Bones ain't here, I'm in charge."

"Yeah, yeah, the old Navy buddies run the show." Corey barked a rueful laugh. "But that doesn't change the fact that Maddock will be upset if he thinks we half-assed this."

"Okay, fine. We'll do it systematically," Willis said, his voice dripping with sarcasm. "But I want to start with this grid right here, just a bit away from the wreck. This is the direction the current would carry anything that spilled as the hull fell apart. We can work outward from there." Willis saw Corey about to raise an objection. "Just because Maddock always starts at the top left doesn't mean we have to."

"I'm not anal, I'm meticulous," Corey said, in perfect imitation of Maddock.

"He don't try that line on me. He just calls it being thorough."

"I get why he does it, but I like your plan better." Corey paused. "As long as you'll be the one to tell him."

"I ain't worried about Maddock. I'm the only person of color on the crew. I'm an affirmative action hire."

"Bones is a person of color," Corey said absently, his attention already back on the charts.

Willis folded his arms. "Seriously? When Bones makes jokes about his race, everybody thinks it's hilarious. I drop a line like that, and nothing?"

"I thought you really were an affirmative action hire," Corey said. "God knows you didn't get this job on your merit."

Willis blinked, then burst out laughing. "Screw you, nerd boy. Takes us to the grid point. Me and Matt will go get ready to dive."

"On it."

Willis' instinct proved to be correct. While they didn't find any treasure, they did uncover some promising artifacts, including a handful of coins that might help them identify and date the wreck. Maddock would be pleased with the results, if not Willis' methods.

By the time their oxygen began to run low, they'd gathered in a satisfactory haul. Maddock would be satisfied with what they'd found, if not exactly happy. They wanted to find treasure. Needed to find it.

Back on board, they took their find below deck and began the process of sorting through and preserving the artifacts. They'd be kept in salt water for the short term until they could be properly prepared for sale.

"What do you make of the coins?" Matt asked.

Willis squinted at the coin he held in his palm. It was an imperfect circle, blackened with age. He could make out the faint outline of a figure in profile. On the obverse side, what might be a torch.

"I don't know much about these; not the way Maddock does. My money's on Greek."

"Well, it's all Greek to me," Matt jibed.

Willis gazed flatly at him. "I know I've told you before. If Bones ain't around, there's really no need to try and fill that void."

"The only void is between your ears," Matt said.

Willis was formulating a suitable counterattack when he felt the deck vibrate. The roar of the engines filled his ears and the boat began to move.

"What the hell?" Matt said, looking up at the ceiling.

"Something's got to be wrong."

They made their hurried way above decks. Willis could tell right away that Corey had turned *Sea Foam* around and was heading back toward shore.

"What's going on?" he asked as he rushed into the cabin.

"Look at the sonar." Corey's face was ashen beneath his sunburned cheeks.

Willis looked at the display and his heart skipped a beat.

"What the hell is that thing?"

Something was bearing down on them. Something big and fast, moving underwater at breakneck speed.

"I can't think of what could have a profile that large," Matt said from over Willis' shoulder. "Have you ever seen anything like that?"

"That big? A submarine maybe."

"That's no sub." The engine whined. Corey was taking it right up to the red.

"How long can the engines hold up?" Matt sounded tense.

"Not much longer at these speeds."

Willis watched the sonar. Gradually, the thing, whatever it was, began to fall back, but it continued to pursue them.

"It ain't giving up."

"Then we'll have to persuade it," Matt said.

"With what? We ain't got any torpedoes here."

"Rifles?"

Willis considered this. Even a high-powered rifle was unlikely to deter something as large as the thing that was coming after them. Still, any port in a storm.

"Maybe if it surfaces we can hit it in the brain pan or something. I guess it won't hurt to try."

Willis and Matt took up arms and positioned themselves at the stern. They couldn't hear much over the roar of the engine and the rush of wind in their ears. Corey called out to them that the thing was closing in.

"It's catching up to us! God, this thing must be thirty meters long!"

And then Willis caught sight it. It was only a brief glimpse, but he was certain about two things: it was a living creature and it was massive. A wave of shock passed over him. It was big enough to be a whale, but a whale didn't move like that. So that the hell was it?

"Hold your fire," Willis said.

Matt didn't lower his rifle. "Why?"

"You see the size of that thing? I don't want to piss it off unless we absolutely have to. Maybe it just breached because it's about to change direction or something."

"Sort of like that time you said maybe that wasn't really an Adam's Apple on that girl we saw in the bar?"

"Hey, she turned out to be cool. She was a Lions fan. Bought me a beer."

Matt smiled. The situation was too tense for anything more. Then his eyes went wide and he pointed.

"My ten o'clock. Look!"

In the distance, a tall dorsal fin cut through the water. Willis had spent enough time at sea to be able to gauge the distance and know that what they were seeing was a very large shark. Not a monster, but a damn big specimen.

"That's got to be a great white."

"I hated that band," Matt said.

Willis grinned. "You and me both, cuz."

"But that isn't what we just saw."

"No, it is not." Willis narrowed his eyes, scanned the surface of the water. Where had it gone?

And then it happened.

The water around the shark began to boil, and then something surged up from the depths and struck the great white hard enough to send it flying into the air amidst a geyser of foam. The shark flew ten meters, struck the water, and was immediately engulfed in a crush of giant tentacles. They wrapped around it like a cocoon and took it under. It was over almost as quickly as it started. They waited, watched, but it didn't return.

"Did that really just happen?" Matt said.

"I ain't been drinking. Have you?"

"Coffee and water."

They were so stunned that they barely noticed when the sound of the engines fell to a normal level and *Sea Foam* slowed.

"Why are we slowing down?" Willis shouted.

"It broke off the pursuit, headed south," Corey called. "No idea why."

"We know why," Matt said, finally lowering his rifle. "It was hungry but it found easier prey."

They returned to the cabin and quickly recounted the sequence of events to Cory.

"Maybe you misjudged the distance and it was actually just a small shark being eaten by a large octopus?" Corey ran a hand through his short, ginger hair.

"It was definitely a great white," Matt said. "The markings, the sharp point at the tip of the dorsal fin. Even if it were small for its breed, that would still have to be an impossibly large octopus. If that's what it was."

"And it knocked that shark around like a beach ball,"

Willis added. "What the hell can do that?"

"I don't know," Corey said, still watching the sonar out of the corner of his eye. "But I think I'm done with treasure hunting for the day."

Willis nodded. "I heard that." He leaned against the bulkhead, breathed deeply, and tried to clear his head. How could they possibly protect themselves from a monster like that?

"I just feel sorry for whoever it decides to snack on next."

18

Andros Island

Maddock and Rae arrived at Blue Descent shortly before the start of the day's competition. Rae was eager to get there, feeling she'd left Kyle unsupervised for too long already.

"Bones is keeping an eye on him," Maddock reminded her.

"Really? Then why is Kyle here and Bones nowhere to be found?" She pointed in the direction of the dive platform, where Kyle stood, waving to them.

"I'm here." Bones came striding along the shore. Usually unflappable, deep concern marred his face.

"What's going on?" Maddock asked.

Bones looked around nervously. "Can I talk to you for a second?"

The men excused themselves and wandered away from the crowd until they were out of earshot. Maddock listened as Bones told him the whole story about the woman he'd met, her odd behavior, and their sudden parting. He went on to explain how he'd subsequently been unable to track her down.

Maddock was surprised. "She must have done a number on you if you went looking for her. Usually it's the other way around."

"That's just it. At first I thought it was her I couldn't stop thinking about, but then I realized it feels more like a craving. I think maybe there was something in the water she gave me."

"Bones, maybe you ought to see a doctor."

Bones shook his head. "Nah, it's already fading away."

He fell silent and Maddock decided to wait him out.

If his mood was dark enough, Bones considered any sort of probing question a form of interrogation. Best to let him do this at his own pace. Maddock was certain there was something deeper at play here.

Out on the platform, Val was giving instructions through a megaphone. The support staff was swimming to their places in the blue hole, and the contestants were getting ready. Kyle was attempting to do Tai Chi.

"He looks like a sleep deprived flamingo," Maddock said as the young man wobbled on one foot and flapped his arms, trying to keep his balance.

Bones forced a smile. "He's a good dude, though."

"Yeah, he means well and seems harmless enough. More a danger to himself than others."

"It's the unintentional harm that worries me." Bones' smile vanished. "It's weird, but I almost feel like something's tugging at me but I can't tell the direction I'm being pulled."

"Well, you do have that ability with taco trucks."

Bones apparently wasn't in the mood to laugh. He lapsed into silence again as the divers took their places and the first event began. There wasn't really much to do once the competition began other than stand on the beach and wait for each contestant to resurface. While the diver was underwater, an electronic voice counted out the seconds the diver was under.

The first diver emerged to applause. A voice came over the public address system and announced that he'd just set the Australian record for a free immersion dive with a depth of ninety-nine meters. Lots of cheers, including the other contestants. Although prizes would be awarded in the male and female divisions of each discipline, most divers were focused on setting national records for their home countries or beating their personal bests. Few of them seemed to feel they were truly in competition with one another.

"Alexei's not here," Bones said.

"You're right. I wonder what happened?" The man had seemed quite gung-ho the previous day.

"I heard there were some disappearances last night. I hope he wasn't one of them." Bones cleared his throat. "There's something I've got to tell you. And I just need you to shut up and listen with an open mind."

"Don't I always?"

"Rarely." Bones reached into his pocket and took out a folded sheet of paper.

"What's that?" Maddock asked.

"I told you to shut up. When I couldn't find Thel and I heard about the missing persons, I decided to stop by the police station just to check. As it turns out, this time every year somebody shows up at the station looking for a friend who was last seen with a gorgeous, green-eyed redhead."

Maddock had a few objections, but held his tongue. *Bones is right about me. I'm not good at listening when the things I hear don't seem to make sense.* Something else was bothering him. The story rang a bell.

"You know what? Rae and I visited the pirate museum today, and the curator told us a story about Riddick Blackwood. Supposedly he discovered the Fountain of Youth somewhere in the Bahamas. Since then, he reappears from time to time, supposedly looking for girls for his harem. I guess he takes them back to the Fountain where he keeps them young and beautiful forever."

Bones' jaw dropped and he swayed on the spot for a moment. Maddock seized him by the arm.

"You're not well. Do you really think this girl slipped you something?"

"All she gave me was water," Bones said hoarsely. "And there didn't seem to be anything wrong with it."

Maddock grinned. "If you're lucky, it was water from

the Fountain of Youth."

"Dude, the person I talked to has made the legend a pet project. He's identified the missing girl she calls 'Patient Zero.' A college student who disappeared back in the seventies."

"And she discovered the Fountain of Youth?"

"Screw you, Maddock." Bones returned the paper to his pocket.

"Hey, I'm sorry. Just messing with you. Let me see what you've got."

Before Bones could reply, Rae's voice rang out above the crowd.

"Way to go, Kyle!"

"Crap, we missed his dive," Bones said.

"We'll fake it. He won't know the difference."

They hurried over to Rae, who was applauding and bouncing on the balls of her feet. She'd removed her shirt, and wore a red string bikini top. The amulet rested between her breasts, flashing silver in the midday sun.

"So glad she wore a bikini top," Bones said.

Maddock frowned.

"Don't tell me you disapprove."

"She obviously forgot there's at least one person who will kill to get his hands on that amulet. We should have found a safe place for it."

"I can hang onto it," Bones said. "That way she doesn't have to put her top back on."

Maddock rolled his eyes. "Bones, it's a wonder you're still single."

"You say that like it's a bad thing."

Out in the water, Kyle completed his post-dive protocols and then swam over to greet them. He was grinning from ear to ear.

"World record!" he shouted.

"Oh my God, that's amazing!" Rae cried. She waded out into the water to greet her brother, but when he reached her, he grabbed her by the arm and pulled her down beneath the surface.

Just then, a low rumbling sound filled the air. Maddock looked around.

"That sounded like thunder, but everything is clear."

"That wasn't thunder," someone said. "I felt it under my feet. Like an earthquake or something."

"There are underwater tunnels and caverns everywhere down there," Bones said. "It's like Swiss cheese. Seismic activity isn't that unusual."

Maddock cocked his head. "How did you know that?"

"I know stuff."

Rae climbed out of the water dripping from head to toe. Her sodden cutoffs had slid partway down her hips. Maddock caught a glimpse of string bikini, then forced himself to look away before she caught him ogling her.

"Tell me you guys hooked up," Bones said quietly. "I won't believe you but I still want to hear it."

"I don't have a towel so you'll have to do." Rae wrapped her arms around Maddock and squeezed him tight, soaking the front of his shirt.

"It's worth it," Maddock said, giving her a quick hug before he turned his attention to Kyle. "You said you set a world record?"

"That's right. Free immersion, ninety-seven meters." He nodded vigorously, his wet brown curls slapping his forehead.

"Didn't the Aussie just make it to ninety-nine?" Bones asked.

"I broke the women's world record," Kyle said.

Rae covered her mouth to stifle her laugh. Pity welled in her eyes.

"I'm not saying I'm a world record holder. Just that I broke a world record."

Maddock forced a smile. "That's a good way of

looking at it."

A commotion out in the middle of the blue hole drew their attention. People were shouting. Contestants and support staff were abandoning the platform and swimming for shore for all they were worth.

"Everyone get out of the water!" Val shouted through her megaphone.

"What the hell is going on?" Bones asked.

The surface of the blue hole roiled as bubbles surged up from somewhere in the depths.

"There must have been a collapse, just like you said."

Only Val remained on the platform. She moved to the edge, looked down in the water, and let out a scream. Moments later something struck the platform from down below with such force that Val was sent flying through the air. The platform flipped, instruments and equipment flew in every direction. Val landed flat on her back in the middle of the blue hole. She surfaced a few seconds later but submerged again.

Maddock and Bones were already in the water, swimming to her aid. They were halfway there before anyone else realized what had happened.

Val's head bobbed above the surface again. Her lips moved, but she made no sound. She seemed to be struggling for breath. They were halfway there when her eyes went wide and she was yanked beneath the surface so suddenly and with such force that Maddock wondered for a moment if she'd ever been there.

Maddock dove and plunged deep beneath the surface. Far below, he saw a dark shape, inky black against the shadowy depths of the blue hole. It moved impossibly fast, seeming to grow smaller by the second. And then it was gone.

A few others caught up to them and they made a quick search, but they didn't find Val. Maddock had known their efforts would be fruitless. Whatever had smashed into the platform had carried her away. He was certain of it.

"I hate to say it, but we're not going to find her," he said to the others. "I think we should get back to shore before that thing comes back."

"What do you think it was?" Koharu, the diver from Japan, asked.

"I didn't get a good look at it," Maddock admitted.

"Maybe it was the Lusca," Bones said as they all began to swim back to shore. "It's a cryptid. A local legend."

"I know. The guy at the pirate museum told us about it. It's a giant octopus with the head of a shark."

"You mean, like the amulet?"

"I think so."

Rae was waiting on shore with Kyle, tears streaming down her face.

"You didn't find her?"

"No. I'm sorry."

She fell into Maddock's arms and sobbed against his chest. Maddock squeezed her tight and stared out at the blue hole. The water was calm again, it surface strewn with remnants of the shattered platform. He had no idea what to make of the attack.

Silence descended upon the assembled participants. Everyone seemed to be in shock. Finally, the remaining organizers took charge. One of their number left to contact the authorities while the others made sure no one was injured. Finally, they announced that the competition would be suspended until further notice.

"Suspended? This thing is over," Bones said quietly. He stopped suddenly. "Holy crap."

"What is it?"

"The paper I was going to show you. It's a copy of a newspaper clipping from the disappearance I was telling you about. It was in my pocket." He extracted the sheet and carefully unfolded it. It was wet, but the ink had not smeared. "The thing is," Bones continued, "the girl in this picture doesn't just look like Thel. It could be her identical twin."

Maddock took the sheet from him and stared at the picture. The young woman was every bit as beautiful as Bones had said. But there was something familiar about her. And then he remembered. He stopped in his tracks.

"I've seen this girl before."

"You have? Where?"

Maddock turned and pointed into the blue hole.

"Down there."

19

Echard checked his watch. It was almost one o'clock. The dive competition ought to be well underway by now, which meant he should have more than enough time to search Alexei's motel room. He'd watched the place for an hour and there had been no sign of the Russian. The coast ought to be clear.

He left the coffee shop, crossed the street, and made his way to the door. It was a cheap-looking place, a one story cinder block building, much like any roadside motel in America. But the paint was fresh, the building in good repair, and the landscaping inviting. Not a bad place for someone living on a budget. He rapped sharply on the door.

"Housekeeping!"

He waited, but no sound came from inside. There was no telltale rumble of the air conditioning unit, a must in this climate. After one more knock just to be sure, he picked the lock and entered.

There wasn't much to see. Alexei kept the place neat and clean. No dirty clothes lying about, not even a stray coffee mug or food wrapper.

He made a quick search of the room and came away with nothing. That couldn't be right. Everywhere Echard went, the museum, the library, even the local storytellers, Alexei had been there, too. They had to be on the same trail. What was more, the man had already become friendly with Maddock and Bonebrake.

"School teacher, my ass," Echard murmured. "Who are you, really?"

He supposed it was possible that Alexei was merely an amateur archaeologist, or maybe a cryptid hunter, but instinct told him otherwise. There was something here.

He just needed to find it.

He moved to one corner of the room, closed his eyes for a few seconds, and when he opened them again, tried to see the room with fresh eyes. What stood out?

And then he spotted it.

Specks of dust lay on the center of the bedspread. He moved closer and saw it was plaster. His eyes drifted up to the air conditioning vent that hung directly above the center of the bed. He smiled.

"Gotcha!"

He climbed up onto the bed and quickly unscrewed the vent. It came free easily. Echard peered inside and saw a small bundle inside a Ziploc bag. Smiling, he retrieved it, then replaced the vent.

Inside were a notebook, a folder containing copies of newspaper articles, and an old book of local legends. He riffled through the magazine articles and quickly set them aside. Nothing there he didn't already know. Next was the book of legends. Scanning the table of contents, he again saw nothing that was new to him.

Echard decided to keep it anyway. Even if he had no use for it, taking it might hinder Alexei's efforts. It would mean letting the Russian know that someone else was on the trail, but that could possibly be a good thing. Let him start looking over his shoulder and see how he liked it. Also, the book might make a good bargaining chip if need be.

The notebook was written in Russian. Echard was just closing it when he heard the sound of a key in the lock. He hastily clicked off the bedside lamp, then drew his knife. Maybe it was housekeeping, but there'd been no warning knock. It had to be Alexei home early.

The door opened slowly. Too slowly. And then he saw the reason. Alexei's right calf was heavily bandaged and he was limping badly. In the semi darkness, he didn't notice Echard hunched down on the other side of the bed, only a few feet away. When he turned to lock the door behind him, Echard sprang.

He wasn't fast enough. Alexei caught a glimpse of him, and despite his injured leg, he dodged to the side. Echard's stab, which had been aimed for the Russian's kidney, sliced him across the stomach instead.

Alexei was unfazed. He lashed out with a right cross that rattled Echard's fillings as it caught him on the jaw. He staggered, and Alexei followed with a roundhouse kick aimed for the head. But his defensive reflex proved to be his undoing. The kick transferred his full weight to his injured right leg, and he fell heavily to the floor. He hit his head hard and his eyes went glassy.

Echard pounced, mounting Alexei's chest and pressing his knife to the Russian's throat. Alexei looked at him through misted eyes. His fingers twitched, as if he wanted to go for Echard's throat. But he thought the better of it and relaxed.

"Wise decision. Now, tell me who you work for."

"Boca Ciega College," he said in a hoarse voice.

"Killing you would be inconvenient, but not that big of a deal. I know who to bribe around here." Echard made the words as icy as he could manage. "So don't piss up my leg."

"I do not know this American idiom, but I think I understand. I work for myself on this."

"So you're a professor by day and an archaeologist while on vacation? What are you? The Russian Indiana Jones?"

Alexei actually smiled. "That is what my girlfriend calls me. I think I am more handsome."

"You're working for the Russian government. Admit it."

"I would never give the Water of Life to any man." Alexei sounded scandalized. "Think of all the evil that could be done. What if Hitler had it, or Stalin?"

"Or the Clintons," Echard added.

Alexei frowned but then made a tiny nod. "That would be bad, too."

"Tell me what you know. And make it fast. My hand could slip at any moment."

"I believe the Water of Life is somewhere in the islands but I do not know where it is. No clue."

"You're lying."

"Everyone I talk to tells me the same things I find in old newspaper clippings. Some say it is legend, others say monster guards it, still others say a pirate guards it. But no one knows how to find it."

"What happened to your leg?"

"Sand shark bite. I was dangling my legs into the water like a fool." Alexei winced. "Please. We can work together. No reason to compete. I only want the satisfaction of finding it."

"You expect me to believe that if you find the Fountain of Youth, you'll just walk away."

"Not fountain. Water of Life."

"Fine. Whatever you want to call it." Echard considered the proposal. Could he trust Alexei? The man seemed sincere enough. "If you're not in competition with anyone else, why all the cloak and dagger?" Seeing the Russian's forehead crinkle, he went on. "I'm talking about secrets. Why did you hide your notes in the ceiling?" Instinctively, he glanced up at the vent.

Alexei chose that moment to fight. He grabbed Echard's wrist in one hand and his throat with the other.

Echard was ready for it. He sliced the Russian's jugular, then covered his mouth as his life's blood flowed freely.

It was over quickly and soon the big Russian lay dead on the threadbare carpet.

Echard had to move fast. He washed his hands and cleaned his knife under the bathtub faucet, making sure to wash all the blood down the drain. Next, he gathered Alexei's research, intending to take it all. And then he had an idea.

He placed the folder on the bedside table. Then he tore a single sheet of paper from the notebook. In block letters, he wrote *MEET MADDOCK AND BONEBRAKE.* Grinning, he tucked the note inside the folder, right on top where the police would be sure to find it.

"Chew on that," he said, as he left and closed the door behind him.

Whistling a cheery tune, he headed down the street. Things were beginning to look up. Now he just needed to get his hands on the ouroboros.

20

When Maddock and the others arrived at Alexei's hotel room, a police car was parked outside, lights flashing. The door to one of the rooms stood open, the area in front of it cordoned off with crime scene tape. A uniformed officer stood guard, while another was conducting interviews.

"I've had enough of cops for one day," Bones said. After the incident at Blue Descent, they'd been among the last to be questioned by the police.

"Whoa, dude! That's Alexei's room they've got taped off." Kyle pressed a hand to his forehead. "You don't think he's… aw, dammit!"

Rae gave her brother a squeeze. "I'm sorry. I know you really liked him."

"I'll see if I can find out what happened." Maddock approached the crime scene, where a few bystanders were milling about a short distance from the taped-off area.

"Found him with his throat cut," a woman whispered to the man standing next to her.

"He's a Russian. Probably something to do with the mob, or maybe the commies are making a comeback," the fellow replied. "Maybe he's got Cuban connections."

Maddock's heart sank. He'd been holding on to a scant hope that maybe it wasn't a murder, or that if it was, Alexei wasn't the victim.

"Excuse me," he said quietly to the pair. "Can you tell me anything about what happened? I'm sort of a friend. I knew him from the dive competition."

The pair, Henry and Cherie, conveyed their sympathies. They owned the motel, and said that Alexei had been an ideal tenant during his short stay.

"Always polite, didn't make any noise, and most important, he paid in cash," Henry said.

"How long was he here?"

"A little over a week," Cherie said.

"The dive competition just started. I guess he was doing some sightseeing?"

Henry shook his head. "Research. Was asking about local legends, wanted to visit the old storytellers. He was a teacher of some sort so I guess he was writing a book."

Maddock's heart skipped a beat. "What was he studying? Any idea?"

"Sea monsters." Henry threw back his head and laughed. "Can you believe that? A grown man believing in monsters."

Maddock forced a smile. "He's not the only one. My friend over there wants to marry Bigfoot." He inclined his head toward Bones.

"That is one big Indian," Cherie said.

"Put your eyeballs back in your head, woman," Hank chided. "He's too young for you."

"I'm sixty, but I'm not dead yet. As you well know." Cherie gave her husband a peck on the cheek.

"You know, he mentioned something about his research," Maddock said, inventing on the fly. "There was somewhere he was going to go after Blue Descent ended, but I don't recall where."

"He talked about going to Cat Island," Cherie said. "I tried to warn him against it."

"Why is that?" Maddock asked.

Cherie simply shook her head and made the sign of the cross.

"My wife's not religious, but she is superstitious. Cat Island has a dark history. I'll say no more than that," Hank added.

"I hate to ask, but can you tell me anything about the crime?"

"Oh, yes. You lost your friend and here we are acting the fool." Cherie sighed. "He went out late last night. Hank saw him when he was taking out the garbage. We don't know what time he returned, but housekeeping found him on the floor. His leg was bandaged, so something must have happened to him while he was out. Anyhow, he had been murdered."

Hank dragged his index finger across his own throat.

"Any clues as to why he was killed?"

Hank pursed his lips. "Housekeeper found a folder with some of his monster research and there was a note about meeting somebody."

"What was the name?" It had to be Echard.

"One of them was Bonebrake. I remember it because it was so unusual. The other was Murdock or Maddox, something like that." Hank's eyes flitted to Bones then back to Maddock and his brow furrowed. "I didn't get your name."

"I'm Abbot, that's Winslow," he said, providing aliases he and Bones had used in the past. "Thanks for your time."

He made his way back to the others and told them what had happened.

"Alexei was researching sea monsters?" Rae said.

"Apparently."

"So, how did our names get dragged into it?" Bones asked.

"I don't know, but the police already have our names and contact information thanks to what happened at the dive contest. It's not a good look for us to be in two places where people were killed on the same day."

"Yeah, but there's no point in running. They'll just put out warrants for us and have us arrested when we get back home," Bones said. "Might as well face the music." His eyes lit up. "Hey, that's Gomez, the officer who helped me today. The cryptid investigator." He pointed to a skinny young man in uniform who had just finished taking a statement and was now headed in their direction.

Gomez stalked up to them, looking agitated.

"I assume you're Maddock?" He didn't wait for a reply. "You two come with me right now."

He led them away from the crowd and out of sight of the hotel.

"So, you did plan to meet Alexei."

"No," Maddock said. "We came to check on him since he was a no-show at Blue Descent."

"Blue Descent? You mean he was supposed to be part of the competition that turned into a disaster? That's quite the coincidence."

"I agree," Maddock said. "But those are the facts."

"Look, we already heard from someone in the crowd that you found our names at the scene," Bones said. "We've got nothing to hide. That's why we didn't bail."

"I don't know exactly when Alexei was killed, but I haven't been alone since night before last," Maddock said. "Between Bones, Rae over there, and any number of people at Blue Descent, I've got plenty of people who can confirm that."

"And I've got people, including you, who can account for my whereabouts," Bones said.

"Where were you around 1:00 this afternoon?"

"At Blue Descent," Maddock said. "We arrived shortly before things kicked off and didn't leave until just a short while ago when the officers at the scene dismissed us."

"I'm a witness," Rae chimed in, "as is my brother."

"And we were questioned at the scene by one of your officers."

"That's good," Gomez said, jotting down their answers. "I didn't want to believe you were involved. Any idea why Alexei wrote down your names?"

"We got along well," Bones said. "He was with a group of us who went out for a beer last night. Maybe he wanted to invite us out for a drink."

Gomez looked around again.

"Look, Alexei was conducting cryptid research. Sea monsters, specifically. Did he talk to any of you about that?"

Maddock shook his head. "No, but we're former SEALs and have spent most of our adult life at sea, so maybe he wanted to pick our brains."

Gomez nodded, kept on writing.

"You should to be looking at a guy named Echard," Bones said. "He's been skulking around, tried to steal an artifact from us."

"Echard? That could be a problem." Gomez lowered his voice. "Look, I think you should get out of here. You've officially been questioned by the police and provided alibis and witnesses."

"So why is there a problem?" Rae asked.

"Detective Lane plays in Echard's poker game, and the word is, Lane is on a losing streak. If Echard is involved, he might put pressure on Lane to pin the crime on you. I'll confirm your alibis but I won't tell Lane that you were here." He paused. "I'm putting a lot of faith in you two."

"Thank you," Maddock said, shaking his hand.

"You still coming over for that beer tonight?" Bones asked.

Gomez laughed. "A chance to swap stories with a fellow cryptid lover? I wouldn't miss it for the world."

21

Echard was fit to be tied. The reliably malleable Lane was on the verge of growing a spine, and it was making his life difficult. He closed his eyes, squeezed the receiver, and counted to three.

"Lane, it's essential that you keep my name out of this investigation," Echard said.

"I'll do my best. But you have to understand, this is a serious issue."

"You know what else is serious? A cop with massive gambling debts. Do you have any idea how much you owe me?"

"Yes."

"And do you have the money to pay me back?"

The line went silent. Echard waited.

"Still there?"

"You know I don't have the money," Lane said in a sullen voice. "That's why you've gotten away with as much as you already have."

"I have no idea what you're talking about." Echard couldn't help but smile. Lane was a fool, but a useful one. "Now, have you arrested Maddock and Bonebrake yet?"

"Can't do it. No motive and they've got confirmed alibis for the time of death."

"But their names…"

"The fact that their names were written on a sheet of paper isn't evidence of a crime."

"And what about my stolen artifact? Did you recover it yet?"

"The artifact you refuse to describe? That one for which you can't provide any proof of ownership? You're tying my hands here."

"I'm on the verge of tying your hands and your feet

to a block of cement and dropping you into the nearest blue hole." Echard gritted his teeth. He had the stolen CT scan images, but if he showed them to Lane, he'd have to explain how he had come by them. And if it was his word against Raeána's, they'd believe the college professor over him in a heartbeat.

"It's a silver amulet shaped like a serpent biting its tail." That ought to be generic enough to keep an idiot like Lane from putting two and two together.

"Like a sea serpent?"

Dammit! The man was developing a backbone and a brain at the worst possible time.

"No, not like a sea serpent. You'll know it when you see it. Just get it back from them."

Lane sighed. "Look, these guys are highly decorated veterans. And not just the same commendations everyone earns if they serve long enough. If Maddock wore all their medals at the same time he could compete in the joust. And that's just what I was able to find out."

"What does that have to do with a Bahamas police investigation?" Echard was losing patience. His hired guns had failed him and now his leverage against Lane was suddenly insufficient.

"Within an hour of getting my first report back on Maddock and Bonebrake, I received a call from a Commander Maxwell in the U.S. Navy. He suggested I direct all future inquiries to him. Then he dropped a few names, including that of the Governor-General. Oh, and would you like to guess who called me no more than five minutes after we hung up, just to confirm Maxwell's instructions?"

Echard's heart began to race, his skin felt clammy. That was not the kind of attention he needed.

"Okay, fine. Handle those two however you feel necessary, but whatever you do, direct the investigation away from me, or else the Governor-General is going to get another call about you. As will a few reporters."

"That won't be necessary," Lane said tightly.

"Oh, and get my amulet."

A sharp knock came at the door.

"I've got to go. Keep me posted." Echard hung up the phone.

The knock came again. A single rap, ominous.

Echard peered through the peephole. The cheap lens warped his vision, but he could see the person standing there was a bear of a man. He had fair skin, a square jaw, and wore his dark hair in a GI cut. He arms and legs were like telephone poles.

"Can I help you with something?"

The man stared directly at the peephole as if he could see Echard on the other side.

"You called for our help. I just arrived from Utah."

Echard gasped. So they really had taken him seriously.

"Great. Just a second." His numb fingers fumbled with the locks. By the time he opened the door, the man was tapping his foot impatiently.

He didn't wait to be invited in. Echard had to spring to the side to avoid being crushed between the door and the wall.

"I'm Echard."

"Issachar."

What the hell kind of name was that? Then again, a lot of the Dominion guys had weird names.

Issachar looked around the small room and apparently saw nowhere he would deign to sit. He turned to face Echard. Inside the small room, the man looked even more imposing. He stared but said nothing.

"How was your trip?" Echard said, unable to bear the silence for more than a few seconds.

"The flight sucked, but it got me out of an archaeological dig in the Utah desert. I'll take the

Bahamas over that any day."

"You don't look like an archaeologist."

"I'm a consultant. I assess situations and provide support and guidance. Occasionally I get directly involved."

Echard wasn't sure how he felt about that. It sounded like Issachar planned to be hands-off, which was great. But Echard could really use some help with the Maddock situation. Best to bring that up when the time was right. "You're going to love the islands. Best rum in the world."

Issachar quirked an eyebrow. "You drink alcohol?"

"No. Just a joke." He hoped Issachar couldn't see the lie in his eyes.

Issachar didn't laugh, or even smile. "Tell me what you've got."

Echard realized he was holding his breath. This was the moment of truth. What if the man didn't believe him?

"An artifact was recently discovered. I believe it's an item of great power... a power of Biblical proportions, if you will. It all started with a story I heard from an old man on Cat Island." Issachar's expression remained implacable as Echard launched into his story. He then gave a quick summary of his subsequent investigations and the events that had brought the artifact to his attention. When he finished, he handed Issachar the items he'd taken from Alexei's room, along with a binder filled with his own research and notes.

Issachar examined them quickly, but not carelessly. He devoured the information like hungry piranha consuming a carcass.

"This is the artifact?" He tapped one of the CAT scan images.

"That's it."

"Not a lot of detail here, but it looks like a serpent

biting its tail. Kind of reminds me of Jörmungandr, the Midgard Serpent of Norse mythology."

Echard was surprised. He'd judged the man on his appearance and concluded his education didn't extend far beyond the efficient cracking of skulls.

"In the Talmudic works, there's a reference to Leviathan with "its tail placed in its mouth, twisting and encompassing the entire world."

Issachar nodded. "The Zohar and the Baba Batra. The Elder was impressed with your thorough citations of scripture and extra-Biblical texts. I think that's the only reason I was sent. He doesn't like to take chances when there might be a scriptural connection."

Echard gaped. "My information was passed along to the Elder?"

"Yes, but don't get too excited. He's quite skeptical. The scripture mentions sea serpents, but not an artifact."

"I'm working on the assumption that the Leviathan legend overlaps with sea serpent tales from other mythologies." He knew immediately he'd chosen his words poorly.

"Is that how you see scripture? Myths and legends? I thought you were one of us. Or, you once were." His tone added layers of meaning to the words.

"Please don't misunderstand. I've been conducting all my research in the secular world, so their jargon has rubbed off on me. But I do think there's great value in these extra-Biblical stories. Even if they aren't literally true, they often contain nuggets of valuable information."

This seemed to satisfy Issachar. "Just making sure. Obviously, not even the scriptures are literally true all of the time. Sometimes the truth lies in the lessons the story is teaching."

Echard nodded, relieved that they seemed to see things the same, at least in this case.

"But make sure nothing else from the secular world bleeds through into your life."

"I understand."

Issachar's eyes narrowed. His gaze seem to bore into Echard's brain. "You've actually seen this amulet? Not just blurry scans?"

"I haven't seen it up close, but I've seen it from a distance and it's the same."

"And why do you believe the Dominion would want this artifact?"

Echard's heart raced. He had never said this aloud to anyone before.

"I think this artifact will give the bearer power over Leviathan."

Issachar's expression didn't change. "And what would you do with a thing like that?"

"Me? Nothing." Echard left out the other reason he wanted to find Leviathan, or Lusca, or whatever you wanted to call it. "But it seems like the sort of thing we, I mean, you, should have charge of. Would you rather it fall into the hands of the Vatican, or Trident?"

Issachar looked up at the ceiling and slowly began to pace. Echard had to hop onto the bed to get out of his way.

"Assuming this artifact is authentic, and if you are correct about its power, there's potential, to be sure. Imagine the disruption to shipping that could be caused."

"Like, foreign countries?"

Issachar shrugged. "In certain situations, but I'm thinking more about using it as leverage to get things done in our own country. The United States is run by the people who own the members of congress. Corporations, mostly."

Echard caught on right away. "You ask them to exert a little influence. Any company that doesn't play ball, ships containing their merchandise start vanishing in the middle of the ocean. Oops."

"Exactly." Issachar stopped his pacing. "You really believe this thing could control Leviathan itself."

"It depends on which story you believe. One account says control, the other says release." Echard held his breath but relaxed when Issachar smiled.

"Many believe that Leviathan is the serpent alluded to in Revelation. Its return is a sign that the End of Days is coming!"

"And that would be a… good thing?" Echard tried to make it sound like a statement of fact, but he didn't quite manage it.

"It is for those who believe." Issachar tossed the binder onto the bed and rubbed his hands together. "It's time to get down to business. Who else knows about the amulet?"

"Detective Lane with the police department. I was trying to use him to get it back from the men who have taken it. He just thinks it's a regular black market antiquity; he doesn't know anything important."

"Still, that's another loose end we'll need to tie up. Who else?"

"A guy at the pirate museum. Lawson."

Issachar nodded.

"And a teacher named Raeána Franklin, and the treasure hunters who found it, of course. They've been hanging out together."

Issachar's eyes narrowed. "And where might I find them?"

"On their boat, I guess. It's called *Sea Foam*. I've tried to get the artifact back from them, but they've proved tough nuts to crack."

Issachar bared his teeth in a wolfish grin.

"Don't worry. That's the sort of thing I can take care of myself."

22

Sea Foam sat tied up at a remote dock. It wasn't much of a marina, just enough slots for a few tour boats, fishing boats, and space for a few guests. Maddock had been inclined to anchor offshore, but when he heard the tale of the crew's narrow escape, he thought the better of it. He, Bones, and Rae now sat on the aft deck, enjoying the cool evening air and moonlit sea. The remainder of the crew, Kyle in tow, had gone out for dinner and drinks. After their narrow escape, they felt the need to get away from the water for a while.

"You think it might have been the Lusca?" Bones asked.

"Of course I don't," Maddock said.

"Think about what happened at Blue Descent. Something did that. It could have been whatever chased the boat."

"True, but that doesn't mean it's the monster we just learned about. I swear, Bones, is there a cryptid you don't believe in?"

"Yes, but I'm not telling you which one. You'll just have to wonder about it."

They heard the sound of a boat approaching. A familiar face guided a small boat up to the dock. It was Officer Gomez. He tied up alongside them.

"Permission to come aboard?"

"Granted," Bones said. "But only if you brought the beer."

"You said you were providing the beer, but I did bring Jack Daniel's." The young man held up a backpack, the kind college students used to carry their textbooks. "I also brought my binder."

"Good man," Bones said.

They sat around drinking and making small talk until Maddock circled around to the subject that concerned him most at the moment.

"I hesitate to ask," Maddock said, "but can you tell us how things stand with the investigation?"

"I can tell you that you're in the clear for now. Detective Lane made some inquiries. I guess whatever he learned satisfied him. That and you both have alibis."

Maddock raised his bottle in salute. Soon, the conversation turned to the unusual creatures Bones and the officer loved.

"We have rich folklore in the Bahamas. Many fascinating stories and creatures," Gomez said.

"Which is your favorite?" Rae asked.

Gomez considered the question. "There's the chickcharney. It's a cryptid unique to Andros. It lives in the forests, usually in pine trees. I can be feathered or furry, but generally resembles a very large owl."

"How large?" Rae asked.

"A meter tall. It has three fingers at the ends of its wings, three toes, piercing red eyes, and a head that can spin three hundred sixty degrees."

"I dated a girl like that," Bones said.

"It's a touchy creature," Gomez continued. "If a traveler meets the chickcharney and shows it respect, the traveler may proceed on his way and might even be granted good fortune. But the traveler who doesn't show the proper respect will be cursed."

Bones perked up at that. "Awesome! What sort of curse?"

"The usual. Bad luck. Financial ruin. It's said that Neville Chamberlain offended the chickcharney by cutting down one of their forests to build a plantation. The endeavor proved to be a spectacular failure."

"An 'overdrawn bank account' cryptid," Bones said. "Not the scariest story I've heard."

"I forgot to mention, if you laugh at the chickcharney, it clamps down on your shoulders and twists your head in a complete circle." Gomez made a twisting motion with his fists and accompanied it with a cracking sound.

"That's more like it," Bones said.

"I've considered doing that to Bones a few times," Maddock said.

Bones smirked. "You've considered doing that to your…"

"Please don't finish that sentence!" Rae snapped.

Gomez laughed and went on. "Islanders were once so afraid of the chickcharney that they took to carrying brightly colored flowers or bits of fabric to charm the creature and as an offer of respect."

"Any specific historical source for that legend?" Maddock asked.

"What makes you think it's a legend?" Gomez laughed. "In fact, Andros was once home to a meter tall burrowing owl called *tyto pollens* or the Andros barn owl. It is supposed to have gone extinct in the 1500s due to the destruction of its habitat. Its appearance must have been alarming to the colonizers and those they enslaved." He grimaced. "But if a few survived, that could explain the consistent sightings of the chickcharney over the years."

"We should definitely go looking for that." Bones sat up straight, turned to Maddock. "We need brightly colored fabric, so you'll have to bring all your Speedos."

Maddock rolled his eyes. "Quick. Somebody distract Bones with another nonsense story."

"Well, there is Anansi, the spider god and trickster. He is said to be the spirit of all knowledge of stories. Of course, his is an ancient legend, carried over from Africa. Ghana to be precise."

"Tell us more about the Lusca," Rae said.

"I don't know a great deal. For some reason, the old storytellers don't like to talk about Lusca. The most common version of the legend is that it's a giant octopus with the head of a shark. In other versions, Lusca is just a giant octopus. In still others, she is a sea serpent, but no description is given."

"Are there any points of agreement among the various versions of the tale?" Maddock asked.

"All agree that the creature lurks in blue holes, dragging victims to their deaths and consuming their bodies. The lost are never found again."

"Couldn't they just be regular drownings?"

"Possibly, but there are many eyewitness accounts of victims being suddenly and violently yanked down beneath the water. One survivor described the experience. He was swimming in one of the inland blue holes when something grabbed him by the ankle and snatched him. He estimated he was pulled down about twenty meters when the thing suddenly let go of him. Even so, he nearly drowned."

"So the Lusca swims from blue hole to blue hole by way of underwater passageways?" Maddock asked.

Gomez nodded. "Exactly. Long, long ago, the water levels were much lower. Andros and the other islands were well above sea level. Over thousands upon thousands of years, sinkholes were bored into the surface due to acid rain, and then passageways were formed as the limestone within the bedrock was eaten away. Eventually the water level rose, creating complex networks of underwater corridors."

"You told Bones that the passageways that connect to the sea were too small for divers to traverse. How about something malleable, like an octopus?" Maddock asked. "If that thing was real, could it come out to sea by one of those channels?"

"Not if it were as large as the legends say. I don't

know that a giant sea monster could make its way to open water."

"But if any creature could, it's the octopus," Maddock said. "They can squeeze through very small spaces. And they're deadly hunters, masters of camouflage."

"But they don't chase after boats," Bones said. "They lie in wait until they can nab their prey. Which actually fits the blue hole legends."

"If I were an octopus large enough to take down a boat, I might chase after one," Rae said.

"What if a new passageway opened up?" Bones said. "Like if there'd been seismic activity in the area."

Maddock remembered the odd tremors he'd felt, one today and another the day before. "Do you think it's possible?"

"Theoretically. Occasionally, the floor of a blue hole will collapse for that reason, which is why the title of world's deepest blue hole is often up for grabs. One is the deepest for a while, then there's a collapse and a new one takes the crown."

"So we've got this giant octopus thing that's been lurking around the blue holes. Yesterday there's seismic activity and boom! People start disappearing, our boat is chased, there's an attack at the dive contest. It fits," Bones said.

"What's the official line on the incident at Blue Descent?" Maddock asked.

"They're saying it was a shark. They think it somehow got trapped inside the blue hole, which led to its aggressive behavior."

"That was no shark attack," Maddock said.

"Maybe not, but you won't convince anyone on the force that it was Lusca, if that's what you're thinking. You're welcome to try, of course."

"What about other cryptid stories?" Bones pressed.

"Anything unique to the area?"

"Of course, we have the usual legends of mermaids and the like. But if you want a unique story..." Gomez scratched his chin. "There's a legend that Christopher Columbus fought, or perhaps killed, a large serpent."

"That's hardly unusual, is it?" Rae asked.

"In this context, serpent does not necessarily mean snake. It could have been a lizard, dragon, or sea serpent."

"Could it have been a gator or crocodile?" Rae asked.

"Possibly, but they weren't native to the area at the time. Most versions of the legend call it a sea serpent. What stands out to me is that Columbus, a man of the world, thought it remarkable enough to record it."

"But not remarkable enough to record a description or make a sketch?" Bones said.

"As the legend goes, he did keep such records of his unusual finds, but his journal disappeared."

"Any idea what happened to it?" Maddock asked.

"I found one reference that indicates it fell into the possession of Juan Ponce de León."

Maddock and Bones exchanged a glance. The legend with which Ponce de León was most commonly associated with was that of the Fountain of Youth.

"What would Ponce de León want with that?" Rae asked.

"Gee," Bones deadpanned. "What could one explorer possibly want with records written by another explorer?"

"Don't make me dump my drink on your head. But okay, that was a dumb question."

"I think it's actually an interesting question," Maddock said. "Those early explorers weren't just looking for new land. They were searching for ways to leave their mark on history. They believed in things we now consider legends. And when it came to something like El Dorado or The Fountain of Youth, they sometimes guarded new evidence like a dragon hoarding treasure. Colonizers were different. They'd send letters back home sharing all sorts of outlandish tales in hopes of garnering more support for their colony. But to the hardcore adventurer, everyone else was their competition."

"Did Columbus ever search for the Fountain of Youth?" Bones asked.

"Not as far as I know," Gomez said, "but he did claim to have found the Garden of Eden on his third voyage. Some legends connect the two."

"Are you suggesting Columbus fought a Lusca?" Bones asked.

"If he did, he was lucky to have survived. Of course, Columbus also claimed to have seen a giant turtle the size of a whale, so he might not be the most reliable source."

Maddock laughed.

They swapped a few more tales. Gomez was a friendly guy and knowledgeable in his field, if Cryptozoology could be considered a "field."

"What about Cat Island?" Maddock asked. "Someone mentioned it to me today. They got tight-lipped very fast, as if the very mention of the place creeped them out."

Gomez nodded. "If you want to see the darkest side of the Bahamas, that's where you'll want to go."

"Are there any spots on the island where we might learn more about the Lusca?" Bones asked.

Gomez nodded. "I can think of one in particular."

23

The police precinct on Andros had some of the worst security Issachar had ever seen. He found it all too easy to slip in through a second-story window and into a meeting room. He crinkled his nose at the overwhelming odor of coffee. He never touched the stuff.

The room was dark but he could see that the furnishings were cheap, all of the folding plastic variety. Cobwebs in the corners and a layer of dust on the windowsill suggested this room didn't see much use. He took a few moments to listen. His sharp ears picked out a single voice down on the first floor. Probably whoever was working the front desk or minding the telephone.

He slipped out into the hallway and made a quick inspection of the space. A locked records room, and a trio of offices. A light shone through the crack beneath the door marked Detective Lane. He smiled. Perfect!

Issachar gave a quick knock on the door. Not too sharp. He wanted it to sound hesitant, like a nervous subordinate who hated to interrupt.

"What is it?" Lane sounded annoyed.

Issachar knocked again and mumbled something unintelligible.

"What was that? Oh, hold on a moment." Footsteps on tile, and then the door swung open.

Lane's eyes went wide when he saw Issachar standing there. He tried to shut the door, but Issachar forced his way into the small office. He clutched the smaller man's throat with one hand and with the other he held the tip of his stiletto a fraction of an inch from Lane's eye. Lane gave way until he was leaning back against his desk.

"You are going to answer all of my questions. If you

try to fight or call for help, this knife goes through your eye and into your brain. Understood?"

Lane tried to reply, but had to swallow a few times before he managed to croak, "Yes."

"Excellent." Without looking, Issachar reached back with his foot and nudged the door closed.

"First, you're going to tell me everything you know about Stanley Echard."

"He's a low-level hustler. Sells fake amulets, runs a poker game, handles a few bets. That sort of thing."

Issachar didn't like what he was hearing. Gambling?

"What else?"

"I can tell you which bar he frequents. Other than that I don't know anything else about him. I only help him out sometimes because I owe him money. Gambling debts."

"Really?" Issachar quirked an eyebrow. That's what Echard had been getting up to? "And to think he wants back in." He'd instinctively distrusted Echard, and it seemed his gut reaction was the correct one. Of course, that didn't necessarily mean Echard wasn't on to something with this amulet. It was up to Issachar to find out if there was anything to it, or just another of the countless dead-ends he'd encountered during the course of his work.

For years, ever since he'd been admitted into the inner circle, he'd been searching for artifacts of power. He'd been skeptical at first, but the Elder had pointed out that scripture attested to the existence of such items. That alone had been enough for Issachar, but then the Elder had shown him something else.

"The ancients had knowledge we only dream of. We must find it again. It is the will of our Lord."

"Tell me about the amulet."

"Please, could you move that knife a bit? I'm not armed and I won't give you any trouble. I'm easy to work with; just ask Echard."

"Good. I'm just looking for some help." Issachar took a step back and made a show of pocketing his stiletto. Let Lane think they were on the same team. It might loosen his tongue.

Lane stood up straight, gingerly rubbed his throat. "What is it you want from me?"

"First, I want all the information you have on Echard's stolen amulet."

"Echard says it's a silver amulet shaped like a serpent, and he gave me the names of the treasure hunters who he claims stole it."

"Claims?" Issachar asked sharply.

Lane shrugged. "This is Echard we're talking about. The truth is a slippery thing with him."

Issachar's stomach clenched. If Echard had sent him on a wild goose chase…

"Did Echard say why he wanted this amulet?"

"He didn't have to. Black market antiquities dealings are all too common in the islands. Knowing him, he's told his potential buyer that he already has it in his possession. Now he's panicking."

Issachar's temper was rising. How had Echard ever been one of their number? Was any of his information of value?

"Do you know where this amulet came from?"

Lane shook his head. "He's been cagey about it. What I told you is everything I know. I'm not even certain I could identify it if I saw it. That's why I haven't tried to get a warrant to search Maddock's boat. That and Echard doesn't want his name attached to the investigation or the artifact."

"I assume Maddock is one of the treasure hunters. What can you tell me about him?"

Lane hesitated, his gaze flicked to the left for a split second. Both signs of possible deception.

"Other than his name? He's got blond hair, his partner is an Indian. The feather kind, not the dot on the head. Their boat is tied up at a private dock near Staniard Creek."

"What else?"

"Not much." Lane rubbed his chin, partially covering his mouth as he spoke. Another subconscious sign of deception. "They were at the Blue Descent deep diving contest today."

The man was hiding something. For some reason, he didn't want to talk about the treasure hunters. Echard had described the pair as 'a couple of idiots.' Probably another lie.

"Have you questioned the men about the theft?"

"They were questioned." Lane wouldn't meet his eye.

Just then, Issachar's sharp ears caught the sound of footsteps coming up the stairs. He glanced away for a split second.

Lane chose that moment to attack. Moving with surprising quickness, he drove his knee into Issachar's groin. Issachar twisted away, but the strike still hurt like hell. Lane punched him square on the chin.

Issachar saw red. He poured all of his might into a punch aimed for Lane's Adam's apple. He felt his fist drive into soft flesh and rubbery cartilage. Lane fell back against his desk, eyes wide, lips moving, hands pressed to his crushed larynx. He was already dead but didn't know it.

Damn! Issachar had lost his temper again.

The footsteps came closer. Thinking fast, Issachar turned out the lights and locked the door.

Lane had sunk to the floor, his eyes glassy with shock and disbelief. He barely struggled when Issachar removed Lane's belt and looped it around his throat.

There was a soft knock at the door. Lane squirmed, tried to make a noise, but Issachar clamped a big hand over the detective's nose and mouth.

"Detective?" a voice called.

Lane struggled, but to no avail. By the time the person at the door had departed, he had gone limp.

Five minutes later, Issachar slipped back out the way he had come. Eventually, probably sometime tomorrow, the detective would be found in his office, hanged by his own belt. The words I DID IT were scrawled in giant block letters across his desk calendar. Did what? Issachar had no idea, but trying to figure that out ought to keep the Andros police occupied for a while. Long enough for Issachar to deal with these treasure hunters.

24

Gomez fired up the small outboard and steered his boat out into the bay. The cool breeze helped to clear his muddled mind. He'd had a couple too many and was feeling the effects. He knew he shouldn't be boating under the influence but it was a way of life around here. He waved goodbye to Bonebrake and the others. The remainder of the crew had returned from their trip into town, and Gomez had found them an amiable bunch. He hoped Lane would continue to leave them alone.

As he steered out of the harbor and turned south toward Andros town, he let out a jaw-cracking yawn. He couldn't believe how tired he was.

"Just take it slowly and keep your eyes open and you will be fine," he said aloud.

The moon was big and bright, painting the surface of the water in silver. It was a perfect night in the Bahamas. The only thing that would make it better would be if he were bringing a woman back home with him. His thoughts drifted to Raeána. So pretty, so intelligent. But, she had eyes for Maddock, that much was certain. But the man wasn't going to stay in the islands forever. Gomez would bide his time.

Soon, the dull drone of the engine and gentle thump of the boat against the breakers had him on the edge of slumber. His eyelids fluttered and the world seemed to flicker and then go dark.

Thunk!

The boat struck something solid.

"Damn!" He sat bolt upright and looked around. Through eyes now wide open he saw only the open sea. In his slumber he'd veered badly off course. He turned and spotted the lights of Andros Town. Distant, but not so very far. He had more than enough fuel to make it home.

The boat rose and fell, water slapping the gunwale. The sound reminded him of what had jolted him from sleep. He'd hit something. Hadn't he?

He looked around. A cloud drifted over the face of the moon, turning the silvery seascape a dark shade of gray.

He always carried a small flashlight. As a police officer, you never knew when you'd end up in a dark place and in need of a light. Now he fished it out of his pocket, flicked it on, and shone it all about. Nothing. And no damage to the boat that he could see.

"Must have just been a wave. It sounded to me like I'd hit something more substantial because I was half-asleep." He said it with conviction, as if he were a witness on the stand, trying to convince himself. But deep down, he wasn't so sure.

He hadn't just heard the impact. He'd felt it. From the tip of his toes right up to his fillings. The boat had struck something with significant force.

"Or," he said slowly, steering the craft back on course, "something struck the boat."

The thought sent an icy stab of fear down his back. Suddenly, all the evening's conversations came back to him. Every myth and legend suddenly became real to him. He thought about the disappearances, the witness statements about the incident at Blue Descent. What could have struck the platform with that much force? And then he remembered the story Maddock's crew told about their flight from a large, unidentified sea creature. Suddenly, the stories of the Lusca no longer seemed a laughing matter.

He broke out in cold sweat. His heart raced.

"I need to get the hell out of here."

He opened the throttle and steered hard to

starboard. No longer did he aim for the lights of town, but made a beeline for shore. He'd beach his boat and either walk home or sleep on the beach. He no longer wanted to be on the water.

As he piloted his craft, he remembered the countless stories of swimmers gone missing. The many drownings where the body had never been found. Too many. He himself had pointed out to Detective Lane that drownings on Andros were ridiculously high, both in gross numbers and per-capita, compared to the other islands. As was the percentage of lost bodies.

Lane had smiled, amusement sparkled in his eyes.

"Who would you like me to arrest, Gomez? A giant squid? I suppose I could call Scotland Yard and ask if the Loch Ness Monster is at large."

Gomez hadn't bothered to correct him regarding Scotland Yard. Lane thought it all a great joke.

It didn't seem so funny now.

Up ahead, he saw a disturbance on the surface of the water just off the starboard bow. A school of fish swimming fast. Probably fleeing a predator. That thought sent a new tremor running down his spine.

He remembered the most recent report he'd taken. A tourist, a young woman on a mission trip. Clear-eyed and level-headed.

"Something just grabbed me and yanked me straight down. I don't know why it let go, but it pulled me so deep so fast that I almost didn't make it back to the surface."

She had then pointed to sucker marks on her ankle.

Gomez had assured her it had been an octopus and that such incidents were rare and highly unlikely to repeat.

It would be like getting struck by lightning twice, he'd joked.

The dark outline of the island seemed to be just as far away as it had when he'd turned for shore. Off to port, just at the corner of his vision, he saw a dark shadow pass beneath the surface of the water. It was only there for a flash. Maybe he'd imagined it.

"Of course it's your imagination. You're half drunk and nearly asleep." But neither of those was quite true. He was wide awake at the moment and barely feeling the effects of the beer.

Still, he was being ridiculous. Frightened by jumping fish, one of the most commonplace sights on the water? The mind was stronger than any drug. He had swapped stories with Bones and now his imagination had run wild, dredging up old stories.

"He was there and then he was gone."
"Something pulled her down fast."
"He was an experienced swimmer."
"No one believes me but something took her down into the blue hole."

So many stories. They couldn't all be explained away, could they?

But they all had one thing in common—every incident had taken place in a blue hole on the island. Not a single incident at an offshore blue hole, much less at sea. He relaxed a bit. Even if he took his own theories as gospel, the Lusca lived in terrestrial waters, in the blue holes and the many subterranean passages that connected them. But like Maddock had pointed out, some of those passages connected to the sea. If one of them was large enough…

And then, up ahead, the surface of the water roiled.

"What in the hell?"

Something beneath the surface was causing the water to churn. Something massive.

And then he remembered another consistent thread among the Lusca stories. The water always seemed to bubble and churn just before a victim was snatched.

Terror now guiding his hand, he turned the boat

sharply to port to avoid whatever it was that barred his way. He was running south, the island off the starboard side. The lights of home were tantalizingly close.

"Please, please, please," he begged no one in particular. He wasn't the religious sort, but if any particular god wanted to answer his prayer, he'd welcome it right now.

Thud!

Something struck the boat on the starboard side near the stern.

Crack!

This time a sharp blow to the starboard side near the waterline. Gomez felt the cold spray on his face, tasted the salt.

Once again he turned his boat back toward the shore. The boat had a low draft. He could run it right up onto the beach, if only he could make it there.

"Come on, come on, come on."

Thump! Thud! Clank!

That was the sound of something striking the outboard motor with sufficient force to bring it to a slow, sputtering halt.

"This can't be."

The engine resisted all attempts at restarting. Even banging on it with a hammer made no difference. Gradually, the boat slowed until it was drifting on the sea.

He dropped to his hands and knees and crawled to the middle of the boat. Not that that put him much farther from the water than he had been in his seat at the stern, but right now, every inch mattered to him. He drifted there, bobbing on the gentle waves.

All was calm. The gentle breeze chilled his sweat-soaked body. The clouds dissolved and once again the moon bathed the world in its glow.

Gomez's heart hammered.

And then the water roiled again, this time all around the boat. He saw a shadow beneath the surface, massive.

A giant tentacle crept over the bow, another the stern.

Knowing that these were the last moments of his life, he could only manage a cold, mirthless laugh.

"I'm going to need a bigger boat."

25

An hour later, Issachar made his way along the shore in the direction of the small private dock where he'd been told his quarry had tied up their boat. He spotted it immediately, the largest of the handful of boats tied up here. He read the name painted at the stern.

"*Sea Foam*. That's… bland."

He remained in the shadows, not wanting to get too close until he'd adequately reconned the area. He saw no one about except two men sitting on the aft deck, drinking. At this distance he couldn't make out many details. One was big and dark-skinned, the other shorter and lighter-skinned. Lane hadn't given him descriptions of the treasure hunters and the purloined case file had been useless, but he assumed these were the men he was looking for.

Lane had been useless. No helpful information about the artifact or the men who, according to Echard, had stolen it. Issachar hated going in blind. He needed more intel.

The sound of voices drifted across the water. The two men were laughing and bickering. Probably had too much to drink.

Issachar smiled. A couple of drunken treasure hunters should pose no challenge. He would dispose of them quickly and make a search of the boat. If he was lucky, he wouldn't even have to use his pistol. Knife work, quiet and clean.

There was no cover on the dock to hide his approach. Instead, Issachar slipped into the water and swam silently along the dock, keeping to the side opposite *Sea Foam*.

He was about twenty meters away, and debating

whether to burn the boat, take it out into deep water and sink it, or simply set it adrift, when he made out a snatch of conversation that gave him pause.

"...too many seals on this boat."

Issachar frowned. Seals in the Bahamas? That didn't make sense.

"Don't forget the Ranger," another voice said. "I've got him and the three of you to deal with. I feel like I'm on an island sometimes. Literally and figuratively."

Issachar froze. Had he heard that correctly? Neither Echard nor Lane had said anything about the treasure hunters having any sort of military connection. But if there really were three SEALs and a Ranger on board, that changed everything. He took a deep breath and sank beneath the water. He swam under the dock and surfaced on the starboard side of a small boat tied up near *Sea Foam*. He peered over the gunwale and got his first good look at the men on board.

One was a small man with pale skin and red hair. Nothing about him suggested he offered any sort of physical threat. But the other fellow. He was a tall, dark-skinned man with a shaved head and a powerful build and he moved with a the grace of a high-level athlete. Issachar sensed the fellow knew how to handle himself.

A third man now joined them. The tattoo on his left shoulder, a sun, star, and lightning bolt on a blue and green shield, identified him as the former Ranger among the crew. That meant the black man must one of the SEALs, which left two more on board.

Issachar assessed the situation. His 9mm was secured inside a waterproof pouch. If he was fast and didn't miss, he could maybe take out two of the targets. But a pistol shot at this range, while clinging to the side of a boat, was far from a sure thing. And the shots would alert the remaining members crew. He didn't like the odds.

He cursed inwardly. It had been arrogant of him to

assume he could simply wing a mission like this. Damn Echard! This was information Issachar needed in advance.

"Time to cast off," the ranger announced.

"Now?" the red-haired man asked.

"It's almost three hundred kilometers. Maddock wants to be there by morning, check out the place Gomez recommended. Also, he wants to get away from Andros sooner rather than later. Let things cool down a bit."

The ranger turned to look out at the open water. Issachar recognized the tension in his movements, saw the automatic pistol holstered at his hip. These men were ready for a fight.

"I've got to tell you," the man said. "I don't like the sound of this island we're headed to."

What island? Issachar thought. Say the name. Say it!

"Make that two of us," the black man said. "I don't like messing with no black magic."

"Maddock thinks we'll learn something about the artifact there," the redhead replied. He paused. "What about that thing? You think it's still out there?"

"If it is, we're ready for it." The big black man reached down and picked up a rifle. He hefted it and scanned the waters. "Anything pops its head up, I'm busting a cap in its ass."

That sealed it for Issachar. Any remaining thoughts he had of infiltrating the boat and cleaning house evaporated. These men had him outnumbered and they were clearly on alert. He needed a new plan of attack. But where were they headed? A distance of three hundred kilometers would take them to any of several islands, including Cuba. They might even be returning to Florida. For a rash moment he considered stowing away, but there was no hiding place for him.

"All right. Next stop, Cat Island." The redhead

retreated to his cabin.

Issachar grinned. Cat Island! He knew little about the place, save the fact it was large, with a tiny population and lots of remote areas. He had to move fast, but he was confident he'd be able to track them down again. Time to regroup.

It galled him to let his quarry slip away, but he knew it was only for a short while. The men had no idea they would be walking into a trap.

The phone rang. Echard rolled over, flicked on the lamp, reached for the receiver. He hesitated. Who would be calling him this late? He could only think of one person, and if he was correct, he really had no choice but to answer.

It rang again. He sighed and answered.

"Hello?"

"You didn't tell me these treasure hunters were ex-military."

Echard had been right. It was Issachar, and he sounded livid.

"I didn't know," Echard lied.

"There are three former SEALs and an ex-Ranger on board that boat."

"You've got to be kidding me." Echard tried to put as much surprise as possible into his voice.

"Stop bullshitting me," Issachar said. "You are on the thinnest possible ice right now."

Echard held his breath. *When you're backed into a corner, nothing to do but fight your way out.*

"That's not fair. I reached out as soon as the artifact was found. I gave you all the information I have."

"I know about the drinking and the scams you run," Issachar said.

Echard's head swam. This was the worst possible scenario.

"Who is saying that about me?" He was surprised he managed to keep his voice steady, even added in a dash of indignation for good measure. "I'll deny it to their face."

"I'm sure you would," Issachar said.

"Look, I've slipped up a couple of times with the drinking and I'm not proud of it. But who called me a scammer? Was it Lane? That man is as crooked as they come."

"Which is how he ended up in your poker game."

Echard bolted upright. His stomach churned and his flesh was cold and clammy. If his estimation of Issachar was correct, this had suddenly become a life and death situation.

"All I want to do is help the Dominion," Echard said. "If you're not interested in the artifact, I understand."

"Shut up and listen closely. You've got one chance to redeem yourself and I need you to act quickly. And I warn you, you are on very thin ice."

Echard listened, knowing his life depended on following this man's instructions to the letter.

26

Cat Island, Bahamas

Cat Island was located in the Bahamas' Central District. Originally settled by loyalists fleeing the American Revolution, the island was home to cotton plantations for centuries, which had eventually given way to slash-and-burn agriculture. Cascarilla bark, an essential component in medicines, scents, and Campari, was an important export. With a population of just over 1,500, the island was sparsely populated, and drew very few tourists. As they made their way to their destination, Maddock couldn't help but feel they had left the modern world behind. The island seemed quiet, and empty.

Boiling Hole looked very much like any other sinkhole. The surface was a little choppier than Maddock and seen before but otherwise it seemed ordinary. The place was nearly deserted. A couple of tourists stood on the other side of the blue hole, snapping photographs. No one was swimming, and that was fine by him.

"I don't see any sea monsters," Willis said, looking around. Matt, Corey, and Kyle had stayed behind on the boat. Maddock hadn't liked the idea of leaving it unattended, and Matt was more than capable of taking care of business. Kyle, too, had vowed to defend it with his life. Maddock was just happy the surfer wasn't here causing more headaches with his constant misadventures.

"Looking for the creature from the blue hole are you?" An old man with dark brown skin and light brown teeth approached.

"Yes. Do you know much about the monster?"

Bones asked.

The old man laughed a rich throaty laugh. "Oh yes. I've heard many stories. I've lived on this island for ninety years, after all."

"Really?" Maddock was surprised. The man's hair was snow white but his skin was nearly free of wrinkles, and he moved like a much younger man. Maddock would have pegged the guy as being in his late sixties, but with a bad dental plan. "What can you tell us about Boiling Hole?"

"I can tell you all sorts," he said. "But you should buy something, man." He opened a battered leather satchel to display a number of handcrafted items.

Maddock inspected them. Most were Driftwood carvings of sea creatures — dolphins, tortoises, and tropical birds.

"I should get a dolphin for my sister," Bones said. "She loves that crap."

"Really? Even with her career change she still likes girly stuff?" Maddock asked.

Angelica Bonebrake, nicknamed Angel, was Bones' younger sister. She was drop dead gorgeous, but had her brother's twisted sense of humor and had a penchant for brawling. After dabbling in modeling, she had recently embarked on a new career as a cage fighter.

"You know my sister. She's a walking set of contradictions."

Rae frowned. "I'm sorry, but I can't imagine you having a sister."

"Just picture me in a dress." Bones said. "We look exactly alike."

"Don't listen to him," Maddock said. He took out his wallet and showed her a picture of himself, Bones, and Angel. It had been taken at the Cherokee casino operated by Bones' uncle, Crazy Charlie.

"She's gorgeous," Rae said. She looked at Bones.

"Are you sure you two share DNA? Maybe one of you is the milkman's kid."

"If that's the case, I hope it's me. My dad was an ass," Bones said as he continued to poke around in the leather satchel, sorting through the knickknacks.

"Interesting that you carry a photo of your best friend's sister," Rae said to Maddock, a glimmer of mischief in her eye.

"Bones' family sort of took me in after my parents died. The two of them are like my brother and sister."

"Then why are your ears turning bright red?" Rae asked.

"I don't know. It's hot out here." He shot a furtive glance at Bones. The truth was, the memory of that night at the casino was special to him, but he had never told Bones about it, and didn't have any immediate plans to do so. Some things were better kept private.

"Hey, check this out." Bones held up an amulet on a cheap rawhide cord. It was silver, roughly cast, but Maddock could tell immediately what it was supposed to be. It wasn't a perfect match for the amulet they had found, but it was of similar size and shape. And it was clearly an ouroboros depicting a shark-headed octopus biting its own tail.

"Is that a Lusca?"

The old man laughed again. "You like that? I cast it just last week. Only two of them in the world, and both are for sale."

"Why this particular design?" Maddock asked. The similarity between the old man's trinkets and the actual artifact was uncanny.

"I saw it carved on the wall of an underwater passageway down there." He pointed into the water. "I was a good swimmer in my youth. I found a narrow passageway, almost hidden by debris, and just a few meters inside there was a carving of a Lusca shaped like this."

Maddock's heart raced. "Did you go deeper into the channel?"

The old man shook his head. "I'm no SCUBA diver." His eyes drifted to the diving gear Maddock and the others had brought along. He raised an eyebrow, a canny expression painting his face. "You want to know more about the Lusca?"

"Yes, please," Maddock said.

The old man didn't reply, but held up the medallion and waggled his eyebrows. The message was clear. *If you want information, buy something.*

"We'll take two of the dolphins," Maddock said. "And both of the Luscas." He gave one of the dolphins to Bones to give to Angel, and gave the other to Rae. She smiled and thanked him with a peck on the cheek. The spot where her lips touched him seemed to burn, and he suddenly felt like a nervous schoolboy.

Get a grip, Maddock. You're a grown man.

"Your ears are burning again," Willis said.

"So, tell us about Boiling Hole and the monster," Maddock said loudly.

Now that the transaction was complete, the old man, whose name was Cyrus, became much more talkative. Boiling Hole, he explained, got its name from the fact that its surface sometimes roiled as if it were boiling. This was most likely due to the fact that it was connected to the sea by a number of underwater channels. It was theorized that the tides caused the phenomenon. However, superstitious natives tended to blame it on the monster.

"They say the water always boils before the Lusca attacks," Cyrus said. "And so, when the water begins to boil, what is the first thing they think of?"

"Have there been any reports of monster attacks here?" Bones asked.

"Oh, yes. For as long as people have lived on Cat Island, there have been reports of attacks in Boiling Hole."

"Any of them reliable?" Maddock asked.

The man made a face, wagged his head from side to side. "People have disappeared. Many people. But is that the monster or is it the result of diving in dangerous underwater caves? Also, baby sharks, rays, and octopus make their way here from the sea. Some of those might be responsible for at least a few of the reports."

This wasn't sounding promising. "Are there any other places on the island associated with monsters?" Maddock asked.

"There is Big Blue Hole. It is a lake near Orange Creek. As the legend goes, there is a monster there that eats horses and perhaps people. The caverns that connect it to the sea are deadly, the currents powerful. Many of the animals and people that find their way into Big Blue Hole end up being carried out to sea. Or, the monster eats them. Most believe it is merely a legend created to warn people from straying into such a dangerous lake, but who is to say?"

"What about other legends?" Bones asked.

"We have many legends. Many stories. After all, Cat Island is the home of obeah." He said the words in a low tone.

"What is that?"

Willis and Rae exchanged a knowing glance. "Voodoo," they said on top of one another.

"That's right." Cyrus nodded. "So you can imagine the depth and variety of our folk tales. Monsters, witches, magic."

Bones appeared to hesitate. "Are there any stories about immortality?"

Cyrus cocked his head. "What do you mean?"

"I don't know. On Andros we heard a story of a

woman who comes back every ten years or so. She doesn't appear to age."

The man shook his head. "Those stories have not been shared with me. You will have to go to Mermaid Hole for that."

Bones smirked. "I didn't know mermaids had…"

"Please don't, Bones," Maddock said. "Every once in a while you can let one of them pass."

"That's just not my style, Maddock. You know that."

Maddock heaved a sigh and Rae rolled her eyes.

"So, what is Mermaid Hole?" Willis asked.

"It is a lake near Bain town. The lake itself is quite small but there are four deep holes in the bedrock which, it is rumored, lead to the home of a mermaid."

"Is she supposed to be immortal?" Bones asked, perking up.

"There is a storyteller who lives there, Mama Wata. That is who you will have to speak to." Cyrus' demeanor had changed entirely. His replies were sharp, his big smile now only a memory.

"Back to the Lusca," Maddock said, returning to the reason for their visit to Boiling Hole. "What is your opinion? Do you think there's any truth to it?"

"I don't think it's impossible," Cyrus said carefully.

"Suppose it's not only possible, but factual," Bones said. "Any theories you can offer? I love a good monster story."

"All right." Cyrus, looked up at the circle of blue sky visible above the dense jungle that hemmed them in on all sides. He scratched his chin. "I believe that the creature might have once roamed the seas but made its home here. Here among the islands, that is. Eventually, something happened, an earthquake perhaps. And it was trapped inside the caverns beneath Andros, which is why nearly all the most reliable reports originate there."

"You think there's only one creature?" Maddock

asked. "Not a breeding population?"

"I don't see how there could be. If they were many of those things roaming the oceans, I think someone would know."

"So it's a supernatural creature?" Bones asked.

"Supernatural or very long-lived. If it existed."

"We've learned very little about the Lusca. All the stories are essentially the same," Maddock said. He gave the man a quick summary of what they had been told. "Might you be able to give us some information beyond that? Legends, details, anything that is not common knowledge."

Cyrus scratched his chin thoughtfully.

"Some say the Lusca is a thing of the ancient world. When man first began to record history, Lusca was already a legend. How it came to be here, no one knows. It is also said that the Lusca serves no master except for the one who holds the keys."

"What are the keys?"

Cyrus spread his hands, palms up. "I do not know. The knowledge, if it ever existed, was forgotten long ago."

"These keys, do you need both or is it either-or?"

"Again, I cannot say. You now know as much as I do."

"Is there any connection between the Lusca and the Fountain of Youth?" Bones asked. "Or are there any Fountain of Youth legends associated with Cat Island? Or any of the local islands for that matter?"

Cyrus's smile collapsed into a tight-lipped frown.

"The Fountain of Youth is colonizer nonsense."

"Hey, no offense intended, dude," Bones said, hands raised in a placating gesture. "Just curious."

"You should not ask about the Water of Life. It is not a story for outsiders."

"We could send the light-skinned brother away,"

Willis said, eying Maddock. "And Bones, too, if he's the wrong kind of brown."

Cyrus forced a smile. "I must go. I think you will be my only customers here today."

Maddock thanked Cyrus for his time. He regretted that they'd upset the man, but more than that, he hated the feeling that Cyrus had more to tell.

"Before you go, could you point us to the spot where you found the Lusca carving."

Cyrus hesitated, his eyes narrowed. "I'm sorry. It was so long ago." With that, he wished them a good day and hurried off.

"That was weird," Willis said. "I mean, I understand not trusting outsiders, but it's not like you were asking for his bank account number. The Fountain of Youth is just as far-fetched a legend as the Lusca, don't y'all think?" He looked from Maddock to Bones.

"Of course it is," Maddock said. "But perhaps they aren't just legends to him."

"Or maybe we're onto something," Bones said.

"Meaning what?"

"I don't know. I'm just saying, maybe him getting all offended was just a cover for whatever he's really afraid of."

Maddock shrugged. "I suppose anything is possible. Anyway, I'm ready to do some swimming, maybe try to find that cavern he told us about. You guys ready to get wet?"

27

The four of them quickly stripped down to their swimsuits donned masks, snorkels, tanks, and flippers, and jumped in.

As soon as Maddock hit the water, he felt a sudden shock. His first instinct was to attribute it to the low temperature, but it really wasn't that cold. It certainly didn't compare to Florida's spring-fed limestone pool. And then he realized he had felt another of the strange vibrations. He swam back to the surface and looked around for the others. One by one, their heads popped up.

"Did you all feel it?" Willis asked.

"Seismic activity," Rae said. "There must be a lot of it going on. It seems like there's a new tremor every day."

"When did these tremors begin?" Maddock asked. A creeping suspicion rose up inside of him.

Rae shook her head. "I haven't heard anything in the news. I felt one for the first time when we were trying to escape from Echard's hired thugs. And then one at Blue Descent, and again just now."

"And we're not on Andros anymore," Bones said. "I guess whatever tectonic plates are shifting must be impacting a wide area."

"Lucky there ain't been a tsunami," Willis said.

Maddock considered the point. When it came down to it, these tremors didn't feel... normal, for lack of a better term. And he found it weird that the tremors seemed to occur whenever Rae entered the water. She still wore the amulet around her neck. He could see it glinting just beneath the surface of the crystalline waters. Could there be a connection? How could there be?

"Let's get started," he said to the others. "If there's

more seismic activity, we don't want to be down in those caverns should something collapse."

"That's Maddock for you," Willis quipped. "Always a ray of sunshine."

They paired off, Maddock with Bones, and Willis with Rae.

"Remember," he reminded them, "cave diving is dangerous."

"He says to a pair of Navy SEALs and an island girl," Bones mumbled.

"What exactly are you thinking we're going to find here, Maddock?" Willis asked.

"Probably nothing," Maddock admitted. "But I'd like to find the carving Cyrus told us about."

"You think it's real?" Bones asked.

"He must have seen an image of the real amulet somewhere, or else his version wouldn't look so much like it. And given the legends surrounding this place, it seems likely there's a connection. And maybe," he paused, not quite believing what he was about to say, "there's a connection to whatever chased the boat."

"So were looking for evidence of a big scary sea monster. Got it," Willis said.

They made a circuit of Boiling Hole, gradually working their way deeper. As they descended they, marked the size and locations of the various passageways. No sign of the Lusca carving, but Maddock theorized it would be in one of the larger passages. The bottom of the sinkhole was filled with detritus and offered nothing of interest to them, unless they planned on recycling old cans and bottles. After giving it a brief scan, Maddock guided them to what he had identified as the most likely target. It was a passageway just large enough for someone to swim into, but partially hidden from view by roots and debris.

As they swam closer, he shone his light into the

crevice. There it was! A perfect rendering of the amulet Rae now wore around her neck. She held it up for comparison and Maddock gave the thumbs-up. How and why this carving had come to be down here was a mystery. Perhaps it was a mystery they could solve.

It was a tight fit, and as they swam deeper, the walls seem to close in around them. Maddock knew that this was dangerous. It would be easy to get lost, or worse, stuck. But he was with three experienced divers and they would look out for one another. And as intrigued as he was, he wasn't about to let anyone get killed over his own flights of fancy. If the way grew much tighter, they would be forced to turn back before they were in so deep that they couldn't turn around.

No sooner had the thought entered his mind than something up ahead caught his eye. He directed his light toward it and felt the thrill of shock as the beam landed on a grinning skull. They swam closer. He could tell nothing about it, there was no context to guess its age or origin. He had to wonder how a human skull had gotten here without the rest of its body in tow. Could this skull have belonged to the person who made the Lusca carving? That was a stretch. There was no evidence for that. Still, it was unsettling.

They moved deeper and suddenly the narrow passageway opened up into a wide underwater chamber. Here seemed to be a dumping ground, the place where refuse collected on its way out to the sea. He saw chunks of wood, bits of plastic, and bones. Lots of bones. Mostly cow, a few he thought might be goat, and many that were human. Someone less experienced might have overlooked them, but they stood out to his trained eye. Bones and Willis both pointed to indicate that they had seen them too.

Maddock wondered how those bodies had come to be there. Possibly swimmers who had drowned, their bodies never recovered. Maybe scuba divers who had gotten into trouble, but if so, where was their gear? Maybe buried amongst the refuse down below. He imagined the bodies being tugged along by the strong current, battering the walls of the cavern, dragged inexorably toward the sea, only to come to a halt in this macabre ossuary.

He held up his hand. The current didn't feel that strong. And then a disturbing thought came to him. Perhaps the strong currents came and went, like a riptide. An unexpected powerful surge that caught a diver unaware. If the flow of the water were strong and sudden enough, a diver could be dragged into a narrow spot and become stuck, or slammed into a wall and suffer a serious injury. For the first time he appreciated just how reckless it had been to go into this without conducting some advance research. He had no idea what he was leading the group into. Then again, what were the odds anyone alive was even aware of this place?

Bones waggled his flashlight in an impatient gesture and swam on ahead. Cursing inwardly Maddock followed along. Bones was probably convinced that they were looking at the leftovers from a sea monster's meal.

Bones led them through a long, spiraling passageway, the only one large enough for them to swim through. It was wide and Maddock felt the strong current encouraging them along.

Something moved up ahead. Maddock saw it. It was a weird, pulsating blob, moving in a strange, alien way. Maddock saw a long, fat tentacle reach out in their direction. His hand went to his Recon knife.

Not in time!

In a flash the creature shot forward, zipping toward him like a grotesque torpedo. His eyes registered mottled skin, long tentacles. He thrust with his knife, but the thing was already past him. He whirled about, but it was gone. Behind him, Willis gave the thumbs-up.

Maddock breathed a sigh of relief. It had been a regular octopus, a very large one to be sure, but not a creature out of legend. He checked his watch. Even accounting for the current, they had plenty of air left. He gave Bones the thumbs-up and they swam deeper.

Soon they came to a place where the passageway split into two channels. The way to their right curved off in a wide-open channel. Maddock could see marks left by divers on the walls. So they were not the first to come this way. Likely, access to the sea was just up ahead. The way to the left would be a tight squeeze, barely big enough for Bones or Willis to get their shoulders through. Going that way would be a bad idea. What if they went in there and they couldn't get back out again?

Fittingly, as soon as the thought occurred to Maddock, Bones forced his way into the narrow passageway.

A variety of curses ran through Maddock's mind as he made a futile grab for his friend's flipper, but Bones was too fast. Not sure what in the hell the big Cherokee was thinking, Maddock shone his light into the small opening. Relief flooded through him. The passageway was merely an entrance to a much larger chamber. He turned, gave a thumbs-up to the others, and followed Bones.

He had to admit sometimes Bones' recklessness paid off. Like Maddock, no diver with half a brain would have given the passageway a second look. Not with another, infinitely safer channel to traverse. It was apparent that they were the first scuba divers come this way.

First of all, this place was an absolute boneyard. The floor of the chamber was carpeted in human remains. There was no way a find like this could be discovered and not make world news. He wondered what in the hell had happened here. Perhaps some form of sacrifice like the Aztecs?

But that was only one reason he felt confident that this place had gone undiscovered. Because lying strewn about the cave floor were gold coins. He hastily took out his waterproof camera and recorded everything he saw. When he was finished, they began gathering the gold coins. The coins were in excellent condition and Maddock immediately recognize several of them. Given the time period, it had probably been part of a pirate's treasure. He saw the broken remains of a small chest lying nearby. But how had it come to be here? A pirate couldn't have swum this far, and a diver would never leave so much treasure behind.

Looking up, he found his answer. The mirrored surface of the water shimmering above said that there was a pocket of air, perhaps a cave, directly overhead. He pointed up and the others followed his eye line and nodded vigorously. Treasured secured, they swam up to see what they would find.

They were in a cave. As he shone his light around Maddock immediately understood how the treasure chest and come to be here. This place showed evidence of human habitation. He saw broken barrels, a clay jug, and an old fire pit.

"Somebody lived here," he said.

"I think it was that dude." Bones shone his light on what Maddock had initially thought was a pile of junk. He realized now that it was the skeletal remains of a man, wrapped in the remnants of old blankets. "I guess he dropped his treasure into the water and couldn't get it back. That's a bummer."

They climbed out, took off their flippers, and moved closer to inspect the body. Tufts of hair clung to the skull in a circle. The body was wrapped in a moldering robe, and its skeletal fingers clutched a rosary.

"I think he was a monk," Maddock said.

"So what was a monk, or whatever he was, doing down here? And why did he die here?" Bones asked.

"A cave in?" Maddock asked, glancing at a ceiling-high mound of rocks. "That pile of rubble over there could be a collapsed passageway."

"As for why he was down here, you think there's a chance he might have been some kind of inquisitor?" Bones was looking in the other direction. They turned to see two sets of shackles set in the wall. Lying nearby were iron clamps and knives. Implements of torture.

"Sure looks like it to me," Willis said.

"And that explains the bodies down there," Maddock said, pointing to the pool.

"Well now I'm not at all sorry that you lost your treasure," Bones said to the skeleton. "And I hope you really did get trapped down here and starve to death."

"We shouldn't stay down here too long," Maddock said. "Everybody give this place the once over and make sure you're not leaving anything valuable behind."

They found little more of value. There was no more treasure, and aside from the crucifix, there appeared to be no artifacts of interest here. And then Maddock saw a glint of silver. On the third finger of his left hand, the dead man wore a ring—the strangest ring Maddock had ever seen.

The band was a twisting mass of tentacles. Where the signet should be was a shark's head with a tiny blue gem where its eye should be.

"Oh my God," Rae said. "Is that…?"

Maddock nodded. "It's a Lusca." He reached down and slipped the ring off of the bony finger. He held it up for the others to see. It appeared to be made of the same metal as the amulet.

"This can't be a coincidence," Willis said. "That ring and that thing," he pointed to the amulet, "have got something to do with each other."

"I agree," Maddock said. "But what?" He let his eyes drift, go out of focus. It was a trick he'd learned from his father. When you think you've seen everything, try to look at it through different eyes. Sometimes, simply altering your eyesight did the trick.

Sure enough, he spotted something. Lying only inches away from the skeletal hand, half buried in bits of a rotted blanket, lay an old journal. Carefully, he picked it up and opened the first page.

"It's in Spanish," he said. "No time to read it right now. We've really got to be getting back." As he tucked the ring and the journal into a waterproof container and secured it to his body, he couldn't help but wonder. What was the man up to? Why had he apparently tortured and killed all of those people? And what did the Lusca have to do with it?

28

Mermaid Hole did not live up to Bones' expectations. The small lake of dull green water out in the middle of nowhere did not conjure up images of mysterious aquatic beauties. He wondered if Maddock and Rae were having better luck. They'd decided to split up, with Bones and Willis investigating Mermaid Hole while Maddock and Rae paid a visit to the Hermitage.

Things here weren't all bad. Apparently at least a few tourists thought the Mermaid Hole worth a closer look. Right now, three attractive young women splashed around in the water. One of them, a deeply tanned brunette in a bright orange bikini, turned, saw him and Willis standing there, and waved.

"Hey guys! Why don't you two come in for a swim?" she called. Her friends repeated the invitation.

"You know what?" Bones said to Willis. "Maddock isn't here to tell us how to go about our business, so I don't see any reason we can't spend a little time investigating the Mermaid Hole up close while we wait for the voodoo woman to arrive."

Upon arriving, they'd spoken with a few locals, none of whom wanted to talk about Mermaid Hole. Finally, one man had told them that the only storyteller at Mermaid Hole was a woman, a practitioner of obeah.

"You can't find her. She will either come to you or she will not," the man had whispered before hurrying away. The words had unnerved them at the time, but somehow Bones could no longer remember why.

"You know what? You're not as dumb as people say you are," Willis said.

"Who says I'm dumb?" Bones asked.

"Not everybody. Just the people who know you, or

have met you, or have heard mention of you…"

"That's enough. We're keeping the ladies waiting."

The two men began stripping off their shirts when a voice from behind froze them in their tracks.

"You are looking for the witch woman, perhaps?" The voice was deep and carried with it the gravitas of age. But when the two men turned around they were surprised to see that speaker was a small woman. No, small did not begin to describe it. She was tiny, well under five feet tall and probably didn't weight more than eighty pounds. Her russet skin was heavily lined. A red scarf covered her hair, but a few shockingly white strands showed at the temples. She stared up at them through rheumy eyes and somehow managed to make Bones feel very small.

"We're looking for a storyteller," Bones said, embarrassed. He quickly pulled his shirt back on. "Someone who knows the mermaid legends."

"That's right, ma'am," Willis added with the air of a young man who had been caught with his hand in the cookie jar.

"There are no mermaids here, young man, despite what the name might suggest," she said. "But if you want to know about Mama Wata, her I will tell you about."

"What is a Mama Wata?" Willis asked.

The woman sucked her teeth and made a clucking sound. "Silly boy. Mama Wata is the spirit who protects this place."

"Protects it from what?" Bones asked.

The woman quirked an eyebrow. "You sure you want to talk to a little old woman? You don't want to go swimming?"

Bones smiled and shook his head. She gave a single nod, turned and walked away. They assumed they were expected to follow and did so.

The old woman seemed to melt into the tree line.

Bones could move quietly in the woods. In fact, he'd only met a few people who could match his skill, but this woman seemed to drift through the jungle as if she were made of vapor. She made no sound, left no track, and never seemed to change her course, no matter what obstacle stood in her path.

They passed into deep shadow among the swaying palms and thick Palmetto until they lost sight of her for a moment.

"Where did she go?" Willis asked.

"I am behind you."

The words nearly made Bones jump out of his skin. How in the hell had she done that?

He turned to see her seated on a low-hanging limb of a Caribbean Pine. She fitted the curved branch so perfectly it seemed as if it had been grown solely for the purpose of providing her with a chair. He and Willis sat down on a low flat boulder, which meant they were now slightly below the little woman's eye level. She seemed to think this was a great joke.

"Now you boys know how I feel, don't you?" she cackled.

"I suppose so," Bones said.

"You may ask me your questions."

Bones was finding it difficult to formulate questions. There was something unsettling about this woman's presence.

"What is your name?"

"You did not come here to ask my name."

"All right, then. Tell us about this Mama Wata chick."

"She is not a chicken. Mama Wata is a water spirit. She can charm men and serpents. Of course, most of the time those are the same thing, no?"

Bones and Willis chuckled.

"I like you," Willis said.

"Not as much as you would like Mama Wata. All the stories agree she is a seductress. Beautiful beyond what the human mind can conceive. Many of the stories associate her with fertility and sex."

"I like her so far," Bones said. "Does she live in this lake?"

The old woman shook her head. "She lives somewhere down below, deep in the passages that connect all the islands together."

"What does she look like?" Bones asked.

"Part human, part creature of the sea. She can take a woman's form for a short while, but she is never fully human."

"So she is sort of like a mermaid," Bones said. "I don't suppose she has red hair and green eyes?"

The woman laughed. "Mama Wata came here from Africa. Her skin and hair are as dark as the night. Her eyes are golden like the sun. And she sings a song older than language. No man can resist its call."

"You said she is a protector of this place. What is she protecting, exactly? No offense, but it seems like an ordinary lake."

"Not only this place. She protects all the deep places, all the Blue Holes, all the caverns. The waters that provide life."

"Are those girls going to be in trouble for swimming in Mama Wata's lake?" Willis inclined his head in the direction of the Mermaid Hole.

It was only a joke but the old woman took the question seriously. "Not if they do no harm."

"Where does the snake charming fit in?" Willis said.

"Not snakes, serpents."

"What's the difference?" Willis asked.

Bones thought he knew the answer. "Serpents could include sea serpents, couldn't it?" He looked to the old woman for confirmation.

She nodded her head. "Mama Wata can charm the great serpents of the sea."

"She's that good-looking or is it her singing?" Bones asked.

"Only men are foolish enough to be mesmerized by her beauty and her song speaks only to humans." She looked down, her expression dark. "In ancient times, with her ring and her amulet, it is said Mama Wata could control the great Leviathan itself."

"You mean like the creature from the Bible?" Willis asked

"Leviathan, Kraken, call it what you will. The ancients wanted her power. Mama Wata fled the Old World, but they sent men to find her and steal her treasures. They got her amulet but not her ring."

"How did they manage to steal it?" Bones asked.

The woman's dark expression brightened and her eyes twinkled. "One of them was very handsome. Mama Wata is a charmer, but she can also be charmed by the right man. That is her great weakness."

Bones could have sworn he saw her wink at him when she said the last. He shifted uncomfortably.

"What happened to the amulet?" A strange feeling was beginning to rise up inside of him. A ring and an amulet. A charmer of serpents. Things had gone from weird to creepy.

"No one knows what happened to it," she said bitterly.

"Did it look anything like this?" Bones reached inside his shirt and took out the cheap Lusca amulet they had bought from Cyrus. When they'd left Boiling Hole, Maddock had insisted that Bones wear one and Rae the other.

The old woman hissed and bared her teeth. Despite her obvious age, they were straight and white. Probably dentures.

"Where did you get that?"

"Boiling Hole. A man named Cyrus sold it to us. He's the one who sent us here."

The woman cackled. "Cyrus. He came around once, a long time ago, asking about things he did not need to know. He did not come back again." Her expression turned grave. "He should not have made that. It is wrong to profit off of the memory of what was lost."

Bones determinedly kept his eyes on the old woman. Somehow, he was convinced that if he and Willis so much as exchanged a glance, the woman would read his thoughts, and he didn't want her to know about the real amulet. Every instinct told him he should keep that a secret.

"Mama Wata didn't have any way of finding the amulet again after it was stolen?"

"How could she? The link is between the ring, the amulet, and the creature, not between her and the amulet."

"And what happened to the ring?"

The woman hung her head. "Without the amulet it was useless. Eventually she lost it, too. Taken by one of the Christians. Another handsome man with evil intentions."

Bones' heart lurched. Obviously, they were talking about a legend here. Just an old story. But clearly in the amulet and ring, he and Maddock had found something of great value.

"This ring and amulet, where did they originally come from?"

"The place where they were forged is long gone. Sunk beneath the waves. The crystals came from farther away." Her eyes flitted skyward.

Bones frowned. Could she mean that they came from space?

"What happened to Mama Wata?" Willis asked. "Is

she still around somewhere?"

"She still lives. Most have forgotten about her, but here on Cat Island, she is remembered. And here, she has power, if only a shadow of what she once was."

"What about the power of the ring and amulet?" Bones asked. "Could someone use them to control the Lusca?"

"In the water, yes. On the land, they are no more than jewelry."

Bones wasn't sure what to make of the story. It was all too bizarre.

"Did you ever tell this story to a man named Echard? A white guy, always looks and smells like he needs a shower."

"That is not the question you want to ask me."

That was true. It didn't matter if he'd heard the tale from this woman or uncovered it elsewhere. Obviously, Echard had heard the story of Mama Wata, and he was willing to kill for what was apparently an incredibly old and legendary artifact. Something else was now on his mind.

"This might be a strange question, but have you heard stories of a girl who disappears and then appears again years later, still looking the same?"

The woman turned her head slightly and stared at him out of the corner of one eye. "What do you mean?" she said slowly.

At the mere thought of Thel, Bones felt a sudden, desperate urge to tell unburden himself to this woman. As Willis looked on in bemusement, he quickly recounted the story of his initial meeting with the strange and beautiful women, and the ensuing events that had brought them to this place.

"And she looked exactly like the girl in the newspaper photo. And Maddock said the girl in the newspaper looked like the woman he saw underwater.

And I just thought maybe there's a connection." When he finished, he realized he was surprised that he had been talking for so long. Mildly embarrassed, he folded his hands and waited.

"You actually met one of them?" the woman whispered.

"One of what?"

"The Finfolk. You must stay far from them. They are more dangerous than you know."

"Dangerous in what way?"

"They are predators. They abduct humans. I will say no more about it."

But Bones had to know more, much more. He remembered his time with Thel. The sadness in her eyes. How conflicted she had seemed. How the water she had given him had been better than any drug, yet had muddled his thoughts.

She really did roofie me, he thought. *She planned to abduct me but changed her mind.*

"So the Finfolk… They're like a cult or something? They kidnap people and force them to join their religion?"

"No," the woman said flatly. "I will say no more about them. To name a thing draws its attention and can give it power."

Determined to keep the woman talking and hopefully circle his way back around to the Finfolk, he searched for another question to ask. He thought about her comment that the amulet and ring only had power in the water.

"The amulet and ring, what would happen if one of them touched water?" Bones said, remembering a discussion from earlier in the day.

The old woman frowned and then her expression brightened. "Was that what I felt? Has one of them been found?"

"What? No, I just wondered."

"If you are going to lie to me, our conversation is at an end."

"No! Please! We found the amulet in a shipwreck. We didn't know what we had. And ever since then, people have been trying to kill us. One of our friends was murdered."

"Meanwhile," Willis chimed in, "our boat got chased by a giant creature, we don't know what, and people are disappearing out in the water."

"Do you have any idea what's going on?" Bones asked. He didn't know why he craved this woman's opinion. Doubtless she would reply with some hokey legend. But for whatever reason, he was prepared to believe her.

She looked him hard in the eye. For a moment, he worried that she was going to ask him about the ring, too. He knew he would not be able to lie to her. But instead, she closed her eyes and let out a deep, tired sigh. She somehow seemed to diminish.

"The amulet had not touched water in centuries. When it finally did, it called out to the Lusca with tremendous force. So powerful that it caused tremors deep beneath the earth. Three times, to be exact." She held up three fingers.

"That's right," Bones said.

"I believe one of these tremors has released the Lusca from the caverns beneath Andros, where it has been trapped."

"You realize this is hard to believe," Willis said.

She inclined her head. "Is that so? Says the man who came to a witch woman for answers."

"Fair point."

"Suppose, for argument's sake," Bones began, "we believe the Lusca is real and that we accidentally set it loose on the world. Where will it go? What will it do?"

"It will answer the call of the amulet whenever it touches water. It cannot resist it."

Bones frowned. If that were true, then the creature was on its way here right now.

"What about when the amulet is on land?"

"Then it cannot hear the call. It will do what any apex predator does. It will go where it wants, do what it wants, and eat whatever it likes."

Bones took a reckless gamble. "Any chance it will go to the Fountain of Youth?"

"Not the Fountain of Youth, boy. The Waters of Life."

Bones sat up straighter. But before he could ask another question, the old woman held a finger up to her lips.

"People are coming."

The average person would have stood and looked around, but Bones and Willis read her tone of voice and instinctively went to the ground. They listened intently. Bones immediately realized what was missing. He no longer heard the sounds of the women splashing around in the lake. Had they left, or did these new arrivals have something to do with their sudden silence?

He caught a glimpse of someone moving off to the left. Before he could react, a voice behind him spoke in a loud, cold voice.

"Hands behind your heads. Slowly."

Bones was never one to back down from a fight, and he rarely paid attention to the odds. But he also had a wealth of experience in the realms of violence and he knew that the unseen speaker behind them was fully prepared to kill both of them. He could read it in the man's tone, and the fact that this person had taken them unaware meant he had skill. Also, he and Willis could not be in a more vulnerable state right now. The boulder where they'd sat afforded little cover, and neither of them carried a weapon other than a knife. He gave Willis a quick nod, and they followed the unseen man's directions.

"You with the long hair," the voice said. "Listen carefully."

"I guess he doesn't mean you, skinhead," Bones said to Willis.

"Never call a black man a skinhead," Willis said.

The hidden speaker did not take the bait. "I want you to slowly take the amulet off and hold it up where I can see it."

"What? This thing? It's not valuable."

"Don't make me ask again."

Suppressing a grin, Bones complied with the man's instructions. He slowly removed the cheap knockoff amulet and held it up.

"Here it is." He poured as much anger and resentment into his voice as he could.

"Good. Now, toss it toward the sound of my voice. And make sure your aim is true. If you throw it out into the forest, I'll kill you out of sheer annoyance. I'm very jetlagged."

"Look man," Willis said, "ain't nobody going to do nothing. We found this thing in a shipwreck. We cleaned it up, but we don't know what it is, and everybody we asked says it ain't worth nothing. We were hoping we could sell it to the voodoo woman, but even she says it is junk."

With that, Bones tossed the amulet back over his shoulder. He heard a clink as the man caught it. A few seconds of silence and then a scornful laugh.

"Echard. What an idiot."

"On that we agree," Bones said. "The guy is an assclown."

The man laughed again, a cold, angry thing. "Bunch of amateur treasure hunters find a piece of crap trinket, which causes that idiot Echard to start killing people, and I'm the one who has to fly to the middle of nowhere to get it all sorted out. I'm not going to kill you, but neither am I going to tell Echard what I've learned. Let him keep trying to kill you. You morons deserve each other."

Bones and Willis knelt there in silence. Bones found himself gritting his teeth, waiting for the sound of a gunshot, the pain of a bullet striking his flesh. Somehow he didn't really believe it would come. The man they'd encountered was clearly a professional, and professionals didn't kill unless they felt it was necessary.

He waited until the count of ten and looked around. No one was there.

"I think he's gone."

"I didn't hear him come or go," Willis said. "That man is good."

"Please," Bones said as he stood and brushed the dirt off his clothing. "Good? That dude just got outsmarted by Dane freaking Maddock."

29

The Hermitage stood at the top of Mount Alverna, the highest point in the Bahamas. From its lofty point overlooking Cat Island and the sparkling waters of the Caribbean, the abandoned monastery gleamed in the sunlight. As Rae and Maddock made the climb to the top, she filled him in on the background of this historic place.

Monsignor John Hawes, known to locals as Father Jerome, built the monastery in the late 1930s. An architect and sculptor, Father Jerome built the Hermitage in Medieval style using local stone. He intended the place to be his personal retreat. He also built many other cathedrals and convents in the Bahamas.

"This place is actually called Como Hill," Rae explained. "But Hawes renamed it Mount Alvernia because it reminded him of La Verna, a hill in Tuscany where St. Francis of Assisi is supposed to have received the wounds of the cross."

"Do you believe in that sort of thing?" Maddock asked. "Stigmata and the like?"

Rae shrugged. "I don't know. As a scientist, I'm naturally a skeptic, but who's to say what's possible and impossible? How about you?"

"The supernatural is Bones' department, and I include religion in that." Maddock hadn't always felt that way, but some of the twists and turns his life had taken had left him in doubt. "My gut says, there's always a scientific explanation for the weird things we encounter."

"That's how I see it for the most part, but I like to think maybe there's a little bit of the universe we'll never be able to explain. That's one of the things I envy about Kyle. He has a sense of wonder about everything. It's so refreshing."

A sense of wonder was frequently the byproduct of a serious lack of information, but Maddock held his tongue. Rae's attachment to her foster brother was deeper than any siblings he had ever met. Her attitude toward him wasn't going to change.

To their left, a sign warned that this place was the private property of the Roman Catholic Archbishop of Nassau, Bahamas, and that the church was not responsible for injury or damage sustained by persons who enter the property at their own risk. Behind it, an old stone gateway surmounted by a cross welcomed them to Mount Alvernia.

"Is it that dangerous?" Maddock asked.

"Just covering their asses," Rae said. "Insurance company probably required it for liability reasons."

"Why do they need insurance when they've got thoughts and prayers?" Maddock deadpanned.

"You're thinking of Protestants," Rae deadpanned.

As they continued their ascent up the long, winding path, they passed relief carvings of the stations of the cross. According to Rae, these were also the work of Father Jerome.

When they reached the top of the hill, Maddock was surprised to see that the gray stone structure with its gleaming whitewashed roof, which had seemed so imposing from a distance, was actually modest, though not without its charms. The site offered a three hundred-sixty-degree view of Cat Island's lush greenery and the sparkling waters of the Caribbean.

"They call islands like this one the Out Islands," Rae explained. "The tourist industry hasn't ruined them yet."

Rae explained that the island was dotted with abandoned buildings, which made it a choice flyover site for amateur pilots. Just to the south lay the ruins of Armbrister Plantation. From there, Armbrister Creek flowed into Boiling Hole. The area to the southwest was called Old Bight.

"But I've heard it said that it was once called the Old Blight. I don't know where the name comes from, though." She shrugged as if to say, *It's Cat Island. What else would you expect?*

The Hermitage consisted of an abbey, a chapel, a bell tower, and living quarters. Maddock looked them over, thinking.

"Now that we're here, what's the plan?" Rae asked.

"I don't really have one," Maddock admitted. "With its proximity to Boiling Hole, I'm wondering if there's a connection to the chamber we found."

"I don't see how. The Hermitage wasn't built until 1939."

"Maybe there was something here before? Or maybe he chose this site for a reason?"

"Oh, come on. Father Jerome was a humanitarian. Are you seriously suggesting he could have had a connection to a torture chamber that's probably four hundred years old?"

"If I had a nickel for every 'good guy' who turned out to be a dirtbag..." Maddock said.

"I get that, believe me," Rae said. "I have no illusions about a priest or anyone else who holds a lot of sway over other people. But I've found that even the good people outnumber the bad by far, and I've found that even growing up in the foster system, the good people outnumber the bad by far. And I've never heard a single bad story about Father Jerome. Even the people who hated outsiders had at least a grudging respect for him."

"I'm not saying he had a connection to the torture chamber. But what if Father Jerome learned about the torture chamber? He was a trusted priest, so maybe someone revealed it in confession, or simply confided it to him. Or perhaps, as a priest serving in the islands, he was privy to stories of what went on here in the past, some of which were unsavory or even shameful. Maybe he left some kind of record."

"So, we're looking for what?"

"I don't know. Everyone kept journals and written records back then. Maybe he left a clue, something that would only mean something to a person who knew about the torture chamber. Maybe even an artifact of some kind. Just look for hiding places that might have escaped notice all these years."

Rae cocked her head and frowned. "You do know that Indiana Jones is a fictional character?"

Maddock laughed. "Crazy as it sounds, I know from firsthand experience that things like that are not as farfetched as they might seem. Especially when it comes to a powerful organization like the church, which has lots of secrets to hide."

Rae nodded. "All right, Doctor Jones. I'll play along."

30

Echard crouched inside the old monastery and listened as Maddock and Raeána talked. He wondered what they would think if they knew just how close Maddock had come to the truth. He himself had only put the final pieces together after finding notes from Brother Jerome's writings among Alexei's possessions. That had sealed it for him.

They needed only the amulet to master the great Leviathan.

That sentence was burned into his mind. And there, on the photocopied page, had been a rough sketch of an ouroboros in the shape of a Lusca. That had sealed it. He had long believed that the Lusca and the great beast from the Bible were one and the same. And if he could only find the amulet, he would be its master.

He'd spent years searching, collecting story fragments, anything that would bring him closer to his goal. For years that was all he had—fragments of legends, with just enough savory bits to prevent him from giving up entirely. One of those stories had been that of a hero of Ancient Greece who had come to the islands and encountered a great sea serpent. Details were sparse, but the hero had survived by stealing something from the Lusca's master and had encased it in earth to prevent the serpent or its master from finding it. But the ship went down in a storm somewhere in the islands, taking with it the item that had been stolen. But, try as he might, Echard could learn no more about the lost key to Leviathan.

And then Kyle had shown up to return the borrowed sailboat, and he had told Echard about the strange artifact brought up from the bottom by a man named

Dane Maddock and his crew. As soon as Kyle had described the clay egg and the shipwreck that seemed to be from the ancient world, Echard had known that this was the breakthrough he'd been waiting for. The clay egg was obviously the earthen vessel that kept the artifact hidden from the great beast. And now he was so close to having it in his possession.

But he was also in danger.

He rested his hand on the pistol tucked into his waistband. He hoped he wouldn't have to use it.

Issachar had been correct when he guessed that Maddock would show up either at Mermaid Hole or at the Hermitage and had been wise to set traps at both places. Right now, Echard's backups should be closing in. Not that his recruits were known for their reliability, but they loved money and would do almost anything for it.

He couldn't stop staring at the amulet that dangled from Raeána's neck. Echard had never seen it up close, but he'd seen the scans, and they resembled the drawing Alexei had photocopied. He wondered if the Russian had come here searching for answers. If so, he hadn't found them.

As he watched, the pair split up. Maddock headed back down the hill, while Raeána approached the Hermitage. Echard's heart leapt. This couldn't have played out any more perfectly! Now, he only needed Maddock to stay away long enough for him to take the amulet and get out of here. Raeána paused to inspect the bell tower, then entered the monastery.

Echard tensed. The moment was almost at hand. Shooting her would be quicker but it would certainly draw Maddock's attention. The knife would be quieter. He watched her, admiring her grace and her beauty. He'd been infatuated with the young woman since the day they'd met, even though her feelings for him were a bit murkier. Hell, he only put up with her idiot brother in the hope that she would see him in a better light. For such a smart, intelligent woman, she sure was stupid in all matters relating to Kyle.

Raeána came to a halt directly in front of his hiding place. She looked around, brushed a stray lock of hair from her face, and let out a little sigh. The delicate sound sent shivers down Echard's spine. He really didn't know if he could bring himself to kill her.

But he *had* to have the amulet.

He drew his knife and waited.

Finally she turned her back on him and he sprang into action. In a flash, he covered her mouth with his free hand and pressed the blade of his knife to her throat. He felt her tense up to fight, but then freeze the moment the cold steel touched her flesh. He couldn't help himself. He held her close, pressed his body against hers, buried his face in her hair and inhaled deeply. Her skin was so soft and she smelled so good. He had dreamed of this. A shame to slaughter such a perfect specimen.

"Don't cry out or you die. Do you understand?"

She nodded and he removed his hand from her mouth.

"My friend will be here any second, you sick freak." Her voice was strong despite the fact that she stood at death's doorstep.

"All I want is the amulet," he growled, trying to disguise his voice. Even now he didn't want her to think badly of him. "Cooperate and you might live."

Down a short flight of stone steps lay the replica of Christ's tomb on Maddock's right, and to the left was another space carved into the bedrock upon which the Hermitage stood. Some sort of cellar, Maddock guessed. He made a quick inspection of the faux tomb, which was little more than an alcove dug into the rock, and the huge stone disc that was rolled to the side.

He saw nothing promising, so he moved to the cellar. A barred door blocked his way, but the lock was cheap and not intended to keep out a determined person. There didn't appear to be anything of interest here, or was there?

The space behind the door proved to be a small, empty room carved directly into the bedrock. There was nothing here. No trapdoors, no cryptic symbols carved into the walls, not even a brick or flagstone to pry up. Still, he took the time to inspect the space before dismissing it.

"I wonder if Rae is having better luck, or did I just take us on a wild goose chase?" he said to himself. He hoped this hadn't been a giant waste of time.

He only had a moment's warning, a dimming of the light inside the room as someone or something blocked the doorway.

Acting on instinct, he dove to his left. A shot rang out, the boom ear-splitting in the confined space. He tucked his shoulder, rolled, and came up with his weapon at the ready—the pistol he'd taken from one of Echard's hired thugs two days earlier. The high pitched whine of a ricocheting bullet filled the air. He felt more than heard something buzz past his ear and then he heard a grunt.

The man standing in the doorway was a big, greasy-looking fellow with mutton chops and a shaved head. His right hand hung by his side, weapon dangling from limp fingers. He looked at Maddock in disbelief, then his gaze drifted down to his t-shirt soaked with blood from the bullet wound in the center of his chest. He tried to stanch the flow with his left hand, but the effort was futile.

"I've got to hand it to you. That's the weirdest way I've ever seen a man kill himself," Maddock said.

"I didn't mean to," the man said. Then his eyes rolled back and he collapsed.

Maddock wasted no time. This fellow must be working for Echard, and if he wasn't alone, that gunshot would have alerted anyone else in the area of Maddock's position. Hopefully it would also draw them away from Rae.

He relieved the fallen man of his pistol, a cheap Saturday Night Special, then paused to peer out the doorway.

He caught a flash of movement just down the hill. A figure ducked behind one of the stations of the cross. And then a fusillade of gunfire erupted. Maddock ducked back inside as bullets slammed into the door facing, spattering him with fragments of rock.

Another bullet whizzed through the doorway and began pinging around the small cellar like an angry yellowjacket trapped in a mason jar.

"I can't stay here."

Mentally calculating the attacker's position, Maddock readied himself, then reached out and opened fire with the revolver, aiming for the spot where the shooter had been moments before. Then he rolled out the door and ducked down behind a pile of rock.

As he rose up, the shooter fired again. As Maddock had expected, the man had remained hunkered down behind the engraving rather than change his position. Which meant if Maddock could get a better angle, he could get off a clean shot.

Maddock fired again, then scrambled down the steep hill as two more shots rang out in reply. He skidded down the slope, hitting every boulder along the way, then landed on his feet in a thin copse of pine. He dropped to one knee and looked for his assailant. The man still hadn't moved.

Now Maddock could see him better. He might have been the dead fellow's brother. He was a bulky white guy with more tats than hair.

As Maddock watched, the man rose up from his hiding place behind one of the stations of the cross, and peered out. He was still looking up the hill for Maddock and had no idea the tables had been turned.

Hugging the ground, Maddock began to crawl toward his target. He closed the gap quickly, until he was ten meters away. The man still had no idea Maddock had left his position outside the cellar.

Amateur, Maddock thought.

Ordinarily, he'd creep right up on the man and take him alive for questioning, but there was no time. He didn't know where Rae was or if she was in danger. He had to end this quickly.

Carefully, he took aim.

The man must have spotted Maddock from the corner of his eye because he suddenly spun to his right and opened fire.

But Maddock was ready, and at this range he seldom missed. Two shots—a bullet to the gut, a second to the head. That ended that.

He sprinted back up the hill, ejecting his spent magazine and slamming another home as he ran. He hoped there was no gunman waiting for him at the top of the steps. If there was, Maddock would make for a target that was hard to miss.

Thankfully no one was waiting for him when he reached the top. But where was Rae?

He made a mad dash for the monastery with no regard for his own safety. How stupid he had been to agree to split up. He'd been so sure no one else was around.

He burst through the door and looked around. Through a nearby doorway he saw a figure lying on the floor. Rae!

He rushed to her side. She'd been bound and gagged and left lying on her side. A trail of blood ran from a cut on her neck and dripped to the floor.

"Rae! Speak to me!"

Relief flooded through him as she opened her eyes and made a muffled sound. He hastily removed her gag.

"How do you expect me to speak to you with Echard's nasty handkerchief in my mouth?"

"Are you all right?" he asked, touching the cut on her neck. It was just a nick and he breathed a sigh.

"I'm fine, just untie me."

He removed her bonds and she sat up and gingerly rubbed her wrists.

"What happened?"

"Echard was waiting for me. He grabbed me almost as soon as I came in."

"And the amulet?" he asked.

Rae smiled. "He fell for it. I think you were right. He's never seen it up close. As far as he knows, he's got the real item."

"That's a relief. I'm just sorry it meant damage to your perfect neck."

"You're a neck man? That's a first."

"I am now." On an impulse, he planted a kiss on her neck where Echard's blade had scored the flesh. Rae grabbed his face in both hands and kissed him hard on the lips.

"That's for saving my life. I heard shots. What happened?"

He filled her in on what had happened.

"Where did Echard go?"

"I don't know. He went out a back window."

Maddock made a quick search but could not find any sign of the man.

"I'm sorry I led you into a trap for nothing," he said.

"It's all right. Your plan worked. Hopefully that's Echard off our backs."

31

Maddock and Rae knew something was wrong as soon as they reached the dock where *Sea Foam* was moored. The entire crew was waiting for them on the aft deck. Bones was pacing back and forth across the deck like a caged lion. Maddock noticed right away that Kyle was not among their number.

Please, let him be below decks, he thought.

"Kyle's gone," Matt said.

"What do you mean gone?" Rae asked. "You were supposed to be keeping an eye on him."

"We did, but then that girl showed up."

Maddock and Rae exchanged a quizzical look.

"Thel," Bones said. "She was here."

"The girl you hooked up with?"

Bones stopped pacing, folded his massive arms, and made a curt nod.

"Man, when you stand like that, you look like a cigar store Indian," Willis said.

"This really isn't the time," Maddock said. Rae was trembling, whether from fear or anger he couldn't tell. "Why don't you tell us what happened."

"We were just hanging out, doing some fishing," Corey said. "And then this gorgeous girl shows up. We'd never seen her before, but Kyle recognized her as the girl you met. They sat on the dock and talked for a while."

"What about?" Rae asked.

"Don't know. She didn't seem interested in talking to us. Next thing we knew, they were gone."

"You didn't see them leave?" Rae said.

"It was like they were there one moment and gone the next."

"They said he took a drink from her flask," Bones

said.

"And now Bones is convinced she's a Finfolk," Willis added.

Maddock blinked. "Finfolk? The shape-shifting sea creatures?"

"You've heard of them?" Bones asked.

Maddock explained that, in the mythology of the Orkney Islands in Scotland, Finfolk were amphibious, sea-dwelling beings who abducted humans to be their spouses.

"The Finwife would take the form of a beautiful woman, often a mermaid, to lure a potential husband. Finmen would take the form of a handsome sailor."

"In that case, Matt is definitely not a Finman," Willis said.

Rae rounded on him. "Can we be serious for a minute? My brother is missing."

"He hooked up with a fine lady," Willis said. "Nothing sinister about that. And I don't believe in Finfolk, no matter what that old woman said."

"Old woman?" Maddock asked. "I think we all need to compare notes."

Each pair filled the others in on the day's events. Willis described the events at Mermaid Hole, and Maddock filled everyone in on what had transpired at the Hermitage.

"What about the bodies?" Matt asked.

"Hid them in the jungle, covered them up best I could. I doubt they'll be found. And I used the pistol I took off of Echard's hired thug, so if there's a ballistics match to something in the police's system, it won't point to us."

"I don't understand how you can talk about this in the way normal people discuss taking out the garbage," Rae said.

Maddock didn't respond. Her choice of the word

"normal" stung a little, but it was true. Among their crew, only Corey could be considered "normal" where violence was concerned. The rest had been hardened to it a long time ago.

"He did take out the garbage," Bones said. "It's never pretty, but sometimes we have to make hard choices."

"What should we do about Kyle?" Maddock asked. As much as he wanted to agree with Willis' take on the matter, he couldn't. As incredible as it seemed, he was convinced that something sinister was at play here, and that everything was connected. There were too many coincidences to believe otherwise. The amulet and ring, the Lusca, the Waters of Life, the strange water Thel had given to Bones. The dots connected but he couldn't make out the image they formed.

"We have to find him!" Rae said. "This girl is obviously a member of a weird cult that drugs and kidnaps people. She must have dosed him with the same thing she gave to Bones."

"But the Lusca, and the ring and amulet..." Bones said.

"These people are clearly fascinated with folklore. They probably call themselves Finfolk and they absorbed these other stories into their traditions."

"The girl in the old picture looked just like Thel," Bones said.

"It was probably her mother. The cult has probably been around for generations."

"What chased our boat? What killed Val?" Bones demanded.

"I don't know. Right now, the only thing I care about is figuring out where this girl has taken Kyle so we can get him back."

"How could a cult of kidnappers exist under everyone's noses like that?" Matt asked.

"People disappear all the time in the islands," Rae

said. "Their bodies are never found. We attribute some to drownings, others to crime, and the rest we figure they got island fever and took off to the mainland. It's possible, especially on Cat Island."

"Let's assume that Kyle has, in fact, been abducted," Maddock said. "Where do we look first?"

"Mermaid Hole," Bones said immediately. "For hundreds of years the locals have been warning people away from the sinkholes under that lake because of the mermaids. Something's down there. I'm sure of it."

"The Finfolk?" Willis said. "Man, that's crazy."

From the door that led to the pilothouse, someone cleared his throat. Corey stood there, a nervous look on his face.

"Guys, I just tried to contact Gomez, just to get his take on this. He didn't show up for work today, and his boat was found adrift. Lots of damage, apparently."

Maddock winced. Gomez was a good egg.

"What is happening?" Rae whispered.

"It's not complicated. We found the amulet and set the freaking Lusca loose," Bones said.

"There's something else." Corey held up a legal pad covered with notes written in his precise hand. "While Amos and Andy were doing shots last night, I was chatting with a couple of ancient dudes who told me all kinds of stories as long as I kept the beer coming."

Maddock nodded. Corey had an inquisitive mind and carried a note pad and pencil with him at all times. It was one of his quirks.

"Anyway, this talk about Finfolk reminded me of a story." He consulted his notes.

"The first British settlement in the Bahamas was at a place called Preacher's Cave on the Island of Eleuthera, back in the 1600s during the English Civil War. They were refugees fleeing religious persecution from other colonists in Bermuda. They were called the Eleutheran

Adventurers."

"We don't really have time for every little detail," Maddock said.

"Unlike when a certain someone lays out a grid," Willis muttered.

Maddock flashed him a dark look. "Hit the high points, Corey."

"Okay, fine," Corey said. "Storms forced their ship to hit the Devil's Backbone Reef off the coast of Eleuthera. The survivors built a permanent settlement there, and converted a cave into a place of worship."

"Preacher's Cave," Matt said.

"Circle gets the square. Anyway, one of the weird stories about this place is that the colonists captured a woman they claimed was a mermaid. Their minister, a man named Roman, was convinced that she was simply a woman possessed by the devil, so they tried to perform an exorcism on her. Things must have gotten a little rough because she died. A few days later, the colony was attacked by what they claimed were a group of mermen. One colonist was killed and two women abducted. In time, the story made its way back to Europe, and the Catholic Church sent a man to the Bahamas to root out these so-called devil creatures. According to the story, he tracked them to Cat Island, even captured a few. By torturing them, he eventually found the way to their lair. But he never learned their secrets, whatever that means. Eventually, the church tried to cover up the story."

Maddock felt dizzy. Impossible as it seemed, the pieces were indeed falling into place.

"Bones, how rusty is your Spanish?"

"Not as rusty as your French. Seriously, dude. Who takes French?"

"That's the class the pretty girls took at my high school."

"That's the class the prudes took, which is perfect for

you."

"I can read it," Rae said. "I'm not great with the spoken language, but my comprehension is good, especially when I can read at my own pace."

Maddock handed her the journal and she began to page through it.

"I'm just skimming but this is definitely the guy." As she paged through, tears welled in her eyes. "God, he did awful things to them."

"Does it say what secrets he was trying to learn?" Maddock asked.

She flipped forward. "He wanted to command the great beast, Leviathan." Her eyes grew wide. "And unless I'm mistaken, this is a map that will lead us to their lair."

She turned the journal around so the others could see the curving, twisting lines that covered the page.

"So, we've got a map," Bones said, "but no starting point."

"Corey, any idea?" Maddock asked.

"Oh, now you want the details? The only thing that might be a clue is something one of the old guys said. When his buddy said there had been a cover-up by the church, he laughed and said they 'literally' covered it up."

"How does that help?" Rae asked.

Maddock mentally assembled the pieces of the puzzle.

"I think I know where we should start."

32

"**So, you're telling** me the Hermitage was built to cover up the torture chamber?" Bones asked as they crested the hill and approached the old building. The two men, along with Willis and Rae, had returned to the top of Mount Alverna, while Matt and Corey made inquiries at every local business and home, not that there were many of either.

"That's my theory," Maddock said. "It seemed odd to me that Father Jerome, a brilliant architect, put a ton of work into constructing not just a home for himself, but a place of worship at the top of the tallest hill on one of the remotest islands in the Bahamas. And he's got the stations of the cross, all fantastic works of art, plus a church, even a replica of the tomb with the stone rolled away."

"What's your point?"

Maddock ran a hand through his damp, sweat-soaked hair. "This is the kind of place where anyone would come for worship, even make a pilgrimage to. But this kind, generous guy put it at the top of the tallest hill of a remote island with a tiny population. Even today it's not easy to get to. Why?"

"It was his retirement home," Rae said. "He wanted rest and contemplation." Despite her obvious concern for Kyle, she was holding up well.

"Put all this work into something that was just for himself? Doesn't sound like the wonderful, generous guy he was made out to be."

"Covering up horrendous crimes doesn't sound like a nice guy, either," Willis pointed out.

"Agreed, but it happened so long before he built this place. It's almost as if he were trying to consecrate this place after all the evil."

"If that's the case, then where do you think we should look?" Bones asked.

"I don't know. What might be a symbol of cleansing away evil?" Maddock asked.

"The altar?" Rae suggested. "That's where someone would be baptized."

"Makes sense. Willis, you check that out. Rae, I'd like for you to show Bones which window Echard climbed out of."

"Okay, but I don't see how that helps us."

"Echard disappeared awfully fast. I'm playing a hunch."

"Just point to the window, but don't get too close to it," Bones said, understanding immediately.

While Maddock and Rae watched, Bones moved in for a closer inspection of the ground beneath the monastery window. He knelt, looked for a few seconds, and grinned.

"Here is where he hit the ground." He pointed to a spot near the wall. "A lot of rocks here, but he still left a nice trail. Come on."

Bones guided them down the hill behind the monastery. Next, the trail made a sharp turn to the left, rounded the crest of the hill, then came to a halt in a thicket of Caribbean Pine. Bones stood there for a long time.

"What do you see?" Rae asked.

"It looks like he knelt down here," Bones said. "I can see knee prints, and there's a whole bunch of sign, like he was shifting around."

"I'll bet he hid here and waited for us to leave," Maddock said.

"Lucky he didn't ambush us," Rae said.

"Lucky for him," Maddock said. "Where did he go when he finally left this spot?"

Bones narrowed his eyes, gave his ponytail a tug as he sometimes did when he was concentrating. "That way." He pointed up the hill back in the direction of the monastery.

They climbed the hill and found themselves standing beside a sundial set on a stone pedestal.

"This is where the trail ends," Bones said.

"Can't be," Rae said. "He had to have gone somewhere."

"Wherever he went, he didn't leave tracks. Too many rocks." He turned to Maddock. "Any ideas?"

Maddock didn't reply. His attention was fully focused on the sundial. Something about it wasn't right, but he couldn't put his finger on it. Sundials were traditionally engraved with a motto, and this one was no exception.

"And, behold, there was a great earthquake: for the angel of the Lord descended from heaven," he read aloud.

"You quoting the Bible, Maddock?" Willis had returned from his inspection of the altar and had come up empty.

"Just reading the engraving. It's weird. Usually a sundial quote is a pithy saying, something that reflects the personality of the owner. But a quote about earthquakes?"

"That's not even the whole verse," Bones said.

"How do you know that?" Maddock said.

"I grew up in the Bible Belt. I was immersed in that stuff. I didn't pay attention, but a few things filtered through."

"So, what's the rest of the verse?"

"I can't quote it exactly, but I know the angel rolled back the stone."

All eyes turned in the direction of the replica tomb of Christ which stood just downhill from the sundial.

And then Maddock realized what was out of place.

"That's it! The sundial is oriented all wrong. It should point to true north." True north was different from magnetic north, which was what a compass would show. In this part of the world, the gnomon, the part of the sundial which cast a shadow, should be adjusted several degrees east of magnetic north. But this one wasn't remotely accurate. Maddock explained this to the others. "Father Jerome was an architect and a sculptor. Those things require precision."

"Also known as being anal," Bones said, "which Maddock is all about."

Maddock ignored him. "In this case, the gnomon is pointed in the direction of the tomb."

"You said you checked it out," Rae said.

"Maybe I missed something. Maybe one of you will see something I missed."

They made their way down to the tomb and made a thorough inspection. They scrutinized every inch of the tomb, but found nothing.

"Maybe the stone disc rolls?" Maddock offered. He and Willis poured all their strength into the effort, but they couldn't budge it.

"Where's Bones?" Willis asked, mopping the sweat from his brow. "He's avoiding the heavy lifting."

As if in reply, the stone disc began to move. Slowly, almost silently, it rolled to the side, revealing a steep pathway that plunged deep into the mountain.

"Did that do anything?" Bones called down from the top of the hill.

"What did you just do?" Maddock asked.

"If Echard already knew where the hidden door was, he must have had a reason to go to the sundial first. Otherwise he'd have just skirted the hill around to the tomb."

Maddock clapped a hand to his forehead. It should

have been obvious.

"Bones, you're a genius."

He looked up to see his friend grinning down at them from above.

"Can I get that in writing?"

33

They followed a steep passageway that wound down into the earth. The air grew cool and damp, the surface beneath their feet slick with moisture. The beams of their flashlights sliced through the darkness ahead. And then a shape appeared.

Maddock drew his pistol, but relaxed almost immediately.

"It's a statue."

The figure was that of a robed man with long hair and a beard. He stood with his back to them. He held a tablet in both hands, thrust out in front of him. On it was engraved a scripture from the book of *Isaiah*.

In that day the Lord with His sore and great and strong sword shall punish Leviathan the piercing Serpent, even Leviathan that crooked Serpent; and he shall slay the Dragon that is in the sea.

"What the hell is this doing down here?" Bones asked.

"Look at the way he's holding the tablet," Maddock said. "It's like a shield."

"A symbolic repudiation of the great serpent," Rae said.

"Which means we're headed in the right direction," Bones said. Undeterred, he brushed past the statue and headed deeper beneath the earth.

They soon came to a fork. The passageway to the left was clear, the one to the right caved in. Maddock's light fell upon an engraving directly above the blocked passageway. It was faint, but he could easily make out the form a roughly hewn cross flanked by a fig tree and a sword. The image was ringed by words written in Latin.

"*Exurge Domine et judica causam tuam,*" Maddock

read aloud.

"What does that mean?" Rae asked.

"Rise Up, O Lord, and Judge Thine Own Cause! This was the emblem of the Spanish Inquisition. I think we've found the torture chamber."

"Which means Echard went the other way," Bones said.

"Good," Rae said. "I can't wait to see him again."

Echard had never come this far before. Always he had stopped when he reached the bridge. It was narrow, slippery, and the pit beneath it so deep that he'd never survive the fall. Before he had the amulet in his possession, it had always seemed like an unnecessary risk. But now that it was finally in his possession, it was time to claim his prize.

He wore the amulet tucked inside his shirt. For some reason, he felt the need to feel it touching his flesh. It hung there, cold against his skin. Strange it felt so ordinary. He'd expected a transformational experience. Not for the first time he tugged at the collar of his shirt so he could get a better look at it. The blue crystal in its eye glinted and his heart leapt. No, it was just reflecting the glow of his flashlight.

"It probably won't work until you actually meet the creature," he said. At that thought, a shot of adrenaline surged through him, a mix of fear and excitement that made his toes tingle and his stomach clench. He was frightened, but eager.

He'd made the decision to go his own way. His hired goons were dead, and who knew where Issachar was? Hopefully still lurking around Mermaid Hole waiting for

Maddock to turn up. The man was scary, to be sure, and the prospect of crossing the Dominion even more frightening, but what choice did Echard have? Issachar had made it clear that he knew about Echard's unsavory dealings, and that he disapproved. There was no way the Dominion would let him back in. But once Echard commanded the great beast, he wouldn't need them. There would be no stopping him. But first he had to cross the bridge.

Echard ran his light back and forth across the narrow stone bridge. It was scarcely a meter wide, it surface engraved with a serpent's scales. Water dripped from the ceiling.

Echard took a deep breath, then stepped out onto the bridge. He was half-expecting it to collapse beneath his weight. It held, but his foot immediately began to slide. He hissed and drew back as if he'd touched a hot stove.

"I should go back," he said. "Get some safety equipment." He considered this idea but discarded it immediately. Issachar wouldn't remain at Mermaid Hole forever, and if he came looking for Echard, he'd go to the Hermitage. Echard's only hope was to finish what he started.

Trembling, he dropped down on all fours and began to crawl.

Maddock was the last one across the bridge. The crossing wasn't as difficult as he had initially feared. The surface was slick, but they'd come prepared. With the added security of a safety rope, the group had made the crossing quickly. That obstacle cleared, they kept moving.

Soon, they came to another fork. Here, there was nothing to indicate which way they should go. The only difference was that the ceiling of one passageway was tall enough to stand in while the other was so low a person would have to get down on hands and knees to pass through.

"Do we split up?" Bones asked.

"No. I think we should stay together."

"Try one and then the other?" Willis offered.

"Maybe, but I hate to go in blind. Do you see anything?" Maddock looked around. Something caught his eye. One particular spot on the wall in between the two tunnels looked different. As he moved in closer he could tell that someone had smeared dirt over a spot the size of his hand. He touched it. It was still fresh.

"I think Echard covered something up." He took out his knife and began scraping away the damp soil. When he'd cleaned as much as he could, Willis took out a water bottle and washed the rest away.

"Whoa!" Bones said.

Carved into the rock was a bizarre, owl-like creature with a long tail and spindly arms. It had three fingers on each hand, each tipped with large, curved claws.

"That's a chickcharney," Maddock said.

"What does it mean?" Willis asked.

Maddock thought about what little he knew of the creatures. They were proud, easily insulted. And it was important to show them respect.

Acting on a hunch, he moved to the passageway on the left, the one with the high ceiling, and shone his light down its length. Lying on the floor at the very edge of the circle of light, lay what he had initially thought was a pile of rocks. In fact, it was a pile of bones. Running up the side of the wall, just above where the bones lay, was a series of holes about a half an inch across.

"I think this way is booby trapped."

"So we take the low road?" Bones asked.

"The chickcharney demanded respect. Which is more respectful? Approaching on your feet, or on hands and knees?"

"I guess it's the best theory we've got," Bones said.

Just then, they heard a series of loud bangs coming from the tunnel to the right.

"Gunshots," Willis said.

"It's got to be Echard. But what is he shooting at?" Maddock said.

Bones shrugged.

"Only one way to find out."

He dropped to his knees and crawled into the passageway.

34

Echard fled blindly through the cavern, ducking and dodging around piles of rock and debris. What the hell were these things?

He heard the sounds of pursuit behind him. Snarling, he fired a shot blindly over his shoulder.

A flicker of movement off to the right, just at the edge of his vision. They were trying to flank him! Or was he just being paranoid? Maybe they were just curious, and his panic had set them off.

Maybe they're like dogs. Don't show fear.

He slowed to a jog, tried to catch his breath.

Big mistake.

A hot lance of pain pierced his back as something slashed him. He whirled about, opened fire. The thing was gone.

Damn! He started to run again, with no idea where he was headed.

Something snagged his foot and he fell hard to the ground. He got a mouthful of grit, a split lip, and what felt like a chipped tooth for his trouble.

The things were still coming. He could hear the way their claws scuffled across the cave floor. Why didn't they call out? Make some kind of sound? The silence made it all the more unnerving. He hauled himself to his feet and continued to run.

Up ahead loomed a narrow crevasse, just large enough for him to squeeze through. Let the freakish things come in after him. They'd have to come one at a time, and he had his gun.

Something swooped down in front of him and he opened fire. The bullet found its mark, caught the thing right between the eyes. He smiled in satisfaction.

He was almost there. But would he make it?

Several of the creatures were moving to cut off his escape. He raised his pistol and fired.

Click.

The magazine was empty! In desperation he flung his empty pistol at them.

Suddenly, they all stopped running. They cocked their heads, listening to a something Echard couldn't hear. And then they turned and headed back in the direction from which they had come.

Echard was so shocked that he stopped running. He turned slowly, made a complete circle. Impossible as it seemed, they were gone. Echard didn't know what had drawn their attention, but he wasn't about to complain. Relief flooding through him, and he sprinted out of the cavern.

"What the hell is this place?" Willis said.

They were in a large underground chamber, filled with piles of rubble and surprisingly, plant life— creepers, a few low-growing woody shrubs, some scrub pine, and vines laden with dark purple berries. The floor of the chamber was dotted with water-filled sinkholes. Guano dripped down the walls, which were pockmarked by what looked like large burrows. A glowing cloud of mist hung about thirty feet above them, illuminated by a handful of tiny shafts of sunlight streaming down from somewhere high above them.

"It's like a biosphere down here," Rae said. "It's remarkable."

Maddock froze in place. "You don't know how right you are."

Approaching them on all sides were some of the strangest-looking creatures he had ever seen.

They were owls, some of them four feet tall. Their bodies were brown, their faces white, their beaks disproportionately long and sharply pointed. And while they lacked the arms of the legendary chickcharney, their feet were tipped with long, razorlike talons.

"Tyto pollens," Maddock said. "I guess Andros wasn't the only island they inhabited."

"Do they bite?" Bones asked as the semicircle of owls inched closer.

"We gotta get out of here," Willis said. "If we had shotguns I'd take my chances, but all we got is knives and handguns. I don't like them odds."

"I'm going on ahead." Rae brandished the knife Matt had given her. "If Kyle is somewhere down here, I can't turn back."

"I didn't say we give up; just find another path."

"What other path? The one with the booby trap?"

She was right. There was no other way forward. Maddock eyed the advancing owls. They didn't make a sound, which unnerved him. He looked at the others and inspiration struck him.

"Rae, take off your shirt."

"This is really not the time, Maddock."

"Just give it to me. You can have mine if you like."

Rae made a face. "It's fine. I've got a sports bra on." She stripped off her bright orange tank top and handed it to Maddock. It was a measure of the seriousness of the situation that neither Willis nor Bones so much as glanced at her. As soon as she took off her shirt, the birds stopped advancing. That was a good sign. Perhaps Maddock's theory was correct.

"You guys gather up some rocks, baseball-sized if you can find them."

Bones cocked his head. "Are you trying to make a

slingshot or something?"

"Not even close. Cover my back." Maddock turned his back on the birds and began shredding the shirts into long strips, which he then had the others tie around the rocks.

"These are very cute, Maddock," Willis said. "But I don't know what the hell we're supposed to do with them."

"According to legend, islanders carried flowers or bits of bright fabric to charm the chickcharney. And considering the engraving outside the entrance to this chamber, I think it's a safe bet that these things are the source of the legend." He held up one of the rocks, a strip of orange fabric dangling from it. "Bones, shine your light on this."

When the beam of Bones' light hit the orange fabric, the effect on the owls was immediate. They all seemed to stand at attention, their rapt gaze fixed on the orange cloth.

"Here goes nothing." Maddock flung the rock far off to the side. Bones tried to keep his light on it as it flew like an orange comet until it fell somewhere out of sight.

As one, the owls made a mad dash for the rock.

"Let's go. Keep your rocks ready in case they come back. And watch out for water hazards."

They dashed through the cavern, with no idea where they were going. As they ran, more owls appeared, their eerie white faces poking out of the burrows in the cavern walls. A few of them fluttered down to the cave floor. Time and again, Maddock and company were forced to distract the creatures until finally they reached the far side of the cavern, where a narrow passageway provided the only means of egress they had seen.

"Will they follow us?" Rae asked.

"I don't know." Maddock shone his light down the passageway. "It looks like there's another chamber up ahead. You guys go ahead. Once everyone's through, I'll throw the last rock and try to distract them." Maddock hefted the rock and took up a position in front of the passageway.

"Shout when you guys are through."

"Be careful." Rae planted a kiss on his cheek. "Don't be too long."

Maddock waited. More owls emerged from their burrows and slowly approached him, their eyes shining red in the dim light. Closer they crept.

"Are you guys through yet?" Maddock shouted.

No reply.

The owls closed in.

"Bones?" he shouted.

Nothing.

He stole a glance over his shoulder, shone his light down the passageway, but the others were nowhere in sight.

"Doesn't anybody follow instructions anymore?"

With a powerful heave, he flung the rock with all his might back in the direction from which they had come. Once again, the owls moved as a flock, turning and running after the rock. Breathing a sigh of relief, he made his way through the passage.

It wasn't long before the silence up ahead began to worry him.

"Are you guys all right?"

Silence.

Pistol in hand, heart in his throat, Maddock emerged from the narrow passageway into a larger chamber.

It was empty.

35

Bones squeezed his bulk through the narrow passageway and emerged into a small chamber. His body wasn't all the way out when a cold, sharp point pressed against his throat. Many hands seized his arms, stripped him of his weapons, flashlight, and backpack. Someone clamped a hand over his throat. He was hustled along another corridor. Behind him, he heard a grunt and the sound of a fist striking flesh. He tried to turn around to go back and fight, but someone jabbed what felt like a spear into his back, just above the kidney.

"Do not resist and none of you will be harmed." It was a woman's voice.

He relaxed, let himself be ushered along the corridor and into another chamber. Here, a cell had been carved into the bedrock. The three of them were ushered inside and the door slammed closed and locked behind them. Someone lit a torch, illuminating their prison with flickering golden light.

They were in a small chamber dominated by a pool of crystalline water. Bones saw the shadow of something move beneath its surface, and for a moment he was almost happy to be behind the safety of the bars.

A dozen or more of their captors stood staring at them. All but two were women. They were clad in knee-length tunics belted at the waist. Some wore leather jerkins. All wore knives like the one Thel had left behind, and were armed with spears or bows and arrows. As they watched, one of the men, a tall, dark-skinned man with long, braided hair, began dropping their weapons one by one into the pool.

Their leader was a fair-skinned woman with blue eyes and white blonde hair. She smiled at Willis, then turned her gaze on Bones.

"So powerful. So dusky. What are you? A Moor?" There was a hint of Cockney in her accent.

"You've never seen an Indian before?"

"India! I have heard tell of that wondrous place!"

"Native American. Cherokee."

The woman shook her head. "It does not matter. We don't have anything like you here. You will improve our stock greatly. You might even produce a boy!" She reached through the bars and caressed his cheek. "I am Gwyneth. I think you and I are going to be great friends."

Bones grabbed her wrist and twisted her arm.

"I'm not that easy."

Immediately, several spears were thrust through the bars.

"If you want to keep your eyes, hands, and feet, I suggest you release me," Gwyneth said. "Whether you keep them makes no difference to me. You won't need them in order to serve our purposes."

Bones let go of her arm and she took a few steps back. "Even stronger than I thought. Our child will be a great warrior. This one looks promising, too." She glanced at Willis.

"Is my brother here?" Rae demanded.

Gwyneth smiled. "Is he the handsome one Thelxiope brought home? He is a simple boy, but sweet. He will serve us well."

Rae snarled and attacked the bars, trying to get at Gwyneth. Willis pulled her back.

"Easy, now," he warned. "It'll be all right."

"Listen to the negro," Gwyneth said.

Willis flared up immediately. "What did you call me?"

Gwyneth ignored him. "You can all be a part of our family." Her eyes narrowed and she smiled at Rae. "You look like a Moor, too. But this man you call your brother, he looks like an Englishman. But he has the brain of a Scot. How is that?"

"We're not blood relations," Rae said.

"Yet you love him?"

"He's the most important person in the world to me. He needs me."

Gwyneth's condescending smile was filled with pity. "He no longer needs you. He will be safe here for many, many years."

"Let him go. He's innocent." Tears streamed down Rae's cheeks.

"You could be with him," Gwyneth continued. "The way you really want to be. Forever."

"It's not like that," Rae said. "You are sick."

Gwyneth shrugged. "You will have time to consider it. We will not do anything to you until the captain has had his sport."

"Who is the captain?" Bones asked.

"No one you will have ever met," Gwyneth said. "But you will get to know him."

"Who are you people?" Rae's voice trembled with rage.

"We are called the Finfolk, although we are not all kin. Like you and your brother." She smiled. "I once lived on the outside. When I was taken, I wanted to leave, too. But now I am happy that I stayed."

"Did you stay or were you kept?" Bones asked.

Gwyneth drew a clay flask from a pouch at her waist and set it on the floor within an arm's reach of the cell. "In case you get thirsty."

"We are not going to drink that," Bones said.

"Sooner or later you will." With that, she led her people out of the chamber.

When they were gone, Willis turned to Bones. "This is Karma, you know. The way you treat women, it's coming back to bite you now. Bet you wish you'd been more of a gentleman."

Bones turned to Willis. "If you're such a gentleman, what are you doing in here?"

"The sins of the first mate are visited upon the crew."

"What the hell are you talking about? And I'm not the first mate. Maddock and I are partners. That makes me co-captain."

"All right, co-captain, you got any bright ideas on how we can get out of here? Or do you want to find out what it feels like to be a kept man?"

Bones didn't have an answer. The prison cell was medieval in design, and with the proper implement, he could easily pick it. But their captors had left them nothing.

"Just give me time," he said. "I'll figure something out."

36

Four passageways led out of the chamber. Maddock had no idea in which direction his friends had gone. The only thing of which he was certain was that his friends would not have abandoned him. Either they had been driven away or taken captive. His money was on the latter. They had vanished too quickly, too, for there to have been a fight.

"Eeny, meeny, miney, mo." He chose the tunnel to the left.

The passageway led to an underground lake. There was no way across or around it.

"This is why I don't gamble," he said. Cursing his lousy guesswork, he returned to the chamber to try again.

The second passageway led him on a steep climb and brought him out on a ledge looking down on a strange sight. A handsome man, tall with dark hair, clad all in black, sat on a chair in the midst of piles of treasure. Gold, jewels, goblets, strings of pearls. Unopened chests stood all around. The very definition of a pirate's horde. A young woman clad in a scanty tunic sat at his feet, gazing longingly up at him.

In the center of the room stood a pile of coral-encrusted stones. From its top bubbled a stream of water, which cascaded down the sides and filled the deep basin that had been carved around it. Two women bathed in its waters. As he watched, one of the women scooped up some water in an oyster shell and poured it over the other's head. The second woman closed her eyes and let out a groan of ecstasy.

That must be some awfully good water.

There was no sign of his friends, nor of Kyle.

A ledge ringed the chamber. Maddock saw another passageway on the opposite side. He got down on his stomach and began to crawl. The people down below paid him no mind, and he worked his way around with ease. Just as he had reached the other side, the man in the chair looked up. His eyes roamed along the ledge. Maddock froze. The man stared at Maddock's hiding place for what felt like an eternity. Finally, he looked away.

Maddock breathed a sigh of relief and continued on. The pathway led downward now, ending at another underground lake. Like the previous one he'd encountered, there was no way around. This time, however, the passageway continued on the other side of the water.

"There's no way they brought Bones and the others here," he said. He could do what Bones would do, and charge into the treasure room, guns blazing. Try and extract the information from whoever he left alive. He discarded that idea quickly. He was running low on ammunition and no telling how many enemies lived down here.

"...went this way." A voice echoed down the tunnel behind him. Many footsteps came his way. Damn! The man in the treasure room had spotted him.

And now he was trapped.

With no better alternative, he dove into the water. Its icy depths delivered a sudden shock to his system. Once again he felt a tremor run through him, weaker this time, but still enough to rattle his fillings.

The medallion!

Both ring and medallion were tucked into his pocket. And he had just dived into the water. If the Lusca, or Leviathan, or whatever the hell it was, was anywhere close by, he would be screwed. He began swimming for the other side with all he was worth. His clothing weighed him down, but he kept swimming. Behind him he heard shouts and them something struck the water just past his head. A spear!

He dove beneath the surface of the water and changed direction, hoping to confuse the attackers. But did he dare climb out of the water when doing so would leave him exposed? He swam until he felt something brush his foot. That sealed it. He made for the edge of the water and clambered out.

An arrow whizzed past his head and he hit the ground. There was scant cover, only a few stray boulders, and he scrambled to get behind the closest one. He must have been just out of range because most of the projectiles landed in the water, but a few nearly hit their target.

He drew his pistol, keenly aware of his dwindling supply of ammunition, and took aim at the biggest of the lot, a shirtless warrior who stood beating his chest and brandishing a spear. Maddock took careful aim and squeezed off a single round.

The bullet struck center mass. The warrior's cries cut off abruptly. He looked down in disbelief at his wound, blood streaming down his belly. He let his spear fall to the ground. And then, like a falling tree, he plunged forward into the water.

The surface of the lake roiled. The remaining warriors broke off their attack, but before they could move a mass of tentacles burst forth. The Lusca had arrived!

The Finfolk, if that was indeed what they were, broke and ran. The Lusca seized the slowest of their number in two massive coils and lifted her high in the air. She screamed and stabbed one of the tentacles repeatedly with an arrow. The others halted their retreat to fire a single, utterly ineffective salvo at the monster. And then, in a single, deft motion, the creature ripped her in half.

That was enough for the remaining Finfolk, who fled back up the tunnel in the direction of the treasure room.

Bile rising in his throat, Maddock made a beeline for the only passageway on this side of the lake.

He felt something burning hot against his thigh and wondered for a moment if he'd been wounded in the earlier exchange. He glanced down and saw that his right pocket was glowing with a blue light. The ring and amulet! They must be reacting to the Lusca. He stole a glance over his shoulder to see if the beast was coming after him. It had vanished from sight, though the surface of the lake still churned.

He reached the tunnel and plunged into darkness. He'd lost his flashlight during the fight. Which was why he didn't see man waiting up ahead.

His foot caught on something and he fell awkwardly. The breath was forced from his lungs as he hit the ground.

A beam of light cut through the darkness and a voice spoke.

"Maddock. Fancy meeting you down here."

Maddock rolled over onto his back. Through watery eyes, he saw a familiar face.

Echard!

37

"**Will you stop** pacing? You're driving me crazy." Rae sat in the corner of the cell, arms folded, glaring at Bones.

"I think better on my feet," he said.

"You've been on your feet since we got here. Have you thought of anything?"

"No, but feel free to contribute any bright ideas you might have," Bones said. The truth was, although the aftereffects of the water Thel had given him seemed to have worn off, coming to this place had once again stoked a hunger inside of him. The source of the water must be nearby. He could feel it.

"You are very loud, did you know that?" a soft voice said.

Bones knew that voice.

"Thel!"

There she was, and with her…

"Kyle!" Rae sprang to her feet and rushed to the cell door. "Are you all right?"

Physically, the young man appeared to be fine, but gaze was faraway, his movements robotic. The glassy-eyed stared was business as usual, but the way he moved indicated there was more at play here than simply not being the brightest tool in the shed.

"Keep your voice down," Thel warned. "The others think I'm just bringing your friend for a visit. I have other plans." She took out a metal pick and began working at the lock.

"You don't have a key?" Bones asked.

"Obviously not." She flashed an annoyed look at him. "You don't know how much I'm risking to set you free."

The questions began to pour out of Bones. "Who the

hell are you? Why the story about being a recruiter? Why did you ditch me?"

"I am a recruiter in a way. I select men for breeding and I bring them back here." She continued to work at the lock.

"I didn't make the cut?" he asked. He couldn't decide if he was offended or not.

"I wanted to. I really did, but I just couldn't do that to you." She paused, reached through the bar, and caressed his cheek. "You and I have a special connection."

Bones couldn't find the words to reply.

"You didn't want to do *what* to him, exactly?" Rae demanded.

"Sentence him to an eternity of slavery and addiction," she said, her attention back on the lock. "Well, not an eternity, but centuries upon centuries."

"Could you please start making sense?" Rae asked. "Who are you, exactly?"

Thel sighed, her shoulders heaved. "I used to be a college student. I came here on holiday and I met a man. I thought he was the most charming person I'd ever met."

"Until you met me," Bones said.

Thel managed a smile. "Right. Anyway, long story short, next thing I knew, I was down here bathing in the Water of Life."

"You mean the Fountain of Youth?" Willis asked.

"That's not what the Finfolk call it. Since then, I've been one of them. Those of us who are adopted as they call it, are used to bring men into the fold. The Finfolk don't reproduce at a rapid clip and they rarely produce male offspring. I'm told the population used to be more balanced, but back then, the men did most of the fighting, which meant they also did most of the dying. As their numbers dwindled, the true Finfolk remain down here and use the rest of us for recruiting."

"How do you keep from getting caught?" Willis asked.

"People disappear in the islands all the time. None of us goes out more than once a year and we try to be careful about our selections."

"How could you be part of a cult that kidnaps people?" Rae asked. "Don't you have a family? People you care about?"

Sadness washed over Thel's face. "I did, but that was a long time ago. Anyway, I can't leave. If I'm away from the Waters of Life for too long, I'll die."

"How long have you been down here?" Bones asked, already knowing the answer but refusing to believe it.

"Since the seventies. I stopped counting a long time ago."

With a cat-like hiss, Rae reached through the bars and tried to grab Thel. Her fingernails raked Thel's cheek. Thel took a step back, blood streaming from shallow cuts.

"Do you want out of here or not?"

"Yes, so I can kill you for what you did to my brother!"

"I like it here," Kyle said dreamily. "I feel better than I ever have. Look at my skin! It, like, glows. And I feel strong!" He flexed and tapped his biceps.

"What is happening to him?" Rae said.

"The Waters of Life accelerate the body's natural healing abilities. It happens so rapidly that it's almost spontaneous." She took the flask from her hip, opened it, and dribbled some water over the scrape on her cheek. As they watched, it mended itself, healing as if it had never been there. "And based on the reading I've done when I'm up above, I think it affects the telomeres in our body."

"What are telomeres?" Willis asked.

Rae answered. "Telomeres are stretches of DNA and proteins found at the ends of chromosomes. They grow shorter every time a cell divides. Once the telomere grows small enough, the cell stops dividing and eventually dies. If telomeres don't shrink, the body can continue to renew itself."

Bones shivered. Growing up on the reservation, death had only ever been discussed as a great mystery of the spirit, something wondrous. To hear the process of dying reduced down to its nuts and bolts was disconcerting.

Thel nodded. "I don't think it completely stops the telomeres from shrinking. The people who have been here the longest show signs of aging. Gwyneth found a gray hair last year. She cried for days."

"How old is Gwyneth?" Bones asked.

"More than three hundred years. She was one of the first settlers in the Bahamas. The Finfolk took her captive. She didn't mind, though. In her time, a woman didn't have many choices. Down here she's a warrior and a valued member of the community. And she gets to live a very long time. We still have to eat, of course. Fish, seaweed, owl eggs. And we bring back supplies from the surface."

Bones felt dizzy. He gripped the bars of the cell. If the water truly did contain substances that could stop aging as well as heal injuries, the implications were staggering!

"How long can someone live?"

"Some of the Finfolk are thousands of years old. They came here from the old world. Humans don't live as long, but they claim one man lived over nine hundred years. I've yet to see someone die of old age."

Willis gaped. "You know how many sick and dying people you could save with this stuff?"

"No. How many?"

Willis blinked, surprised by the question. "All of them, I guess."

"Exactly. Think about the state of the world right now—the threat of overpopulation, the consumption of resources, the pollution. Now imagine that no one ever dies. They have children who also never die. And those children have children."

Bones understood right away. Without natural deaths, the human population would quickly exceed the world's capacity to support it. Wars would be fought on a grand scale to control limited resources. Population controls would be necessary. But in the end, nothing would stem the tide.

"There's also the problem of the water being the most addictive substance ever. Bones had no more than a sip and I can tell he's still feeling it. If a person drinks too much, they'll never be free from it. They have to be near it, drink it regularly, or they die."

"And how much has my brother had?" Rae asked.

"Not that much. Not yet. The next few days are going to be hard on him, like an addict quitting cold turkey. But he will survive."

"Why lure him here only to release him?"

"Because I know Bones won't leave without him."

"I want to stay," Kyle said without a trace of emotion.

Bones had heard enough.

"Give me that."

He reached through the bars, snatched the pick away from Thel, and began to work at the lock. Thel stood back and watched in silence. A minute later, the lock clicked and he swung the cell door open.

"Don't do anything to her," Bones warned Rae. "We need her help to find our way out of here."

"What about Kyle? He doesn't want to come with us."

"I'll throw him over my shoulder and carry him out of here if I have to."

"And Maddock?" she asked.

"Don't worry. We'll find him."

Seeing no other weapon, he grabbed the torch from the wall. He hoped he got the chance to use it on somebody. To hell with the Water of Life and all the rest of it. They were going to find Maddock and get the hell out of here. And if he had to take a few Finfolk with him along the way, so be it.

38

"**Toss me your** weapon," Echard ordered. He had his own pistol trained on Maddock, finger on the trigger, steady aim.

Maddock had no choice but to comply. Still catching his breath, he slid his pistol toward Echard, who picked it up and tucked it into his pocket.

"I'm impressed that you made it this far," Echard said. "How did you figure out that Father Jerome was the key?"

"A hunch, mostly." Maddock sat up and winced as a sharp pain stabbed into his side. He might have broken a rib. "How did you figure this out?" Maddock grimaced and made a show of favoring his side as he shifted into a more comfortable position. Let Echard think he was out of the game.

"I'm a collector of old stories. Tales of great powers the ancients possessed. Powers that are beyond our comprehension, but are very real."

"You sound like that Grizzly Grant guy on television. The Atlanteans had flying chariots, Moses could zap people with his staff, and Elvis is still alive." He could have gone on. He'd spent years listening to Bones prattle on about it.

"What I would give to get my hands on the staff of Moses. I've known of the existence of ancient world powers for quite some time. And I'm not alone. There are people all over the world who want to get their hands on such things."

"Like the Ahnenerbe?" Maddock asked.

Founded by Heinrich Himmler, the Ahnenerbe was a Nazi think tank which had sponsored expeditions all over the world in search of the very sorts of artifacts

Echard described.

"That's one of them, although they aren't really a major player anymore. If they ever manage to bring you-know-who back, things might change. None of the other Nazis had his charisma."

The average person would have been surprised at the insinuation that the Ahnenerbe was still hanging on, operating in the shadows, but not Maddock. He'd seen a few things in his time and knew that as long as an ideology survived, there would be adherents to its cause. And some of them managed to stick around long past their expiration date.

"I first heard about the amulet from a local storyteller. Once I dug into it, I became convinced that Lusca was simply another name for Leviathan, the great beast of the sea. The more I researched it, the more convinced I became that I was correct. I discovered that the ancients had possessed an amulet that would control Leviathan, or the Lusca if you prefer. According to an obscure legend, a Greek warrior seduced Lusca's master and stole the amulet. Rather than claiming the power he'd rightfully gained, he tried to hide the amulet away. His plan had been to take it to Santorini and destroy it. But his ship sank and the amulet was lost. That is, until you stumbled across it."

Maddock hid his smile. It seemed Echard didn't know about the ring.

"What about the torture chamber?" he grunted, still feigning serious injury.

"It started out as an attempt to deal with the Finfolk. Thinking they were merely a local cult, the church sent an inquisitor, a monk named Titus, to root them out. He began by questioning the locals. Questioning led to torture which eventually led to him capturing one of the Finfolk. It was from her that Titus learned about the great beast and the amulet that could control it."

"Is the Lusca a creature of the Finfolk?"

Echard shook his head. "The Lusca is no one's creature, but it will bend to the will of the one who holds the amulet." He reached inside his shirt and took out the souvenir amulet Maddock had purchased from the peddler at Boiling Hole. "As I understand it, the Lusca was the guardian of this place. It vanished long ago, trapped beneath Andros as it turns out. The Finfolk covet the amulet as much as anyone. If they find me before I find the Lusca, things could get ugly."

"Did you kill Alexei?" Maddock asked.

"I had to. All the work I'd done and some English teacher from Tampa is suddenly on the same path? Hell, he was ahead of me but didn't know it. His research included excerpts from Father Jerome's journal. That was the final piece I needed. Well, that and the amulet which you so kindly delivered into my hands."

"Was Father Jerome in on it?" Maddock was growing impatient. Echard's focus never lapsed, his aim remained steady.

"He was horrified when he heard the stories. He had his doubts about the amulet, but he believed in Leviathan. He also thought the Finfolk were demons, and that the place they lived was the passageway to hell. As far as I can tell, he made it as far as the owls and turned back."

"Why didn't he seal the tunnel off forever?"

Echard shrugged. "Probably knew there was no point. These islands are filled with underground passageways. They'd just find another way out. Besides, he was a man of the cloth, a true believer. He probably thought the best defense was a spiritual one."

"But you put two and two together, stole the amulet, and came down here looking for the Lusca?"

"Exactly."

Behind Echard, the surface of the lake began to

bubble.

"Looks like the show is starting," Echard said. "Don't go anywhere. I imagine my new pet eats a lot."

He gave the amulet a jerk. The cord snapped. Holding it out in front of him like a talisman, he approached the water.

"Where are you?" His eyes searched the depths. "Come to me."

"It has to be in the water," Maddock said. "At least, that's what an old woman told us."

Echard shot a glance back at him, frowned, considered. "Can't hurt to try, I suppose. And don't try to run. I'm an excellent shot."

"Sure you are," Maddock said. But he made no move to flee. He wanted to watch this.

Echard knelt at the water's edge and dipped the amulet into the water. The surface began to churn.

"That's it, baby. Come to papa!"

Slowly, something broke the frothy surface of the lake. It was the head of an octopus, but in his wildest dreams Maddock could not have imagined one this large. Its flesh was gray, its underside white. The mantle, the portion of its body that contained its vital organs, the portion most thought of as a head, came to a point, giving it a snoutlike appearance. Strange markings on either side of the mantle, charcoal gray with triangular white patches, vaguely resembled a shark's open maw. Maddock could see now how the shark-octopus hybrid legend had sprung up.

Echard began to speak to the giant cephalopod as if uttering an incantation.

"Leviathan, great beast of the sea. By the power of the ancients, I command you."

One by one, tentacles emerged from the water. The largest octopus Maddock had ever heard of, the giant Pacific, had an arm span of up to thirty feet. This one had to be well over a hundred, and that was based only on what he could see above the water. It could be even bigger.

"By your might you rule the oceans," Echard intoned.

The tentacles began to sway. For the first time, Maddock truly appreciated the power of these creatures. They were powerful predators, all muscle and sinew, suction cups and crushing coils. He wondered if, like the Pacific octopus, Lusca was also venomous. At the thought he inched away.

Echard continued to babble, waving the amulet. Maddock didn't know what Echard expected to happen, but Maddock didn't want to be too close when it did. He began to inch away. He could have run—Echard was paying him no mind—but something made him stay. Echard was a murderer. He deserved what was about to happen.

The beast was growing agitated, its tentacles whipping about, the water churning. Echard seemed oblivious to it.

"I forgot to tell you!" Maddock yelled. "That's not the real amulet."

Echard whipped his head around.

Maddock took out the authentic amulet and held it up. Its crystal eye glowed bright blue.

"What do you mean?" Echard demanded. Eyes wide with horror, he turned around just as the Lusca wrapped one of its crushing coils around his waist and lifted him high in the air.

"No!" Echard screamed. "Leviathan, I command you to serve me!" He still held his pistol, and he emptied it into the giant creature. Every bullet found its mark, but they were like mosquito bites to the giant creature. Maddock wondered if they'd even managed to penetrate the thick hide.

The creature wasn't listening. It whipped Echard from side to side, snapping his neck. Still holding his limp body by the waist, Lusca took hold of Echard's wrists and ankles and pulled. Maddock had separated plenty of raw chickens in his time and the sound of Echard's arms and legs being ripped from his body reminded him of popping the drumstick out of the joint. His stomach twisted. He'd seen plenty of death in his time, but this was particularly grisly. But it was no less than Echard deserved.

Still, it was time to get the hell out of here.

39

Thel led them through a series of natural passageways. They were small and not easy to traverse. They also seemed to be leading the group in the opposite direction from the way out.

"This isn't the way we came," Rae said.

"That's the point. I don't want to run into anyone."

"What will happen to you when they find out you betrayed them?" Bones asked. He wasn't sure why he cared after the chaos the young woman had caused. Still, he felt connected to her in an inexplicable way.

"I didn't do anything," she said. "You picked the lock. Obviously whoever searched you didn't do a thorough job. Not my fault."

"It's still one a hell of a risk," Bones said.

"Some among our number have lost their humanity, but not me. I'm told that in ancient times the Fins didn't compel people to join their ranks. But as their population dwindled, they decided they couldn't wait around for the occasional mortal to voluntarily join their ranks. That's when they began resorting to force. And then when they came here and discovered the Water of Life, they had their solution. There was no need to force anyone after that. A sip of water and they were more than happy to come along."

"It's still compulsion," Rae said.

Thel nodded. "I know."

"Why my brother? Why did you kidnap him if you know it's wrong?"

"I know you won't believe me, but it didn't happen like that."

"You let him drink the water!" Rae said hotly.

"She didn't give it to me," Kyle said. He'd been quiet

for so long that Bones had forgotten he was there. "I just snagged it and took a chug."

"You did?" Rae gasped. "Why?"

"Bones kept talking about how good it was. I had to try it."

"I thought he'd had too much. The way he was acting I was certain he had passed the point of no return. I thought maybe there was something the Fin could do for him."

Rae laughed. "Why would they do that?"

"His crystal. It's special."

Kyle suddenly pressed his hand to his throat, his eyebrows raised in surprise. "Hey, where is my crystal?"

"It's right here." She pointed to the crystal hanging from her own neck. There was something different about it.

"It's glowing," Bones said.

"It is a thing of the ancients. When I brought Kyle here, I thought I could barter it for help saving him, if any help could be found. By the time I got him down here, it had become obvious that what I observed was not the effects of the Water of Life. It was just… him." She cleared her throat. "Since then, I've kept him confined to my quarters. They think I'm using him for, you know, but really I've just been keeping him away from the water until I could think of a way to get him out of this. I mean, he's truly an innocent."

Bones didn't know what to say. It seemed Thel had a conscience, but that didn't change the things she'd done.

"I know what you're thinking. I don't pretend that I've always done the right thing, but I've done what I had to do in order to survive. You were a soldier. You've done similar. Maybe you did it because your superiors told you to, but that doesn't always make it the moral or ethical thing to do."

Bones nodded. He vaguely remembered spilling his

guts to her the first night they'd met. All the guilt, the demons that had driven him to drink. The nightmares he was still trying to wake up from.

"What were you saying about the crystal?" Willis asked, sensing the tension between them.

"There are ancient powers, mostly forgotten. Those who still believe are met with derision."

"Preach!" Bones said. It wasn't far from comments he had made when friends refused to listen to his legends and conspiracy theories.

"What power does this crystal have?" Willis asked.

"Let's just say that it could be weaponized to terrible effect."

"Really? That thing?" Rae asked. "Kyle always said it had powers."

"All crystals have power," Kyle said. "I actually studied gemstone therapy when I lived in California. I almost got my license, but the dude wanted a thousand dollars."

Thel met Bones' gaze and gave a tiny shake of the head. Her message was clear. She didn't mean the usual New Age crap. What she was talking about was real and it was scary.

Predisposed as he was to believe conspiracy theories, this was difficult to swallow. At least the so-called Waters of Life enhanced existing biological functions. It was something he could wrap his head around. Even a giant octopus, a really huge one, seemed natural in its own way. But the idea that a surfer dude's lucky necklace could be dangerous?

And then he remembered a question that had been nagging at him.

"Say, was that you who Maddock saw down in the blue hole?"

"Blue hole?"

"A couple of days ago at the Blue Descent

competition, he thought he saw a woman swimming deep down in the blue hole. He said she looked exactly like you."

"Hey, I think that chick did look like you!" Kyle said.

"That wasn't me," Thel snapped. She was visibly upset.

"No, it was totally you!" Kyle continued.

Thel raised a hand. "Quiet! This is the way out. Just follow this passageway. Any time you come to a fork, always take the way that goes up. At the end you will have to swim through an underwater channel. It's not hard to find it when you know to look for it."

"Willis can get them out safely," Bones said. "I have to find Maddock."

"No. I can't let you risk it. I'll find your friend and show him the way out."

Bones smiled sadly. "You don't know Maddock. He won't leave just on your say-so. He's stubborn like that."

"No one is going anywhere."

Out of the passageway strode a young woman dressed in a tunic and jerkin. She carried a sword in her right and a sword breaker in her left. Behind her came half a dozen more warriors all armed with spears. Bones couldn't believe his eyes. This girl looked just like Thel, but a few years younger.

Bones took a step forward but Thel moved in front of him.

"Don't do this Aggie," Thel warned. "Just let them go. They won't come back."

"You know the rules, mother. No one leaves. Not ever."

"Mother?" Bones said.

"This is my daughter, Aglaope. She was born a year after I was taken. She's a true Finfolk." There was deep sadness in Thel's voice, but also a touch of pride. "She has recently forgotten that she is also human."

"Being human is not a badge of honor," Aglaope said.

"Look, I don't want to get in the way of a family squabble," Bones said. "It's getting close to beer thirty, so we're just going to get out of your hair."

He took a few steps as if he intended to simply pass the Fins by. When Aglaope moved to block his path, he thrust the torch into her face, then delivered a push-kick to her chest that sent her flying backward into the group of warriors.

One of the men threw his spear at Bones, but he was falling backward, and the throw had no power. Bones caught it out of the air, reversed it, and struck the nearest warrior in the temple, knocking him out.

Still lying on the floor, Aglaope swung her sword awkwardly. Bones deflected it with the haft of the spear. And then he heard the sound of lots of footsteps coming their way. He turned to the others.

"Run!" He gave Willis a shove and they fled into darkness.

"Where are we going?" Willis asked.

"I don't know," Bones said. "Just not back that way."

40

Maddock sprinted down the passageway, leaving the Lusca and the few remaining scraps of Echard behind. He had no idea where he was headed, or if this path could lead him to his friends. At least it would take him away from the monstrosity the lurked in the water.

The way twisted and turned, always leading him back to his right until he was certain he'd come in a circle. Up ahead, a golden glow told him he was approaching a lit chamber. He slowed to a walk and moved forward on silent feet.

He was approaching the treasure room. A massive heap of loot was piled just inside the doorway, blocking him from view. He peered inside. He was looking at the back of the chair on which the man in black had sat. Beyond it was the fountain, now empty. But past that, what he'd been unable to see before, was a blue grotto. The azure waters glowed with a dull light.

Passageways led off to either side of the chamber. One of those had to be the way forward. Left had been unlucky the last time, so he decided to take the right. He'd taken three steps when he heard someone clear his throat.

"It's customary to knock."

The man dressed all in black stepped out from behind a pile of treasure. He was well over six feet tall, nearly of a height with Bones. He wore a doublet, breeches, over-the-calf boots with folded cuffs, and a cutlass at his hip.

"If you're supposed to be the Dread Pirate Roberts, you forgot the mask," Maddock said.

"Black Bart?" the man said. "He was a solid captain, but dreaded? Hardly."

"Never mind," Maddock said. "But why are you dressed like that?"

"I've dressed this way for hundreds of years." The man frowned, ran a hand through his wavy, shoulder-length black hair. "I know it's been a few centuries but has everyone already forgotten Riddick Blackwood?"

Maddock's heart skipped a beat. The man did resemble depictions of Blackwood. But it couldn't be.

"Is this some game you cultists play? You dress up like someone from the past and try to convince us you're immortal?"

The man called Blackwood smiled. "I understand your disbelief. I didn't believe it either when I found this place. But I assure you it is true. I lost count after my one-hundredth birthday, but the others assure me I am more than three centuries old."

"You look good for your age," Maddock said. "I suppose that's the Fountain of Youth back there? Or the Water of Life?"

Blackwood nodded. "I don't understand how it works. It heals wounds, cures illnesses, and slows the aging process. I look a little bit older than I did when I arrived." He touched a patch of gray at his temple. "But I expect to be around for a very long time." He barked a rueful laugh.

"Suppose I believe you. How did you come to be here?"

"I was searching for the Fountain of Youth. I found my way to the Mermaid Hole on Cat Island. There was an old woman I hoped to meet there, but she would not reveal herself to me. But I met someone else, a girl of unsurpassed beauty. She said she could show me the Fountain of Youth. And she did." He laughed again.

"Is all this treasure yours?"

He nodded. "For years I continued to ply the seas around these islands. Never too far away, and I always kept some of the water with me. I could stay away for five days at a time, much longer than anyone else." He gazed with sadness at the closest treasure pile. "It's strange. The first time you take a prize it is an absolute thrill. You feel like a god. The next one is good too, and the next, and the next. Finally you realize that you are only making more and larger piles of the same old thing. It no longer brings you joy but you feel compelled to continue hoarding it. Now I despise my riches but cannot bear to lose a single coin. It's the same with drinking and wenching. It's all like a game of noughts and crosses. Not challenging or even entertaining, but you just keep playing."

Maddock knew that noughts and crosses was a very old name for what Americans called tic-tac-toe.

"Let me get this straight. You feel sorry for yourself because you've spent three hundred years partying with beautiful women in the middle of more treasure than I've ever seen?"

"I'd kill myself if I could, but someone always dumps me back into the fountain. If someone would cut my head off, that would do it, but they won't agree. My seed has produced three true Finfolk, more than anyone else. That's why they keep me around where they dispose of other men fairly quickly."

"What do you mean by true Finfolk?"

"The Fin have gifts humans do not. Most of their couplings with humans produce human offspring. Those are taken to the surface and given to the church. At least, that is what they tell me."

"Is that what they have planned for my friends? To use them for breeding stock?"

"Those are your friends? Yes, I believe that is the plan. They are especially excited about the red Indian. None of them have seen one before."

"What about Raeána?"

"Is that the girl's name? She is to be a special treat for me. I get those from time to time. After that it's up to me to decide how long she lives."

Maddock took a step toward the man, who smiled and drew his sword in a deft, practiced motion. Maddock froze.

"Do you know what I miss the most about my life as a pirate? A good fight! It's better than rum, better than a woman. And they won't let me fight. I'm too valuable."

"Good for you. Now, tell me where to find my friends."

Blackwood reached into the closest treasure pile and withdrew a cutlass.

"Fight me," Blackwood said. "I'll even tell you where your friends are. Down that passageway," he pointed to his left, "take the first and second right turns." He tossed the cutlass to Maddock, then moved to bar the way. "And I'm not letting you pass."

"Doesn't seem like a fair fight," Maddock said.

Blackwood shrugged. "What do you expect? I'm a pirate."

Maddock examined the cutlass. The sheath was gem-encrusted, but when Maddock drew the sword, he found it was plain and serviceable, though the wrappings around the hilt were crumbling. He'd done a bit of fencing, studied kendo, but a duel to the death?

"Why do you care?" Maddock asked. "You've clearly lost interest in life."

"Because fighting is when I feel most alive. We should probably begin. You never know when one of the Fin males will take a fancy to your young girl and try to bypass me in line." Blackwood smiled pityingly. "Don't make me chase you."

If Maddock still had his pistol, he'd have simply shot the man, Indiana Jones style, but that was not an option. He moved into an en garde position.

Blackwood smiled. "Excellent!" He advanced, sword extended. Maddock held his own sword out before him, not gripping too tightly, and they began to circle.

Blackwood made a probing thrust which Maddock easily parried. Blackwood's smile grew bigger.

They continued this cycle of thrust and parry. Each time, Blackwood was quicker, his blade coming closer and closer to Maddock.

Maddock was falling into a pattern. Time to change things up.

He feinted, then slashed at Blackwood's thigh. It was an unexpected move and the pirate barely managed to avoid it.

"Very good!" Blackwood said. "You almost drew first blood. I'll have to focus."

Blackwood attacked with a fury. Thrust, slash thrust, feint low. Then he raised his sword and whipped it around in a circle.

Maddock felt a sharp pain in the back of his head and he moved away. When he touched the spot, he was relieved to see there was no blood.

"You like that little trick?" Blackwood said. "The back of the sword is flat. It makes for a good club. Come now. Let us continue."

Blackwood danced in again with a spirited attack. Maddock mostly fended it off, but came away with a nick on his shoulder. Blood soaked his shirt sleeve. The fight was not going well.

Maddock snatched a handful of coins from a nearby treasure pile and flung them in Blackwood's face. The pirate flinched and Maddock attacked again. Blackwood fended off the attack and backed away from the treasure piles.

"That was not sportsmanlike."

"I thought you were a pirate." Maddock said.

Baring his teeth, Blackwood resumed the attack.

Once again, Maddock came away with minor wounds. But hope was not lost. Although Blackwood was far more skilled with the sword, he was badly out of shape. Sweat streamed down his face. His shoulders heaved.

"Sitting on your ass drinking rum is bad for the lungs, isn't it?"

Blackwood nodded. "I used to practice regularly, but I grew bored with that. They weren't real fights. This one is."

As Maddock expected, Blackwood's onslaught was furious. The pirate needed to end this while he still had the strength to fight. He danced back, made Blackwood chase him. Blackwood's attack grew more reckless. Time and again the tip of Blackwood's sword missed his throat by inches. But the pirate was slowing down, and as he grew more tired, his movements became easier to anticipate.

"Have you always been that thick around the middle?" Maddock taunted.

Like most vain men, Blackwood didn't deal well with outright mockery. He took a wild swing meant to remove Maddock's head from his body.

Maddock saw it coming. He ducked beneath the strike, sprang forward, and drove his shoulder into Blackwood's gut. His sword clattered to the ground as he scooped Blackwood up in a double-leg takedown, forced him back to the edge of the water, and slammed him to the floor. He quickly moved into a mount position and began to pummel Blackwood, who tried to put up a spirited defense, but he was exhausted. Blackwood covered his head and tried to turn away from the rain of fists and elbows. Maddock let him turn over, then snaked an arm around his neck and sank in a chokehold.

Blackwood didn't give up. He kicked, clawed, even tried to gouge Maddock's eyes, but in the end, his body went limp. Maddock stood, retrieved his sword, and looked down at the man who, moments before, had tried to kill him for sport.

"Now, what the hell do I do with you?" he said to the unconscious form. He wasn't about to saw the man's head off. He wasn't a Jihadist. But to leave Blackwood alive?

Before he could make up his mind, he heard the sound of running feet. And then Bones, Willis, Rae, and Kyle burst into the treasure chamber, followed by a host of Finfolk.

"Maddock!" Bones said. "About time you showed up."

41

There was no time to think. The only thing that mattered was survival. They dashed behind a pile of gold as arrows zipped through the air and clattered off the stone walls.

"Nice sword," Bones said.

"Thanks. Riddick Blackwood gave it to me. Where'd you get the spear?"

"Stole it from Thel's daughter. It's a long story." Bones froze, then looked around. "Thel! Where did she go?"

"How about y'all shut up and help me fight?" Willis was grabbing anything heavy and easy to throw and hurling it at the Finfolk. A goblet caught the nearest warrior on the bridge of the nose. She let out a curse, dropped her bow, and pressed her hands to her face.

"I think it's been a long time since they've been in a real battle," Bones said. "They should have flanked us by now, but they're hanging back."

"We're still the 7th Cavalry and they're the Sioux."

Bones frowned. "You do not really expect me to spend the last moments of my life pretending I'm General Custer?"

"Of course not. I'm Custer. You're just some random soldier."

"Screw you, Maddock. You got a plan?"

Maddock climbed up onto the treasure heap for a better look. Bones was right. The Finfolk were hanging back, content to keep Maddock and the others pinned down by their archers. With that thought, he ducked as someone took a shot at him.

"It's like they're waiting on something, or someone."

"Then you should do something before that

happens," Bones said.

And then Maddock had an idea. A stupid, crazy, reckless idea. But if it worked...

"Can you two cover me?"

"We can't exactly lay down suppressing fire," Bones said. "But we'll give it a shot." He hefted his spear.

Maddock took a deep breath. "On three. One... two... three!"

Bones let out a war whoop, clambered to the top of the treasure heap, and hurled his spear at the ranks of Finfolk. The others threw everything they could get their hands on.

With the enemy momentarily distracted by flying gold, Maddock made a mad dash across the treasure room. He was tired from his fight with Blackwood and weakened by blood loss. One of the Finfolk, a blonde woman in leather armor, spotted him and moved to intercept him. Before Maddock could react, another group of Finfolk burst into the chamber. They were led by a red-haired woman. Maddock knew from the old newspaper photograph that this was Thel.

Thel charged directly at the blonde woman, who bared her teeth and snarled.

"Traitor!" the woman said. "I knew you weren't one of us."

"You've forgotten what it means to be human, Gwyneth!"

"And you don't seem to realize that you are no longer one of them." Gwyneth pointed straight up.

Maddock kept running. Even with the support of Thel and her contingent, they were still badly outnumbered. His plan needed to work.

As he ran, he slid the Lusca ring onto his finger and slipped the amulet around his neck. Each was hot against his flesh and burned with brilliant blue light.

Out of the corner of his eye he saw Willis and Bones,

armed with short swords and Templar shields, join the fight in support of Thel and her allies.

Thel and Gwyneth were engaged in a furious duel. He saw Gwyneth thrust and Thel dance away. And then he was flying through the air. The world seemed to slow down around him. The world reduced to a series of snapshots. Arrows flying. Bones slamming his shield into the face of a Finfolk warrior. Kyle had jumped onto a man's back and was pounding his head with a fist-sized rock. As each blow struck, he shouted, "Smash!"

And then Maddock hit the water. This far below the surface, he'd expected it to be frigid, but it was as warm as bathwater. Blue light swirled around him. A low rumbling filled his ears, rising to a crescendo. Alien thoughts filled his mind. He felt a ravenous hunger, a boiling rage. He thrashed around, fought to swim to the surface. What was happening to him?

And then the Lusca was there. A monstrous, dark behemoth that seemed to suck in the light. Maddock's vision began to flicker as if he were rapidly changing television channels.

He saw the Lusca bearing down on him.

He saw himself floating in the water.

Again and again the images changed until he finally realized what was happening. He was seeing through his own eyes and through the eyes of the Lusca. As unbelievable as it was, the legend had proved to be true. The amulet did control the Lusca.

Control! That had been the entire point of this. He focused all his thoughts on the creature, concentrated on seeing only through its eyes. Once again he saw himself in the water, but this time the image didn't flicker.

Surface, he ordered the Lusca.

The Lusca rebelled. Maddock tried again to bend it to his will, but it was like trying to wrap your arms around a tornado. His ears rang and sharp pain stabbed his eyes. Now he wanted nothing more than to break the connection before it drove him mad. He pressed his hands to his temples and tried to scream. Water poured into his mouth and he began to choke.

Once again his vision flashed between two consciousnesses. Through the eyes of the Lusca, he saw the havoc it wrought in its rage. Its grasping tentacles caught up the Finfolk, crushed the life out of them. Sections of ceiling crashed down onto the combatants. Thel now dueled with a woman who looked like her doppelganger. The daughter Bones had mentioned?

And then he saw through his own eyes. He was sinking. He knew he ought to try to swim, but he lacked the will.

A shape appeared in the water, small, but growing larger.

It was a woman. She was tiny, not even five feet tall. Her skin was a rich brown, her eyes sparkling green. Her long, silver hair spread out around her like a halo, and her scales shimmered like mother of pearl.

Scales?

She seized Maddock by the front of his shirt, pulled him to her, and kissed him full on the lips.

He could breathe again!

Lips still pressed together, they swam to the surface.

"Silly boy," the woman said, holding him at arm's length. A human cannot control the great beast. Give me my ring and my amulet."

She didn't wait for him to comply. Instead, she tore the jewelry from him and slipped them on.

She closed her eyes.

The effect was instantaneous. The Lusca knew its master. It ceased its thrashing about, even released Kyle, whom it had just seized. The young man stared in disbelief as the coil slid back into the water and the great beast sank out of sight.

Silence reigned. The survivors had stopped fighting and taken shelter from the mad monster. Many lay dead on the ground.

Maddock swam to the shore and looked around for his friends. Bones and Willis appeared from the shadows. The big men looked like something out of a horror film. They were spattered with blood from head to toe. He didn't see Rae.

He had only a moment to wonder where she was before someone let out a roar of anger.

He turned to see the blonde warrior standing in the fountain. She was naked, and all over her body, cuts and gashes were turning to angry red scars, which faded to pink and then vanished. All this happened in the time it took for her to clamber out of the fountain and grab a fallen sword. She advanced on Maddock.

"I'll kill every one of you…"

She didn't get to finish the sentence because, as with every other human, it was impossible to form words once the head was removed from the body. She still managed a step and a half before her headless form collapsed at Maddock's feet. Standing behind her was Riddick Blackwood.

"You beat me," he said. "But now you owe me your life, so I'd say I'm ahead." He winked.

In that moment, Maddock understood the legend of Blackwood's irresistible charm, how despite his depredations, he could make people love him. He laughed.

"I could have killed you but I left you alive."

"Call it even?" Blackwood held out his hand to shake.

"We can call it even, but I don't trust you enough to shake your hand."

Blackwood sheathed his sword. "Wise decision."

"Maddock?"

"Rae!" Maddock whirled about to see Raeána staggering toward him, an arrow protruding from her stomach. He ran to her and caught her before she fell.

"I got shot," she said. Her voice was weak.

"It's going to be all right." His hoarse voice turned the lie into a barely audible gasp.

"We can put her in the fountain," Thel said.

"I'll help. Give her to me." Kyle rushed to Maddock's side and scooped his sister up in his arms.

"What's going to happen?" Maddock said.

Thel bit her lip. "The Water will heal her, just like it did for Gwyneth. For all the good it did her." She kicked the blonde woman's head into the water. "But she will never be able to leave again. Not for more than a few days."

So Blackwood had been telling the truth! He still wouldn't have believed it if he hadn't seen Gwyneth healed before his eyes.

"I don't know if I want this," Rae said as Kyle carried her to the fountain.

"I won't let you die. You've saved my ass a dozen times and this is the first chance I've had to return the favor."

Tears flooded Rae's eyes. "I don't want you to be alone."

"I won't be." And then, still holding his sister in his arms, he plunged into the fountain.

Rae cried out in pain and began to thrash. Maddock made a move to go to her aid but Thel grabbed him by the arm.

"She will be all right, but he should have taken the arrow out first. It's more painful when the body forces it out on its own."

Rae's cries of pain lasted only a few seconds. Then she sprang to her feet, hands on hips, and began scolding her brother.

"Don't you know what you've done? Now you're stuck down here forever."

Kyle splashed water in her face.

"Are you kidding? This place is awesome. I mean, all I ever wanted was to chill and have a good time. It's not like I'm planning a career on Wall Street. And I can still go up top and surf can't I?" He looked at Thel, who smiled.

"From time to time you can." She turned and addressed a knot of Finfolk who stood off to one side. They were all that remained of Gwyneth's warriors. "Things are going to change here. No more kidnappings. No more treating our number like prisoners. If anyone cannot accept that, speak now. Your heads can join the others."

For the first time, Maddock realized how many headless corpses lay on the ground. No quarter had been given in this fight.

No one had the stomach to fight. The survivors, including Thel's daughter, who had come off worse in her duel with her mother, made their way to the fountain for healing, then set to disposing of the bodies.

Thel pulled Bones aside for a quiet talk, then she and her daughter departed.

"That family's going to need some counseling," Willis said.

"What was up with you jumping into the water?" Bones asked. "We needed you in the fight. You're just lucky the Lusca didn't eat you, too."

"I had a little help," Maddock said. He pointed to the water where the strange little woman waited. Her elbows resting on the rocky ledge, her arms covered her bare breasts. "You can't see it underwater, but she's got scales down there."

"Webbed feet, too," the woman said.

Bones frowned, his lips moved, and then his

expression brightened. "It's you! But you're young and hot!"

The woman laughed. "I told you that you would like Mama Wata. Now, you boys must say your goodbyes. This is no place for you."

Maddock nodded. This was the moment he had been dreading. Rae was seated at the edge of the fountain, her fingers trailing through the water. He sat down beside her and she managed a sad smile.

"I'm sorry," she said.

"Don't be. It's my fault. If I hadn't brought you down here..."

"You didn't bring me. I came to find my brother." She pressed a finger to his lips before he could reply. "It's done. Let it go."

He nodded. "I'm sorry we didn't get to know each other better."

"Goodbye, Maddock."

They kissed and then he stood. She seized his hand.

"Do you know what Junkanoo is?"

"The street parade?"

She nodded. "If you ever wanted to say hi, there's a good chance you'll find me at the parade."

He smiled. "It's a date."

He couldn't bring himself to look back at her as he returned to his friends, who stood talking to Riddick Blackwood and the woman who called herself Mama Wata.

"Maddock, this dude says he's the real Riddick Blackwood," Bones said. "But he's never heard of Jack Sparrow."

"Don't mind Bones. Thanks for saving my life."

"And thank you. You made me realize I don't want to die. I just need a little variety." He glanced up at the ceiling. "I would love to go up top for a drink, but I wouldn't know where to begin."

"Come on up with us," Maddock said. "First round is on me."

Blackwood looked down at his pirate garb. "I don't think I'm dressed for the occasion. But I hope our paths cross again some day. Today was literally the most fun I've had in a hundred years."

"You boys come here," Mama Wata said sharply. Maddock, Bones, and Willis obeyed immediately. "Kneel down where I can see you." She eyed them individually, as if taking their measure, then nodded as if making up her mind about something. "Close your eyes. I will give you my blessing."

Maddock closed his eyes. He felt the touch of her fingertip on his forehead. She drew a shape there and his entire body tingled.

She pulled his head down close and whispered in his ear.

"Forget."

EPILOGUE

The sun was just peeking over the horizon when the three men returned to *Sea Foam*. Matt was dozing in a chair on the aft deck. He sprang to his feet when Maddock cleared his throat.

"Where the hell have you been? We looked everywhere and couldn't find you. You guys are never leaving me behind again!"

"Dude, chill," Bones said. "We got lost in some caves. Only just found our way out a little while ago."

Maddock's memory was hazy but what Bones said sounded correct.

"Where's Rae? And did you find Kyle?"

"Yeah, he was lost in the same caves. They going to take the ferry back," Maddock said. "We had a fight. She's too obsessed with that brother of hers."

"Sorry, man. That sucks."

Corey appeared on deck, rubbing his bleary eyes. "Did I hear you guys say you got lost? For almost twenty-four hours? That's amazing. Bones is never going to live that down."

"Dude, you once got lost walking home in our own town."

"I was drunk," Corey said. "Anyway, where's the ring and the amulet? And did you find the Lusca?"

Maddock frowned. Hadn't they found… something? His thoughts were murky.

"It was all just a legend." The words came to him unbidden. "The artifacts were a matched set but that was the only thing special about them. Rae is going to see to it they get into a museum."

Corey and Matt exchanged bewildered looks. Matt scratched his head.

"And Echard?"

"Found him down in the caverns. He'd taken a bad fall and was on the verge of death. He admitted he was a black market antiquities dealer. That's why he wanted the amulet."

Matt seemed to be having a hard time taking all of this in.

"Let me see if I've got this straight. Echard's dead, Rae and Kyle are safe, there's no sea monster, and we've got nothing to show for all our work?"

"I wouldn't say that." Willis emptied his pockets, spilling double fistfuls of gold coins onto the deck.

"Where did you get that?" Maddock asked.

"I don't know. Found them along the way."

"In that case," Corey said, "I'd say this expedition was a success."

Maddock nodded. "Let's find a place to fuel up and then we'll head for home."

Two hours later, *Sea Foam* was cutting through the water, headed in the direction of Key West. Maddock sat sprawled on the deck, an unopened bottle of Dos Equis in his hand. His head was killing him and try as he might, he couldn't picture any of the events since the group had left the boat in search of Kyle.

A shadow fell over him. He looked up to see Bones standing there.

"Pull up a chair." Maddock slapped the deck beside him.

Bones sat down and gazed up at the sky.

"I feel like there's a bunch of stuff I ought to remember, but I can't."

"Same here. What about Willis?"

"He wanted some rack time. Said his head was killing him."

"I know the feeling." Maddock closed his eyes and rubbed his temples. It wasn't any better when he opened them.

"Stuff doesn't make sense," Bones said. "Kyle left with Thel, but she wasn't there when we found him, and he didn't say anything about her, did he?"

Maddock shook his head. "Why didn't we ask?"

"I don't know. And I remember being lost in the caverns, but how did we get down there in the first place?"

"Well, we started out…" Maddock realized he couldn't remember either.

"And how do you know the Lusca is just a legend? We just wandered around the caves for almost a day."

Maddock didn't have an answer, only a strong conviction that the monster didn't exist.

"And there's one more thing." Bones reached into his pocket and took out a golden figurine. It was a winged being holding a fiery sword. "I thought it was an angel, but look at the face."

Maddock frowned. The thing had the head of a serpent.

"It's got a tail, too," Bones said, turning it around. "And the weirdest part is, I don't remember where I got it."

"That's not unusual," Maddock said. "You're so light-fingered you sometimes steal without even thinking about it."

"Hey, I haven't done that in a long time. And we're not talking about cool dishes from the Japanese restaurant. This is a freaking golden idol and I've never seen anything like it before."

"Neither have I," Maddock admitted. Strangely, he didn't even care.

"And when I look at it, I get pissed off and want to throw it into the ocean."

"In that case, give it to me. That's too much gold to throw away."

Bones made to hand it to him but changed his mind and pocketed it again.

"Sooner or later I'll figure it out. The memory has to come back to me sooner or later, doesn't it?"

Maddock nodded. "Absolutely. One day, you'll remember."

THE END

FROM THE AUTHOR

One of my favorite things about writing the Dane Maddock Adventures is the research that goes into the books. (Don't tell my younger self that). I love making use of "real" mysteries and legends, as well as actual people and places. Contest is loaded with these, and I would be remiss if I did not acknowledge the work of author M.L. Behrman, whose book, *Mojave Mysteries*, provided a wealth of story material.

ABOUT THE AUTHOR

David Wood is the USA Today bestselling author of the Dane Maddock Adventures and several other books and series. He also writes fantasy under the pen name David Debord. He's a member of International Thriller Writers and the Horror Writers Associon, and also reviews for New York Journal of Books.

Learn more about his work at www.davidwoodweb.com or drop by and say hello on Facebook at www.facebook.com/davidwoodbooks.

Made in the USA
Coppell, TX
20 November 2019